How could a house cast a spell over her?

Zady had dreamed of living in a place like this.

Aware that she'd never be able to afford one on her income, she associated having a house with finding Mr. Right, followed by Baby Right. Now Nick dangled the lure of living in this minipalace rent-free.

Nevertheless, the psychic price was too high. No sane woman would agree to a second job as nanny to Mr. So-Wrong-She-Couldn't-Imagine-Anyone-Wronger-Unless-It-Was-Dwayne. Yet here Zady stood in the cold air of an early February night feeling utterly enchanted by the scent of jasmine and the twitter of night birds.

She kept picturing her goddaughter, Linda, toddling happily about with Nick's son, Caleb, in the cheerful kitchen, clouting each other over the head with blocks, screaming and then cuddling with her while muffins in the oven perfumed the air. Exactly who would be baking those muffins, she had no idea.

She must be delirious. Or under a spell.

Standing close enough to shelter her against the chill breeze, Nick radiated persuasion.

"I'm only asking you for six months," he said. "Will you agree to move in for that long?"

Dear Reader,

Nurse Zady Moore is struggling to move past a failed relationship and some spectacular misjudgments. The last thing she needs is an entanglement with Safe Harbor Medical's newest obstetrician, Nick Davis.

Nick's trying to sort out the best way to care for his three-year-old son, Caleb, born out of wedlock and living with maternal grandparents since his mother's death six months earlier. Not only has Nick made mistakes, he has a look-alike cousin, the doctor who recently hired Zady as his nurse. She knows where her loyalty lies—with Marshall, not reputed playboy Nick. But fate, and love, have other plans.

I introduced Zady in *The Baby Bonanza* as the estranged twin of ultrasound technician Zora. Since the sisters reconciled and Zady moved to Safe Harbor, I decided to explore how she overcomes her muddled past and finds love. In the process, I discovered a complex relationship between cousins Nick and Marshall, who demanded that I write their stories, too.

There's a complete listing of the series along with recipes from earlier books on my website, jacquelinediamond.com. Welcome to Safe Harbor!

Best,

Jacqueline Diamond

THE DOCTOR'S ACCIDENTAL FAMILY

JACQUELINE DIAMOND

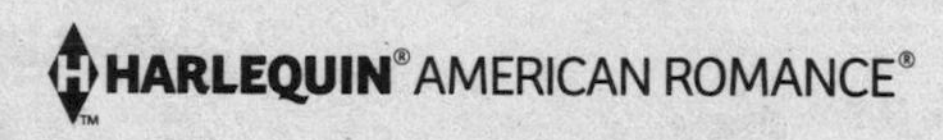

ISBN-13: 978-0-373-75584-4

The Doctor's Accidental Family

This edition published by arrangement with Harlequin Books S.A.

For questions and comments about the quality of this book, please contact us at CustomerService@Harlequin.com.

Printed in U.S.A.

The daughter of a doctor and an artist, **Jacqueline Diamond** has been drawn to medical themes for many of her more than ninety-five published novels, including her Safe Harbor Medical miniseries for Harlequin American Romance. She developed an interest in fertility issues after successfully undergoing treatment to have her two sons, now in their twenties. A former Associated Press reporter and columnist, Jackie lives with her husband of thirty-five years in Orange County, California, where she's active in Romance Writers of America. You can learn more about her books at jacquelinediamond.com/books and say hello to Jackie on her Facebook page, JacquelineDiamondAuthor.

Books by Jacqueline Diamond

Harlequin American Romance

Safe Harbor Medical

The Holiday Triplets
Officer Daddy
Falling for the Nanny
The Surgeon's Surprise Twins
The Detective's Accidental Baby
The Baby Dilemma
The M.D.'s Secret Daughter
The Baby Jackpot
His Baby Dream
The Surprise Holiday Dad
A Baby for the Doctor
The Surprise Triplets
The Baby Bonanza

Visit the Author Profile page
at Harlequin.com for more titles

To Ari and Claire

Chapter One

Any minute now, she'd saunter into sight along the walkway, her reddish-brown hair brightening the gloomy January evening and her smile outshining the leftover holiday lights still draping the roof of the extended-stay motel. Shrugging into his sports coat, Dr. Nick Davis peered out his window at the opposite row of units.

No sign of her yet. It was 5:20 p.m., almost time for him to leave.

He'd moved into the Harbor Suites a few days ago, just before starting his position as an obstetrician at Safe Harbor Medical Center, and he'd noticed the woman right away. Identifiable by her blue-flowered nurse's uniform, she arrived home just as Nick was departing for his evening office hours, which were followed by overnight duties in Labor and Delivery.

Tonight, he planned to catch her eye and give her a friendly nod. Nothing too personal; just enough of an acknowledgment to pave the way for later conversation. Laying the groundwork, so to speak.

His cell rang. An emergency? A glance at the readout produced an irritated groan: Grandma Elaine. Elaine Carrigan wasn't *his* grandmother, but the title fit her.

"Hello, Elaine," he answered.

"Nick! You aren't with a patient, are you?" Her voice had a thin, wavering quality. Maybe it was his imagination, but she sounded especially edgy.

"About to head to the office. Is Caleb okay?" Nick glanced at the large, framed photo of his three-year-old son on his coffee table. One of the few personal notes in the bare-bones apartment lined with his unopened boxes, it touched his heart afresh. Those innocent, eager brown eyes were much like Nick's, and the nearly black tumble of hair was like Bethany's.

Caleb had been an accidental blessing who'd transformed his father's life. If Nick had had his choice, the boy would have moved in with him after Bethany had passed away six months ago. However, in view of Nick's bachelor habits and the boy's painful loss of his mother, Nick had agreed that he should stay, for now, in his familiar home with his grandparents an hour's drive away.

Until this week, Nick had worked at a clinic half an hour from the Carrigans. Although he'd hated to move farther from his son and accept longer hours, the pay in his new job should enable him to achieve important goals: putting a big dent in his medical school loans and saving to provide a home for Caleb before the boy reached kindergarten age.

His arrangement with the elder Carrigans had gone smoothly until early last month, when they began occasionally postponing his weekly visits with vague excuses. Nick had always considered them reliable, unlike their daughter, but he was beginning to revise that opinion. Still, they'd celebrated Christmas together, a happy holiday for the child they all loved.

"He's fine," Elaine said. "I'm calling about Sunday."

Nick's jaw tightened. "There's no problem, is there?" He had arranged an afternoon get-together with his son.

She gave a low cough. "His best friend from preschool is having a birthday party on Sunday. Caleb brought home an invitation yesterday and that's all he talks about. We could insist he skip it, of course."

Nick knew his son loved birthday parties, and he didn't wish his visits to have unpleasant associations. Also, he'd witnessed a few meltdowns lately that in somebody else's child might be described as temper tantrums. With the boy still in a fragile emotional state, it would be unwise to push too hard.

"When does it start?" He might be able to squeeze in a pancake brunch.

"Ten o'clock," Elaine said.

"On a Sunday?"

"They attend church early, and that's when they're free. Why don't you come Saturday morning instead?"

"As I explained, I don't finish my shift until 8:00 a.m. on Saturdays and I'll be exhausted." Especially since this was his first week on the new job, and he hadn't yet acclimated to his schedule. "How about Saturday afternoon?"

"My nephew and his wife from San Francisco will be here, and Caleb adores playing with their little girl. You could join us, I suppose, but mostly he'll be busy with his little friend."

Nick tried to contain his exasperation. Lately, negotiating arrangements for his weekend visits seemed almost as tricky as trying to establish peace in the Middle East. He didn't recall Elaine acting this difficult in the past, but after the holidays she might be clinging extra hard to her grandson.

Through the window, he spotted the pretty red-haired nurse approaching on the walkway. Their encounter, which he'd been looking forward to, would have to be postponed or he'd be late. His evening patients, most of whom were referrals meeting him for the first time, deserved the assurance that Nick cared enough to stick to his schedule.

His son deserved to know he cared enough to maintain regular visits, too. Bethany had never been good at keeping to a routine, and as a result, Nick had been lucky to see his son a few times a month. Since her death, however, he'd resolved to provide a stable influence. Also, at three, his son had become old enough to enjoy longer outings.

"I can't skip a whole weekend with Caleb." Holding the phone to his ear, Nick stepped outside into the crisp air. "I'll be there Sunday night even if it's only for an hour."

Elaine caught her breath. He could almost hear her thinking fast. "I'll tell you what. Saturday evening, my nephew and his wife plan to take the children to a puppet show in north Orange County. Why don't you go with them? It's halfway between us. I can email you the details."

"That'll be fine." Locking the door, Nick conceded that, while he preferred to be alone with his son, this was a reasonable compromise. It might be extra fun for Caleb, too. "Thanks, Elaine."

"My pleasure." She sounded relieved.

What was going on with the Carrigans? Next weekend, Nick resolved to ask her. They all had to work together for Caleb's benefit.

Turning, he discovered that the nurse had paused to chat with a neighbor. The delay offered a second chance. Nick could afford to carry out his original plan as long as he didn't stop for any lengthy flirting, which he hadn't intended, anyway.

He cut across the sparse lawn between a couple of squatty palm trees intent on shedding as many fronds as possible. Pacing his steps, he reached his target just as the neighbor disappeared into a unit and the nurse took out her keys.

At close range, she was taller than he'd guessed, perhaps five foot six, and he caught an appealing whiff of flowers. Sharp, intelligent gray eyes fixed on him questioningly.

"Hi, there," Nick said casually. That was her cue to nod or smile or both. Instead, she froze, keys in hand, blinking at him.

Some people didn't react well to the unexpected. "We haven't met before," he said to bridge the silence, and extended his hand. "I'm Dr. Davis." While using his title could seem pompous, it might reassure her that he, too, worked at the medical center.

Another blink. "The hell you are!" she snapped, ignoring his outstretched hand. "Now, if you don't mind?"

He was blocking her path, he realized. "Sorry." Too stunned to figure out how else to react, Nick moved aside at the same moment as the nurse. After an awkward shuffle on the sidewalk, he cut his losses and stomped across the grass toward the parking lot. Behind him, he heard her door open and slam shut.

Sliding into his old blue coupe, Nick replayed the conversation, baffled. He'd said hello and introduced himself, and she'd answered, "The hell you are."

The hell he was what? A doctor? True, he hadn't yet put on his white coat, since he'd rather not risk soiling it. And he sported a few days' growth of stubble, but why should that have provoked her response? Nick liked the casual effect of the beard, and Dr. Mark Rayburn, the administrator, hadn't objected during their interview.

Rayburn *had* initially chosen another doctor for this position, Nick conceded as he exited the parking lot. He'd landed the job after his rival discovered over the holidays that she was pregnant, and decided against taking on such crazy hours.

Still, he'd been the runner-up. He assumed plenty of OBs had applied to the prestigious facility, which over the past half-dozen years had been transformed from a community hospital into an internationally recognized fertility center.

Nope, he decided as he cruised along the quiet residential streets en route to the hospital. His rough jaw wasn't enough to warrant a slammed door.

Maybe the woman simply hated doctors in general. In that case, why had she become a nurse? Or did her blue-flowered uniform indicate something else? Perhaps she worked at a strip joint whose themed attractions included nurse-doctor seductions.

Better idea: quit thinking about her and move on.

The medical complex came into view, dominated by the six-story hospital with its graceful curving wings. Beside it, along the circular driveway, stood the medical building where, during his early-evening hours, Nick shared office space with several fellow obstetricians.

Scaffolding and signs warned of construction at the third low-rise tower, a five-story former dental building recently purchased by the hospital to expand the men's fertility program. It should also, Nick had heard, contain enough remodeled medical suites to liberate the younger obstetrical staff from their cramped quarters.

By the time he parked, it was still only a quarter to six. What a joy to live within a mile of his workplace, he mused as he got out.

Through the early-winter darkness, lights shone from the medical building. Nick entered to see the elevator doors sliding open. He quickened his pace.

Then he spotted its sole occupant, an all-too-familiar woman. The same woman who'd just snubbed him outside his apartment.

How had she zipped over here and gone upstairs? At second glance, he saw that she'd also done a quick change into slacks and a loose top.

Nick halted so fast he stumbled and nearly collided with her. "Excuse me," he muttered.

"No problem." She smiled, which gave her face a softer cast. On further inspection, Nick registered that her hair had grown several inches and her figure had gained a matronly heft.

Obviously, this wasn't the same woman. Waving apologetically, he said, "You startled me. I think I just met your twin."

"Zady?"

They really *were* twins? "She didn't introduce herself."

"Well, that's who she is, Zady Moore. I'm Zora." The young woman extended her hand, which he found firm and warm. "Zora Moore Mendez, to be precise."

"I'm Dr. Nick Davis. I only started working here two days ago, so I haven't met many people," Nick explained. "I'm an OB."

"Oh, your suite is on the third floor." She appeared well informed. "You might have met my husband, Lucky Mendez. He's Dr. Rattigan's nurse, on the fourth floor."

Joining a staff meant learning a lot of names and faces. Doctors had to be adept at memorization to master human anatomy and keep prescription medications straight, and fortunately, Nick had been blessed with an unusually good memory. He didn't need it to identify Dr. Cole Rattigan, though. The renowned urologist headed the men's fertility program here, and was overseeing the transformation of the new building.

"I don't think I've met your husband, but I'm sure I will," Nick said. "Do you work here, too?"

Nearby, a second elevator discharged more people. He ought to hurry, but he hoped for a clue that might account for Zady's rude reaction.

"I'm an ultrasound tech on maternity leave," Zora said. "We have two-month-old twins."

"You must have amazing stamina," Nick told her.

"Why do you say that?"

"No dark circles." He wasn't flattering her. Having stayed up for the past couple of nights, he appreciated how well rested she looked.

"Helpful housemates," the woman said cheerfully. "They're babysitting right now while I bring dinner for Lucky, since he and his doctor are working late."

"I'm sure they're busy these days." It didn't appear that

Nick was going to find out anything more, and he had to go. "Nice meeting you, and your twin."

Zora shared a conspiratorial smile. "I'd say you have a twin of sorts, too."

A possible explanation? Nick went on high alert. "Who's that?"

Her head tilted in surprise. "The other Dr. Davis."

"The other…?" Then it hit him—the explanation for that cute nurse's decidedly unattractive response to him.

Nick should have done a lot more research before he decided to come to Safe Harbor.

Chapter Two

Zady took a late lunch on Friday due to her doctor's busy schedule. A brilliant urological reconstructive surgeon, Dr. Marshall Davis commanded respect bordering on adulation. Since he'd joined Safe Harbor Medical two months ago, patients had flocked to him, putting a heavy load on his office nurse—Zady—as well as his surgical staff.

Zady didn't mind the challenges of the job; she was grateful for it. The man had chosen her from a long list of applicants, and consistently inspired her to do her best. This post might be more stressful than her previous position with a urologist in Santa Barbara, north of Los Angeles, but she took pride in it and it meant a lot to her.

In the cafeteria, she plopped a salad onto her tray and, while waiting in line to pay, surveyed the airy, chatter-filled room for friends. Not that she had many yet, but her twin, Zora, had introduced her to a few people. She'd met others when they greeted her in the hall by the wrong name, and she explained the mistake.

Mistakes. Her sister had phoned her last night to tell her about her encounter with the *other* Dr. Davis. Zady's cheeks heated with embarrassment. Despite her initial shock at being approached by a man who strongly resembled her boss—and then hearing him claim the same name—she should have known better.

After all, *she* had an identical twin. Yet, having done a bit of internet research on her boss, Zady knew the doctor was an only child. And also unmarried, not that she pictured him in a romantic light. Marshall Davis was cool, remote and precise, as a surgeon should be.

According to Zora, the stranger was apparently Marshall's cousin, which explained the strong resemblance. Zora had also heard from her husband—who kept an ear to the ground—that the men didn't get along. Fortunately, they worked in different departments.

Speaking of her brother-in-law, there sat Lucky at a table across the room with his friend and landlady, Karen Wiggins Vintner, a financial counselor. The forty-something Karen, black hair clouding around her thin face, was talking animatedly.

After paying for her salad, Zady started forward, then paused as a lanky male figure crossed her path, her iced tea sloshing in her glass. *Taller than his cousin,* she registered.

"I didn't mean to… Oh, it's you." Nick Davis broke stride, oblivious to having cut off a couple of lab technicians. They circled past, keeping their no-doubt unflattering responses to themselves. "Startling you seems to be a habit of mine."

How had she ever confused him with *her* doctor? That casual air, the smile playing around the corners of his mouth, the way his gaze lingered on her…totally relaxed, but also unwelcome. She recalled what Marshall had said this morning when she mentioned running into his cousin.

"Nicholas is a playboy," he'd commented briskly. "Got a girl pregnant a few years ago and didn't bother to marry her or support their kid. You're too smart to fall for a loser like him."

"You bet I am," she'd answered.

"What should I bet you are?" The object of her mental digression continued blocking her path.

Had she spoken out loud? Zady couldn't believe she'd been so indiscreet, but she must have. Instead of answering—since he had no right to eavesdrop on her private thoughts, even if they had accidentally become audible—she countered with, "What are you doing here? You work nights."

Nick favored her with what many women would consider a heart-stopping grin. "Apology accepted."

"I didn't..." But she *had* been embarrassed when she realized how bizarre her reaction must have sounded last night. "Okay, I was rude."

"Twice." Arms folded, he remained in place, ignoring the heads swiveling toward them. The cafeteria was gossip central, and Zady figured she'd better defuse the situation quickly.

"Sorry." For good measure, she added, "Sorry for the second time, too," and gauged the distance between him and the nearest table. Too narrow to squeeze through without spilling her tea.

"That's it?" This guy couldn't take a hint.

"Are you under the impression that I owe you something?" Zady wished she had the power to shift objects, specifically him. *Telekinesis*, that was the word. If she did, she'd move him across the room to the patio where a group of doctors were enjoying the sunshine that bathed Southern California even in January.

"Courtesy," the man said. "Friendliness to a stranger in a strange land."

"I prefer a more traditional approach to strangers," Zady told him. "Like shooting them with an arrow. Or running in the opposite direction."

"Is that an invitation to give chase?" The twinkle in his eye nearly melted her defenses.

But Zady refused to be played for a fool. A man who'd abandoned his pregnant girlfriend and their child really was a loser. Besides, she knew on which side of the cousinly divide her loyalties lay. A nurse's duties to her doctor went beyond merely following orders.

Instead of dignifying his comment with a reply, she said, "You never answered my question about what you're doing here in the middle of the day."

Glancing toward the patio, Nick nodded to someone on the far side of the glass doors. "I was invited for informal introductions. Due to my last-minute arrival on staff, I gather I'm a little off the usual welcoming schedule."

Outside, the hospital administrator, Dr. Mark Rayburn, waited with a rather strained smile, Zady noted. "Gee, I guess I'll have to let you go. What a pity."

"See you around, stranger." With a teasing twist of the lips, Nick sauntered off.

Why did he enjoy ruffling her feathers? Zady wondered as she headed for Lucky's table. Not that she hadn't enjoyed it, in a perverse manner.

Aware that their interaction had been thoroughly observed, she struggled to smooth out her features.

Except for his nosiness, her brother-in-law was a great guy, she reflected, taking a seat between him and Karen. Not only was he handsome, with dark coloring she credited to his Hispanic heritage, he was also a terrific husband to her sister. Zady would be a happy woman if she could meet someone like him, although preferably minus the elaborate tattoos peeking out from beneath the sleeves of his navy nurse's uniform.

"Enjoy your little chat with the new OB?" Judging by Lucky's amused expression, he'd heard from his wife about Zora's encounter with Nick last night. While Zady would hate to return to the days when she and her twin had barely been on speaking terms, she did *not* care to discuss her reactions to the annoying second Dr. Davis.

To her relief, Karen cut in. "I have you listed for setup for the party," she said, consulting her phone. "We've invited the guests for 2:00 p.m., so you should arrive by noon. It's a week from Saturday, you'll recall."

"It's on my calendar." Mentally, Zady placed the context: a dual-purpose party to be held at Karen's large house. The celebration would serve as an informal reception for Karen and her anesthesiologist husband, Rod Vintner, who'd married in a small ceremony on New Year's Eve. It would also be a joint thirtieth birthday party for Zora and Zady.

Karen's five-bedroom house was home to quite a clan: in addition to Karen, Rod and his two school-age daughters, Lucky, Zora and their twin babies also rented rooms, as did an older nurse.

"Why isn't Zady baking?" Lucky asked. "She's famous for her apple pie." He'd eaten several slices at Thanksgiving.

"I thought you hated anything to do with a kitchen." Karen peered questioningly at Zady.

"I do, sort of." Her forkful of salad hovered in the air. "I hate catering to people. My ex-boyfriend and his snotty kids treated me like a slave." Since the recent breakup of her decade-long relationship, she'd avoided ovens and stoves, except when she had a chance to compete with Zora. They'd both baked pies for Thanksgiving—or rather, that had been the plan. Zady's sense of victory over her superior crust had crumbled when she discovered her sister had sent Lucky to the supermarket to buy her pecan pie.

While her companions continued their party planning, Zady stole a peek at the handshaking ritual on the patio. Nick's easy manner with her had changed to short nods and taut body language. Perhaps he was intimidated by the presence of bigwigs like the fertility chief and the head of the men's program.

With the administrator at his side, Nick moved to the next table, where the slightly less exalted staff members rose to say hello. Perfunctory greetings faded as, across the table, his cousin uncoiled to face him.

Dr. Nick Davis and Dr. Marshall Davis had similar builds, tall and muscular. Zady noted a strong resemblance in other ways, too, from their brown hair and straight noses to their folded arms.

"You can almost smell the testosterone, can't you?" Lucky murmured.

Zady grimaced. "I'm surprised Nick chose to work here, considering their antagonism."

"I'm fairly sure neither of them was aware they both planned to join the staff," Karen said.

"Where'd you hear that?" Lucky, usually the first with the gossip, sounded slightly miffed.

"My lips are sealed."

"Pillow talk," he said in disgust. "Rod heard people yakking in the operating room."

Karen chuckled. "It kills you that my husband picks up scoops without even trying, doesn't it?"

"It's not fair," Lucky replied. "He has nothing to do all day but stand there monitoring his equipment and eavesdropping."

"Maybe he'll move on." When both companions frowned at her, Zady clarified, "I mean Nick. Now that he's discovered his cousin's here, he ought to leave."

"Be careful what you wish for," said her brother-in-law. "The obstetricians thanked their stars when he jumped into the job. They were taking turns delivering babies every night until he signed on."

"Why do you dislike him?" Karen asked Zady.

"I don't." She searched for an honest response and discovered she wasn't sure *how* she felt about the man, and that troubled her. "Marshall doesn't care for him, and that's good enough for me."

"You have a lot in common, though," Lucky said.

"Such as?"

"You both live at the Harbor Suites." He grinned. "I'm sure you'll be borrowing cups of sugar back and forth.

Wait—no kitchen stuff. Okay, cups of laundry detergent. And who knows where that will lead."

"To piles of dirty clothes, if borrowing his detergent is my only option," Zady said. "Besides, I'm only staying at Harbor Suites until I find an apartment."

Which wouldn't be easy. Rentals in the area were too expensive for her to live alone. And although the nurse who rented a room in Karen's house had offered to move out so Zady could join her family, she'd declined. Living there would bring too much intimacy between the sisters. *Way* too much.

"I'm sure he plans to rent a place, as well," Karen said. "Once that happens, I doubt you'll run into him much."

"I guess not. But Safe Harbor's a small town." Even smaller than Costa Mesa, just down the freeway, where Zady had grown up.

"If it's meant to be…" Lucky let the words trail off.

"Don't stop there. Keep having fun at my expense."

"I'm trying." He sighed.

Zady checked her watch. Although she hadn't been out of the office for an hour, she'd finished eating. She could see that Marshall wasn't done his meal, but she wanted to prep his next patients so he'd waste no time on his return.

"Gotta go." She finished her milk with a gulp. "Later, guys." They chorused their farewells.

In the corridor, she was surprised to see Nick. How had he finished eating so quickly? Perhaps he hadn't stayed for lunch, she reflected.

"You weren't waiting for me, were you?" She braced for a flip response.

"Actually, yes." Nick showed no trace of his usual humor. "You didn't tell me you work for my cousin."

"I didn't even know you had a cousin."

He moved aside to let an orderly push a gurney past them. "That was last night. During our conversation earlier today, you did." With a wave of his hand, he dismissed his own comment. "Not your fault. As I'm sure you've gathered, Marshall and I aren't on good terms. It would be unfair to put you in a position of conflicting loyalties."

"Is that what I'm in?"

He ignored the question. "The two of us should keep our distance."

But you're the most interesting thing that's happened since I got here. Now, where had that thought sprung from? True, Zady had lain awake last night reviewing their interaction in light of her sister's revelation, and, a short while ago, she'd relished their verbal sparring. The guy had a quick wit and delightfully teasing manner, although until this moment, she'd considered Nick simply an attractive nuisance.

But if he took this divided-loyalties business seriously, there was no sense arguing. "Agreed."

Despite the flat overhead lighting, shadows touched his eyes. He couldn't have grabbed more than a few hours of sleep since his overnight shift. "It isn't personal. I just prefer that we lay our cards on the table."

"And give them the royal flush," she finished.

"Apt image," he said. "Well, see you around. Or not." As he departed, Zady waited a few beats to avoid the awkwardness of exiting together.

That was that. No more Nick Davis to bump into, trip over and match wits with.

As she walked toward the staff entrance, she reluctantly acknowledged the unpleasant emotion stirring inside her.

Disappointment.

Chapter Three

"You don't have to allow relatives in the delivery room if you'd rather be alone." Nick regarded young Mr. and Mrs. Wang sympathetically.

The wife, seven months pregnant, sat on the examining table in a skimpy hospital gown, while her husband shifted uneasily from foot to foot. Nick would have preferred to have this discussion in a less sterile setting, but he could hardly invite them into his office, which was a former storage closet.

In the week since he'd arrived at Safe Harbor, he'd adjusted fairly well to the overnight schedule. It was harder to double as counselor and lifestyle coach during his two hours of evening consultations, but these appointments brought in extra income and helped him build a patient roster for the future.

"Do we have to let them into the waiting room, either?" asked the husband. "Her mother drives me crazy."

"And his mother drives *me* crazy," added his wife.

"I can issue orders to keep family members in the main lobby," Nick suggested. "It would be simpler if you talked to them honestly, though."

"They'd be horrified." Mrs. Wang shook her head, brown hair tumbling around her shoulders. "I have a PhD in business administration, but around my mother and mother-in-law, I feel about five years old."

"They always cite Chinese traditions," said her husband. "I think they make them up just to torment us."

"Outline your reasons for desiring privacy during the

birth," he said. "Then share them in writing so your parents have a chance to think them over before reacting. And don't forget that family can be an important source of love and support for new parents."

The couple thanked Nick for his advice, and he urged them to contact him with any further questions.

Although he struggled to look wise and fatherly, he felt like a phony.

When Bethany had delivered Caleb, she and her parents hadn't allowed Nick anywhere near her. As for *his* mother, under the circumstances, there'd been no question of inviting her to the hospital, but he wouldn't have done so, anyway. His mom could be charming, but also self-centered and unpredictable. Still, she'd adored her grandson, although she'd died of lung cancer a year after Caleb's birth.

For all her flaws, at least his mom had stuck around during Nick's childhood. His father, who experienced severe mood swings, had kept the household in turmoil until he left for good when Nick was ten. His later, sporadic attempts at reconciliation had ended in disappointment when he failed to appear as promised or talked nonstop, rambling from one topic to another. Yet he'd refused to accept treatment for bipolar disorder.

By the time the Wangs departed, it was nearly eight, and he had to report to the hospital next door. Nick checked the text messages in his phone. According to the charge nurse in L&D, three women had been admitted. All had been seen by obstetricians and labor was progressing normally, with none close to delivering.

He could afford a few minutes to relax. With the Wangs receiving follow-up instructions from evening nurse Lori Sellers, Nick finished entering his notes in the computer and went to drink what would be the first of many cups of coffee tonight. Caffeine kept him alert, but he'd become inured enough to it that he could fall asleep instantly whenever he had a chance to lie down.

In the break room, he found one of his suitemates, Dr. Jack Ryder, eating a slice of cake left by the daytime staff. "Surprised to see you here this late," Nick said, eyeing the last piece set out on the counter.

"I had to perform emergency surgery this afternoon. It put me behind. I offered to let patients return this evening rather than reschedule for a later date, and some of them did." Jack, a handsome fellow oblivious to his impact on the hospital's female staff, indicated the remaining slice. "Help yourself. There's no one else here. Adrienne hightailed it home to relieve her babysitter."

Dr. Adrienne Cavill-Hunter, who'd formerly held down the overnight shift and still maintained evening hours, was married, with a six-year-old son. Nick appreciated sharing an office with fellow parents; Jack had a four-month-old daughter with his wife, a surgical nurse.

As he dug into the cake, Nick considered asking his colleague's advice about his uneasy feelings regarding the Carrigans. The puppet show on Saturday had been fun, and Caleb had snuggled happily with his father at the ice-cream parlor they'd visited afterward. Elaine's nephew and his wife, a couple in their late thirties, had proved likable, as had their little girl.

Yet, twice the couple had changed the subject when Caleb mentioned his grandparents. While Nick didn't wish to act paranoid, his instincts told him the Carrigans were keeping him in the dark about something.

However, he decided against raising the subject with Jack. His fellow obstetrician didn't know the people involved, nor did he necessarily have any relevant experience.

"I've been meaning to talk to you." Jack's statement broke into his thoughts.

"Shoot."

"It's about the office situation. Adrienne believes it's too early, but if we wait, we may lose our chance." Jack stuffed his paper plate into the trash.

"Too early for what?" Nick wasn't keen on hospital politics. Still, he felt a natural affinity for the colleagues who, in some cases, had to work odd schedules and share inadequate office space due to overcrowding.

"The Porvamm." At his blank reaction, Jack explained, "That's our nickname for the Portia and Vince Adams Memorial Medical Building."

That name rang a bell. "The dental building."

His colleague perched on the arm of a couch. "It's got five stories. You'd think there'd be plenty of room to go around, right?"

"Sure." Nick peered into the staff refrigerator on the chance that there might be additional, overlooked treats. No such luck.

"The upper floors will house labs, operating suites and so on for the men's fertility program," Jack told him. "We all hope there'll still be space for the rest of us, but we can't assume. We're forming a committee to encourage Dr. Rayburn to set aside a floor for ob-gyns, pediatricians and neonatologists. Are you in?"

"I'd like to know more about it." Caution paid, especially for a guy who'd been on staff only a week.

"Okay." Jack cleared his throat. "You aren't close to your cousin, are you?"

"That would be an understatement. Why, is he involved?"

The other doctor nodded. "Considering that he just arrived in November, he's already throwing his weight around plenty. Buzzing in Cole Rattigan and Mark Rayburn's ears about making sure there's room for future urology fellows."

"He'd rather leave offices empty than fill them with current doctors who're already overcrowded?" That sounded like Marshall. The spoiled product of a privileged upbringing, he looked down his nose at anyone who wasn't part of his group or, in this case, his medical specialty.

"So you're with us?"

Nick tapped his watch. "Listen, I'm interested, but if I don't get moving, the L&D nurse is going to send out a search party."

"Speaking of parties, you should get better acquainted with the rest of the staff." Jack accompanied him toward the hall. "We're having a get-together Saturday afternoon in honor of my uncle's recent marriage. Anesthesiologist Rod Vintner. You've met him?"

A mental image formed of a slender man wearing a fedora, his short graying beard and mustache neatly trimmed. "Dr. Rayburn introduced us. He's a funny guy."

"Hilarious, mostly at my expense." Jack smiled. "I'll email you the details."

"Thanks. I'd enjoy that." Nick hadn't yet promised to join their committee, but he hoped the invitation stemmed from more than simple politicking. And he *was* eager to widen his circle of acquaintances.

Although he'd grown up and lived until recently only a half hour's drive from here, most of his old friends had marched down the aisle and now socialized as couples.

When it came to dating, Nick had learned caution from his disastrous relationship with Bethany. Since his move, the only woman who'd caught his eye was Zady. How frustrating to run into her not only at the Harbor Suites but also at the supermarket and around their residential motel, and he couldn't do more than say hello.

Even at a distance, he noticed appealing quirks, like her habit of mumbling to herself and then halting with a guilty start. And the ironic slant of her mouth when she regarded him promised peppery rejoinders—if only she'd talk to him.

All the more irksome that he was avoiding her because of his cousin. Nick had learned from Adrienne about a rumor going around the hospital that he'd abandoned his pregnant girlfriend and their son. Only Marshall would spread such a dishonest tale. And although tempted to broadcast the fact that his cousin was a lying snob, Nick had simply told his suitemates the truth and left it at that.

Once people got to know Nick better, it should be easier to counter Marshall's attempts to undermine him. Working nights made that difficult, so the invitation for Saturday was appealing. With his regular visit to Caleb scheduled for Sunday, Nick should have a pleasantly busy weekend.

His thoughts shifted to the evening ahead. Each time he held a newborn in his hands, a sense of wonder swept over him. What more could a man ask than to participate in miracles all night?

Humming tunelessly, he quickened his pace toward the elevator.

HAD THERE EVER BEEN a cuter baby boy in the history of the world? Zady wondered as she gazed down at her nephew, Orlando, snuggling in her arms and wrapped in a hand-crocheted blanket. Two months old and already he could yawn and gurgle with the best of them.

Guiltily, she glanced up at Karen, who was greeting guests. Although Zady had fulfilled her responsibility of setting up the dining room buffet table, she felt as if she should be doing more. Instead, she hadn't been able to resist when her sister laid Orlando in her arms.

The landlady seemed oblivious to Zady's guilty vibes. No one else glared at her, either. Lucky and Zora were welcoming friends, while Rod's daughters, Tiffany and Amber, circulated with trays of appetizers. At thirteen, Tiffany showed signs of developing into a beauty, while eleven-year-old Amber retained a childish playfulness. As they passed their father, Rod helped himself to the treats, proclaiming it his duty to serve as official taster.

Standing in the den of Karen's house, Zady reveled in the waves of love that surrounded her. Unfortunately, the joyous feeling faded at the memory of a blow she'd received this morning.

She'd figured she was completely over Dwayne, her faithless ex-boyfriend. Sure, he could be devilishly sexy, but she'd been a fool to stick around when he kept postponing marriage and children, pointing out that he already had three from his former marriage.

Then he'd cheated on her, impregnated his girlfriend and crowed about becoming a father again. Zady had finally found the strength to dump the guy and, along with him, the decade she'd invested in him.

But this morning, a mutual acquaintance had posted pictures of Dwayne's newborn baby son online.

How could a kid with such rotten genes be so adorable? Not as cute as Orlando, of course, but still… Babies were deceptive. Men were deceptive. Hearts were the worst of all.

Tears stung Zady's eyes. Here it was, her thirtieth birthday, and she had neither a husband nor a baby. Worse, her gut told her it was largely her fault for making really bad choices.

She could use a friend to pour out her troubles to, but everyone here really belonged to her sister, and despite their renewed closeness, Zady didn't feel comfortable unloading her misery on Zora. As for Zady's closest friend from up north, a fellow nurse named Alice Madison, she now lived with her husband and baby in the Los Angeles area, but responded to Zady's communications with brief, impersonal messages.

Whatever the knack was for developing intimacy, it seemed to have bypassed Zady entirely. If only she could find a guy she related to easily, who didn't try to take advantage of her. A guy something like Nick…but with better references.

Keeping her face averted to hide her distress, Zady slipped from the den into the kitchen. Mercifully, it was empty, but any minute someone might wander in, so she carried little Orlando into the pantry. If anyone spotted her, she'd pretend he'd been fussing and needed a spot of quiet.

Sorry for the slander, she mentally wafted to her nephew. Oh, heck, why bad-mouth an innocent child? She'd claim she'd come to fetch a can of olives.

As she'd anticipated, footsteps tromped into the kitchen. "Why shouldn't I have invited him?" That might be Jack Ryder's voice, Zady thought, and wondered who he was discussing. "It's Rod's wedding reception, and he doesn't care."

Care about what? She nearly asked the question aloud. Maybe she should reveal her presence before the conversation went any further.

However, a woman had begun speaking. "This gathering isn't just for Rod and Karen." That must be Jack's wife, Anya. A bubbly surgical nurse, she had once shared an apartment with Zora. "It's also Zora and Zady's birthday party."

What does this have to do with us? Despite the rudeness of listening from the pantry, curiosity held Zora in place.

"Fortunately, it's a big house and people can socialize with whomever they like," Jack retorted cheerfully. "Now, where's that dip?"

"I'm guessing in the refrigerator." The heavy door opened. "Here it is, just like Karen said. Now, I still don't understand why you invited—"

"So we can get better acquainted." Jack sighed. "Okay, truth is, I suggested he join our committee. We need someone who won't be afraid to stand up to Marshall."

What committee and how did this involve Marshall?

Zady owed it to her doctor to discover what might be afoot. And her curiosity was growing by the minute.

"The sooner you present your case to the administration, the less chance of this whole business turning into some ridiculous feud," Anya continued.

"If Marshall weren't so greedy about office space, we wouldn't have to fight him on it," Jack grumbled. "Reserving two entire floors for urologists!"

Now Zady understood the issue. But the dental building had been acquired specifically to expand the men's program. Aside from the fact that he was currently forced to share a suite with several other doctors, Marshall had every right to insist that the Porvamm be used as intended. She wouldn't hesitate to tell Jack that, either, except that a nurse, especially a new one, would be unwise to wade into doctors' politics.

In her self-absorption, Zady had almost forgotten the infant in her arms. With timing that bordered on sabotage, Orlando let out a squawk.

"Hey! Is someone in the pantry?" Male footsteps approached.

Elbowing open the door, which she'd left slightly ajar, Zady emerged. "I was in here fetching, um…" What had she planned to use as an alibi? Her brain refused to cooperate.

Anya paused in removing plastic wrap from a bowl of onion dip, her face a study in confusion. Her tall, handsome husband showed no such uncertainty. "You were spying!"

Zady's mother had always said that the best defense was a good offense. "I needed a moment alone, that's all. How should I know you guys would barrel in here and start discussing state secrets?"

Jack scowled but cast a guilty glance toward the dining room, from which drifted the hum of conversation. "I suppose I shouldn't have brought it up with people around, but I never imagined Marshall's nurse would be lurking with big ears."

"What if Lucky had heard?" Zady retorted. "He works with Cole, and I'm sure they don't keep secrets from each other. *Or* from Dr. Davis."

"She's right," Anya chimed in.

Thank you. Zady decided she shared her sister's high opinion of Anya.

"Will you rat on us when he gets here?" Jack demanded.

"Marshall's coming today?" Zady hadn't expected to run into her boss.

"I assume so. Surely Lucky invited him." Zora's husband, who'd recently earned a master's degree in nursing administration, was helping Dr. Rattigan and Dr. Davis coordinate the growth of the men's program. "You shouldn't blab everything to him."

"How would you like it if your nurse kept *you* in the dark?" she asked.

"He'd hate it." Anya caught her husband's wrist. "Why don't we end this discussion before the whole world gets involved?"

"They soon will be anyway," Jack muttered.

Great. Zady would rather not make enemies, she reflected as the couple exited with the dip. Perhaps she should ask Zora's opinion before informing Marshall. But how unfair to lay that burden on her twin.

Also, Zady had vowed to forge her own path, and this struck her as the kind of tough choice she shouldn't shrink from. Loyalty to Marshall mattered. Too bad it stood between her and his cousin, whom she'd run into twice this week, at the supermarket and in the laundry room.

Each time, her traitorous brain had reacted with a snap of admiration for his tousled good looks. It would be a relief when he or she, or both, found a better place to live.

Orlando, who'd been fussing softly, quit beating around

the bush and let out a wail. Instantly, nursing supervisor Betsy Raditch appeared. "I'll take him," she volunteered, holding out her arms.

Since grandmotherly Betsy doted on babies, Zady relinquished her nephew without a qualm. "Thank you."

"My pleasure." Beaming, the older woman carried off her tiny charge.

In breezed Tiffany and Amber to refill their trays from an array of hors d'oeuvres on the table. With Orlando gone, Zady wished for a task to focus on, but the girls already had the serving job covered.

As if on cue—or perhaps due to the often-rumored psychic link between twins, which had never been much in evidence until now—Zora popped in. "Let's open presents!"

"I love watching people open presents," Amber enthused. The deaths of her mother and stepfather in a car crash last fall had left a mark, but she and her sister were adapting well to sharing a home with their father and his new wife.

"Your parents should go first." Zora assumed the pile of wrapped packages in the living room was mostly for the newlyweds.

"Oh, they requested no more gifts. They already received a ton of stuff." A grin lit Zora's face. As usual these days, she radiated happiness. "Enjoy, sis! Those are for us."

"Those are for us?" Zady asked simultaneously, unintentionally matching her twin's phrasing.

"You guys are cute." Tiffany gazed from Zady to Zora. "You're like reflections in a mirror."

"I'm chubbier these days," Zora said cheerily. "Breastfeeding and all."

"And you have more freckles," Zady teased. That had been the subject of arguments between them during their teen years.

"She smiles more, too," Amber noted.

"She deserves to." Zady draped an arm around her sister's shoulders. "Okay, let's—" She flinched as the doorbell rang.

That must be Marshall. With an unpleasant jolt, she realized that telling him about the plot might spoil everyone's mood. Best to get it over with quickly, like ripping off an adhesive bandage. "I'll answer that."

"Why you?" Zora inquired.

"Because I'm faster," she retorted, and took off for the front of the house.

No one else had responded, probably because the front door stood partly open and most guests just walked in. But Marshall had a more formal personality. No wonder he remained on the porch, an appealing figure with his dark, brooding air.

Zady stopped short. She'd done it again. This wasn't Marshall, it was Nick.

What was he doing here? And why did she experience a rush of warmth when his startled gaze met hers?

He cleared his throat when he saw her. "I didn't realize you'd be here."

"I had no idea you were coming, either." Despite the many reasons why he was bad news, Zady nearly added, "I'm glad you came."

She was saved—or thrown under the bus—by Jack's sudden appearance at her side. "She knows about our plans," he told Nick. "And she intends to spill it to Marshall, so don't trust her."

"That's the last time I ever hide in a pantry," Zady blurted, and marched off, leaving Jack to show Nick around. Not even the sight of her sister gesturing toward a pile of presents could restore her high spirits.

Well, not quite.

Chapter Four

At the sight of Zady, a thrill skittered along Nick's nervous system, and he didn't miss the welcoming glint in her eyes, either. As his fellow MD prattled on about the committee and Zady's alleged spying, he experienced a surge of annoyance, not at her but at Jack for inserting a wedge between them.

Although not crazy about Zady's allegiance to Marshall, Nick rather admired her initiative in hiding in the pantry. He disliked doing what people expected, possibly because while he was growing up people had often expected the worst of him. So he appreciated the same irreverent trait in others.

Still, the situation emphasized the gap between him and the lively nurse. He'd never intended for his lifelong one-upmanship with Marshall to turn into a Hatfields versus McCoys feud, even though it *was* unfair to deny Nick's colleagues their share of office space.

"As to your committee, I haven't agreed to anything until I learn more," he reminded Jack when the man paused for breath.

"I figured I should warn you."

"Consider me warned." It was counterproductive to snap at the guy who'd invited him today, but because of Jack, Nick had lost his chance at a private conversation with Zady. She'd joined her sister in the center of a dozen or so well-wishers, beneath a banner reading, Happy 30th Birthday!

"Speaking of warnings," Nick added, "you told me the party was for your uncle."

"It is, among others. Does it matter?"

More than you can imagine. "Never mind." Nick tried to smile, achieved a grimace and cleared his throat. "I can't wait to meet your wife."

"Anya's right over here."

While shaking hands with a charming woman who struck him as a sensible counterweight to her husband's enthusiasms, Nick made a quick survey of the living room. The striped sofa, gleaming curio cabinet and formal raised dining room reinforced his impression of elegance. As he drove up, he'd admired the ocean view and the blue-trimmed white house that dominated the block.

Impulsively, he muttered, "Beautiful place. Must be nice to be rich."

"Karen?" Anya said. "She's not. She inherited the house in bad shape. To pay for refurbishing, she had to take in renters."

Kicking himself for being judgmental, Nick said, "I shouldn't leap to conclusions. But now that she's married an anesthesiologist, surely they can afford to keep the place to themselves."

"Rod's practically broke." Jack shrugged. "He spent years fighting for custody of his daughters, whom he lost to their billionaire stepfather. That would be the late Vince Adams, who endowed the Porvamm to the hospital."

"And now, here we are." A red-haired girl in her early teens presented a tray filled with stuffed mushrooms. "Is this the cute new doctor Zora's been talking about? Hi, I'm Tiffany Adams."

"I'm Nick Davis, and thanks for the compliment." He'd have extended his hand, but hers were already occupied. Instead, he selected an hors d'oeuvre.

"Sorry for gossiping," Jack said.

"I forgive you. Don't do it again, cuz." After a mock attempt to kick his ankle, the girl moved on.

What an interesting group, Nick mused. He'd heard that Tiffany and her younger sister, who must be the flame-haired kid also passing out treats, had inherited a fortune, but they didn't act snobbish. There was nothing wrong with money as long as you didn't let it inflate your ego or corrupt your values, as it seemed to have with Marshall and his parents.

A shout of laughter erupted around the gift table. Zady and Zora were performing an impromptu baton-twirling routine with a pair of canes, no doubt a gag gift implying they'd become decrepit with age. Karen, watching beside her husband, gazed anxiously at a nearby lamp.

The twins halted amid giggles. "You'd better keep these." Zora handed both canes to Rod. "As you can see, we're a menace."

"Sorry, Karen," Zady added.

"No harm done," responded the bride.

Observing the sisters together, Nick was again struck by the similarities of coloring, height and mannerism, but also by the differences. Thinner, with reddish-brown hair a shade lighter than her twin's, Zady had a more reserved manner and a trace of sadness around the eyes.

What was bothering her? Her gaze kept returning to the pink-blanket-wrapped baby girl nestled in Lucky's arms. Longing to be a mother, too?

Ironically, Nick had had a son before he'd even thought about fatherhood. In the three years since then, Caleb had changed him. If only he could offer his son an ideal home, with two happily married parents, but that hadn't been in the cards. Now Nick was determined to provide the boy with as much stability as possible, but it was proving an uphill battle.

Elaine Carrigan had led him through yet another song-

and-dance routine about tomorrow's meetup with Caleb. She'd seemed especially reluctant to have Nick visit their home. Only when Nick demanded straight out that she tell him what was wrong had she backed down and suggested he arrive after lunch for a play session.

The couple owned a large house in a semirural setting. Bethany had cited her desire to raise their son there as one of several reasons for rejecting Nick's offer of marriage, and the Carrigans had emphasized how much Caleb loved the place when they'd urged Nick to let him stay with them after Bethany's death.

But what was going on now? Had the house become unsafe, or were they trying to edge him out of the boy's life? Worst-case scenario: they planned a bid for custody and, by reducing contact, aimed to portray him as an indifferent father.

Tomorrow, he'd find out.

Across the room, the twins were laughing again as they displayed the contents of an over-the-hill survival kit: fang-like teeth, bottle-thick glasses and Halloween-worthy black wigs. They called out thanks to the eminent Dr. Cole Rattigan.

When Nick had met him at the hospital, the man had inclined his head with royal coolness, leaving an impression of arrogance. Today, however, he beamed at everyone. No doubt both his attitude and the funny gift owed a lot to the elfin woman with him, also the object of the twins' gratitude. That must be his wife, Stacy.

An older woman with graying dark hair brushed past Nick to scoop wrapping paper and ribbons into a trash bag. She was clearly the other housemate he'd heard about, a nurse. "Ready for cake?" she asked the birthday duo.

"You bet, Keely." Thanking everyone again, Zora piled the gifts neatly, while Zady silently gathered the remaining wrappings. Struck by her reticence, Nick recalled that these were her sister's friends. While everyone appeared to welcome her, he wondered if she, too, felt like an outsider.

Most of the residents and guests trooped into the den, where Nick had seen a cake on display. Only he and Zady lingered in the living room.

"I'd have brought a gift if I'd realized it was your birthday." He bent to lift one end of the coffee table as she raised the other.

"Like we need more gag gifts?" She indicated a spot where the table legs fit into carpet indentations. "Don't worry about it."

Nick helped lower the piece gently. "You should go blow out candles and help cut the cake."

"Those big-number three and zero candles? Zora can manage. As for cake-cutting, when my brother-in-law sees dessert, everybody better clear a path."

"It's your birthday," he reminded her. "I'll finish straightening here. Go eat."

Zady's wry gaze met his. "I'd rather wait till…"

When she broke off, Nick guessed the rest. "Till Marshall arrives?"

"Yes. I'd like to get that out of the way."

"The tattling part?"

She blew a strand of hair sideways off her cheek. "Yeah. The part where I metaphorically stab you in your evil heart. Does that sum it up?"

"I haven't yet thrown in my lot with the conspiracy," Nick responded mildly. "Although I do agree that space should be allotted to other doctors."

"That's not my problem." Zady planted hands on hips. "Anything else?"

Nick had trouble organizing his thoughts with her standing there, her face animated and her knit top stretching over her breasts. "Yeah. You look really cute."

"How condescending!"

"Have trouble accepting compliments, do you?"

"Only from the devil's minions." She laughed.

"Hey, I'm a good guy. Mostly." Judging by the noises from the den, everyone had dug into the cake. Nick was too busy enjoying the conversation to care about dessert. "I deliver babies night and day. Well, night and sometimes day if we're busy." He'd stayed until 10:00 a.m. once this week.

Zady studied him. "Why *do* you work such long hours? It must interfere with your swinging-bachelor life."

"Is my cousin trotting out that old 'He's a playboy' crap?" In all honesty, Nick was partly to blame for the image. At a family gathering years ago, he'd called Marshall a stuffed shirt and bragged about his own playboy antics—mostly invented—while sailing to the top of his medical school class at UCLA.

He'd been aware that his successes, which resulted as much from a top-notch memory as from hard work, had been a sore spot with his cousin. A year older and proud of his admission to Harvard Medical School, Marshall had assumed he should be superior at everything. Instead, he'd struggled with his studies until he hit on his true talent as a surgeon.

"Let me guess. Your goal is to get rich enough to buy your own hospital," Zady said.

"Don't forget the private fleet of jets." Okay, enough teasing. Nick could see from her dubious expression that she half believed him. "I don't come from wealthy parents like my cousin. I'm paying off med school and supporting a son. I have a three-year-old—no doubt he mentioned that."

"In passing."

"What did he say, exactly?"

"That you weren't involved with raising your child." Her guarded tone implied she was softening his cousin's comments.

"I'm as involved as I can arrange." No more light tone.

"Caleb's mother died six months ago in a boating accident. I let him stay with his grandparents, but I visit every week. However, during the last month, they've become—"

Although he wasn't sure why he'd started to confide in her, he felt a flash of irritation when the doorbell interrupted. If that was Marshall, Nick doubted he'd get a further chance to explain. Still, he appreciated being able to correct a few of Zady's false impressions.

In fairness, Marshall had no doubt only repeated what he'd heard from his mother, who must have drawn what she considered a logical conclusion from the fact that Nick didn't marry the woman carrying his child. Neither his cousin nor his aunt was likely to give Nick the benefit of any doubt.

"I'd like to hear more, if you're still speaking to me," Zady said before hurrying to answer the door.

How much more should he share? Well, Nick *could* use feedback about his current concerns. He'd hate to misinterpret the Carrigans' behavior and antagonize them needlessly. However, once Zady told Marshall about the forces allied against him, he would raise the drawbridge and release crocodiles into the moat.

Luckily, I know how to swim and dodge at the same time. Nick only regretted that the barrier between him and Zady, which had lifted briefly today, would once again slam into place.

DESPITE HER PLAN to share what she'd learned, Zady found that difficult as she welcomed her doctor into the house. His expression guarded, Marshall squared his already straight shoulders beneath his dark blue jacket and handed her two gifts decorated with satiny paper and elaborate bows.

"Happy birthday."

"Thanks." Zady cast an uneasy glance toward the living room, but Nick had vanished. "Come in."

Now what should she say? She could hardly blurt, *"By the way, while I was lurking in the pantry sulking about my ex-boyfriend's baby, I eavesdropped on a plot."* How melodramatic.

Also, what Nick had said about his son gave her pause. While she doubted Marshall had been deliberately untruthful, he'd gotten his facts wrong. That was unrelated to the conspiracy, but was it wise to choose sides?

"Everybody's in here." The gifts in her arms, she led him to the den.

The sight of Dr. Rattigan drew a smile from Marshall. Pleased to see him unwind a little, Zady introduced her boss to a few people en route to joining his supervisor. After he seemed settled, she and Zora opened his gifts.

The boxes contained expensive skin-care products. "Ooh, this smells wonderful!" Zora exclaimed. "Zady and I can have a beauty day."

"These are fabulous," Zady agreed.

Marshall ducked his head. "The department store clerk recommended them. I'm afraid I'm no expert on gifts for ladies."

"You did great." Lucky approached carrying slices of red-velvet cake with cream-cheese frosting. "Here you go, Dr. Davis. Zady, you, too."

There was plenty of cake left, she noticed, and remembered that Nick hadn't had any. Where *was* he?

Ah, there, hanging back near the kitchen. One of the Adams girls, trying to squeeze past, bumped him and giggled loudly, drawing everyone's attention.

If someone had whacked Marshall with a rod, he couldn't have reacted more strongly. At the sight of his cousin, every muscle in his body stiffened.

Zady might have responded pretty much the same had she run into Zora unexpectedly before they reconciled last fall. Their dysfunctional mother had pitted them against each other their entire lives, but once Zady moved back to the area, she and her sister had quickly seen through the lies. Whatever misunderstandings—or well-grounded enmities—lay between these cousins probably had deeper roots.

The men nodded in mute acknowledgment. Zora broke the tension by declaring that the wrappings were too lovely to throw away. "You never know when they'll come in handy. Maybe for a craft project."

Zady joined her in folding them. "I'm sure we'll reuse them."

Leaving his untouched plate on a side table, Marshall hurried to pick up a bow that had dropped to the carpet. "I'd hate to leave a mess," he explained, handing it to her.

"Thanks," she said. "But you should take it easy. You're a guest."

"If something needs doing, I'd rather take care of it immediately," he replied.

The doctor was uncomfortable at social gatherings, Zora reflected. Perhaps that explained why, according to hospital gossip, he didn't have much of a private life. *Which is none of my business.* "Enjoy your cake. Unless you haven't eaten any real food yet?"

"Oh, there's food?" He glanced around.

Zady was directing him to the dining room, when the usually bashful Dr. Rattigan cleared his throat loudly. "While everybody's here, I have an announcement."

The conversations died down. Amber and Tiffany stopped joking with their father, and Jack froze, as if fearing Cole might hand out the office suites willy-nilly.

"This won't be officially announced until tomorrow, but I believe that Luke's family and friends ought to hear it first." Cole was the only person Zady knew who referred to Lucky by his formal name. "He's being promoted to director of nursing for the men's fertility program."

Cheers broke out. "Way to go!" and "Well deserved!" flew through the air. Zora rushed to hug her husband, and Betsy—director of nursing for the hospital staff—called congratulations to her newly elevated colleague.

Lucky started to speak but had to try several times before the words flowed. "I can't tell you how much this honor means to me. It's been a long haul for a guy who started his career as a security guard and an ambulance driver. To have Cole Rattigan believe in me is a dream come true."

"We all believe in you," Karen called.

"Don't overdo it," Rod declared. "He still has to wash dishes later."

Encouraged by his friends, Lucky clasped his hands in a victory salute. On his right arm, a tattooed dragon wriggled menacingly. On the left, a cartoon woman whose armor emphasized her physical bounty waved her sword at the beast.

"Dare we hope he'll get those ugly tats removed?" Marshall muttered so low that Zady doubted anyone else heard.

Don't you realize he's my brother-in-law? Although she wasn't crazy about the tattoos, either, the remark struck her as inappropriate at a moment when they were celebrating Lucky's achievement.

She recalled Nick's comment about Marshall's privileged upbringing. Much as she admired her doctor, it must be hard for him to understand what an achievement it was for a guy from a poor neighborhood in LA to earn his RN and then his master's degree in administration, studying at night while working days.

When the crowd around Lucky thinned, Marshall moved forward to shake his hand. He did have good manners, she mused, but that insight into his thinking had left a sour taste. Zady decided that whatever confidence she wished to impart to her boss could wait—or she might stay out of this altogether. Since Marshall was already guaranteed a large suite in the remodeled building, he wouldn't be directly affected by the administration's decision.

The grumbling in her stomach reminded her that it was nearly four o'clock. Having skipped lunch, she wandered through the kitchen into the dining room, where, despite earlier depletions, there were still plenty of cold cuts and side dishes.

The only person in the room, Nick, stood filling a pita pocket with hummus. As she watched, he tucked in thin-sliced ham and several pickle chips, finishing it all off with a squirt of mustard.

"I hope your medicine cabinet's stocked with antacids." She took a paper plate off the stack.

"It's fun trying new food combinations," he responded, and added sliced black olives to the mix. "Speaking of food, have you spilled the beans yet?"

"Excuse me?" Zady spread mayonnaise on whole wheat bread before layering on corned beef and Swiss cheese.

"Have you told my cousin about the big conspiracy? I've been waiting for him to glower in that winning fashion of his." Edging alongside her, Nick smelled of coffee and spicy mustard. "Try that stinky cheese over there." As he spoke, he plopped a hunk of it into his already stuffed pita.

"Can you wait a minute? I'll have to leave the room once you start eating that," Zady said.

"I'm not the person who bought it," he remarked cheerily. "What did you stock for Marshall's palate? I don't see escargots. How about some pâté de foie gras? I can hardly pronounce it."

"There's nothing wrong with French cuisine unless you're a reverse snob." She sliced her sandwich diagonally in half. "Well, maybe that pâté." She'd read that its manufacture involved cruelty to geese.

"You pegged me right, I'm a reverse snob." A sexy chuckle tickled her ear. "I'm low class and proud of it."

She added potato salad to her plate. "To answer your question, I've decided to stay out of office politics."

"Sensible of you." Following her example, Nick went for a serving of potato salad, then topped it with chives and salsa.

"You doctors should bring your issues into the open and discuss them like adults."

"That assumes we *are* adults." He hesitated. "Listen, I have a favor to ask."

"Does it involve eating stinky cheese?"

He shook his head. "It involves driving across the county with me tomorrow to visit my son." His tone had lost its teasing lilt.

What a strange request. "Why?"

"I need an objective observer for a tricky situation." Nick had switched gears so abruptly that Zady found herself bracing for a punch line. Instead, he explained, "Caleb's grandparents have been stalling me whenever I try to visit, and I'm not sure what's behind it. His grandmother has become, well, unpredictable."

She was no expert on kids, nor was she eager to be on closer terms with the second Dr. Davis. Still, the request sounded genuine. Like her, he had few friends in Safe Harbor, and it showed that he placed a lot of trust in her. How could she say no if it meant helping him to see his little boy more?

"I suppose I could ride along," Zady said.

"And possibly distract the little guy if I need a minute alone with Mr. and Mrs. Carrigan?"

"Sure. I like kids." Zady hadn't meant to volunteer for babysitting duty, but she wanted to find out more about Nick's son.

"It would mean a lot to me." Reaching across the table, Nick plucked a radish from a bowl and added it to her plate. "A token of my esteem, madam."

"I'm overwhelmed."

They were grinning when Marshall emerged from the kitchen. He broke his stride, his high cheekbones coloring.

Oh, great. He probably assumed they were flirting, which they weren't—exactly. Zady nearly rushed in with an explanation, but they'd been discussing Nick's private business. Also, what she did on her days off didn't concern Marshall.

"See you around," she told Nick, and, with a smile for her boss, carried her food away to eat in peace.

Chapter Five

Keenly aware of the proximity of other people, Nick kept his voice low as he faced his cousin across the dining room. "Don't take it out on her."

"Don't take what out on her?" Marshall frowned at a cabinet full of showy china, then—with an expression of distaste—plucked a paper plate off the stack. Funny how easily Nick tracked his cousin's reactions, even though they'd avoided contact these past few years. "You mean I shouldn't blame her because she's on good terms with my cousin? As always, you assume I'm an ogre."

As always, I'm probably right. That would sound childish, Nick conceded. "I had no idea you'd joined the staff."

"Same here." With surgical precision, Marshall formulated a sandwich, trimming off edges of meat and cheese that lapped over the crust. "I've admired Cole Rattigan for years. Anyone would leap at the opportunity to join his program and play a role in its growth."

Leaning against a wall, Nick started to bite into his pita, but he'd overfilled it. To avoid smearing his face, he returned it to his plate. "My motives were less noble. I applied for the overnight labor-and-delivery shift, plus evening hours, to pay for my student loans." He paused, unsure whether to reveal more.

"Is that a slam?" Marshall asked, measuring a small, rounded serving of carrot salad.

"How would that be a slam?"

"You resent my financial advantages," his cousin said.

"I'd love to be debt-free," Nick conceded. "I'd also love

to have had a father like yours who supported his family instead of abandoning them. That doesn't mean I resent you for either."

Marshall's eyes narrowed. Had Nick unwittingly stepped on his toes with such a plain statement of fact?

"I hadn't considered your perspective." Marshall gazed distractedly through the window toward the wetlands that bordered Karen's property.

Above the brown-and-green expanse, a pelican took flight, and Nick recalled reading that the estuary was a bird sanctuary. Its decomposing vegetation was also the source of a rotten-egg smell he'd noticed outside. Mercifully, it either didn't penetrate the house or he'd quickly grown accustomed to it.

His cousin continued, "But you haven't considered my perspective, either."

"Enlighten me."

"My dad may have paid the bills, but he spent almost every waking minute running his company." The late Upton Davis had founded a medical-device firm to market his designs. "I wish he'd spent more time with me. But you're right. I was lucky I didn't have an alcoholic father."

"Dad's primary problem wasn't alcoholism, it was being bipolar." Nick didn't mean to defend the man. "Not that that's an excuse. He failed in his obligations and I'm still picking up the pieces."

Marshall shrugged. "The bottom line being, we're colleagues now."

"And since we are, let me clear up a misconception." No sense allowing ignorance to fester. "Whatever you may have heard, I did not abandon my son. I've helped support Caleb for the past three years and visited as often as his mother and my schedule would allow. Now that she's dead, I have legal custody, although at present he's staying with his grandparents."

"You have custody of your son? I apologize for misinforming Zady." Marshall's face revealed an unexpected glint of longing. "And you named him Caleb after our grandfather? That's excellent."

When Nick had suggested it before the birth, Bethany had merely added it to her list of possible names. He was grateful she'd chosen it. "Too bad Grandpa didn't live to meet his namesake."

His cousin swallowed. "You're a lucky guy."

"Yes, I am." It had never occurred to Nick that Marshall might envy him for being a father. Perhaps the man's steely surface and superior attitude didn't tell the whole story.

The drift of people into the adjacent living room discouraged further conversation. Jack Ryder quirked an eyebrow at Nick as if to ask what he and Marshall had been discussing.

Did this dispute about the dental building have to spark armed us-against-them camps? Well, perhaps where he and his cousin were concerned, a certain amount of antagonism was inevitable.

Taking his leave, he carried his bulging pita into the kitchen to eat over the sink and dispose of the mess.

Zady had had a point, he reflected, and not only about fixing smaller sandwiches. Staying out of office politics was a prudent policy, not that he would necessarily adopt it.

He hoped for more of her good advice tomorrow. Six months ago, allowing the Carrigans to keep his son had been the best course for the boy's well-being, but that had changed.

WHAT DID YOU WEAR on a not-date with an attractive man while avoiding a wrong impression, especially when you weren't sure what the right impression was?

Zady laid out several pairs of pants, then removed the jeans because the little boy's grandparents might disapprove. Then again, no matter how strongly Nick assured them Zady was merely a friend, they'd undoubtedly compare her to their daughter's sainted memory. They must still be grieving deeply.

She studied her remaining choices. Navy slacks and a print blouse struck her as too much like a uniform. What about tan slacks and a red, blue and tan–striped shirt? Should she pair it with a red sweater or a tan one?

She could use feedback—not Zora's, since Zady wasn't about to spread the word that she'd be accompanying Nick. She missed the easy exchanges of opinion she'd had with her friend Alice Madison. They used to consult each other about all sorts of issues when they worked in the same medical building in Santa Barbara.

Zady picked up the phone. It ought to be possible to reestablish ties, since Alice's new address in Culver City was less than an hour's drive from here. They might even meet for lunch occasionally on weekends.

Several buzzes later, her friend's voice responded with a puzzled "Hello?"

Hadn't she recognized Zady's number? "It's me, Zady."

A pause, then a lackluster "Hi."

Judging by her friend's uncharacteristic lack of energy, all was not well. Zady felt foolish for calling about such a trivial matter. Her heart squeezed at the possibility that anything might be wrong with Alice's little girl, Linda, who was Zady's godchild. A health problem would also cxplain why she'd received only a perfunctory email thanking her for the doll playhouse she'd sent at Christmas.

"How are things?" Zady asked.

"Not good." Alice took a shaky breath. "Bill and I may be splitting."

"You can't!" *Great response.* "I mean, he seems like such a nice guy."

In her late thirties, Alice had recovered from an early divorce and become a radiant bride, marrying a physiotherapist who shared her goals and showered her with affection. Pooling their medical expertise and interest in health, they'd launched a company that put on lifestyle seminars and sold health supplements and portable exercise equipment.

"We thought moving to Southern California would be fantastic for business, and it has been," Alice said. "What we didn't count on was the amount of work it would be. Add a toddler to the mix and we hardly ever have a free moment. When we do, we argue."

Tucking the phone against her shoulder, Zady changed into the tan pants. "This is a temporary glitch. You can work through it."

"Bill set up a month's worth of seminars around the Western states without consulting me." Alice sighed. "He says he can handle it by himself, but if I'm not there, things will fall apart. This tour is too much for one person to coordinate. I told him to cancel it until Linda's older, but he insists we have to strike while the iron is hot."

"That's hardly a reason to divorce him." Discovering that she'd buttoned her shirt crooked, Zady started over. She'd promised to meet Nick in less than fifteen minutes.

"He's high-handed and condescending," Alice burst out. "I assumed we'd be true partners. Instead, he acts as if he's the boss and I'm the employee."

Zady could hardly suggest Alice learn to tolerate such a situation. Still, she couldn't encourage her friend to abandon her marriage, either. "Sit down with him and figure out a compromise. Your little girl needs both her parents."

"You really love her, don't you?"

"Of course!" Zady said. "I just wish I could spend more time with her."

"You wouldn't...do anything, would you?"

"Do anything?" Then it hit Zady what she meant. "Of course not!"

Nearly four years ago, after Alice had learned that her body was no longer producing viable eggs, she'd wept on Zady's shoulder. She'd have been content to adopt and Bill had agreed, but as the only child of high-achieving parents, he'd longed for a baby to carry on his family's genetic heritage. And Alice wanted to provide one.

As an obstetrical nurse, Alice had colleagues who had been willing to waive their usual fees for the in vitro procedure, but she and Bill would have had to go into debt to pay for an egg donor. Without hesitation, Zady had volunteered, and the process had brought the women even closer.

When their baby girl was born, Zady had been thrilled to be chosen as godmother. Alice and Bill had considered her part of the family, welcoming her offers to babysit Linda.

After they moved to the Los Angeles area, she'd driven down from Santa Barbara occasionally to babysit on weekends when they were tied up with seminars. But these past few months they'd grown distant. Zady had assumed her move to Orange County would help, but now she understood why Alice had been reluctant to confide in her.

"I know you counted on us to raise Linda as a married couple." Alice's voice trembled. "But this is beyond my control."

"I would never interfere." Zady had signed legal papers surrendering her rights. And much as she loved her goddaughter, she was in no position to raise a child unless there was no other option.

"I'm glad you called. It's been hard for me to get any perspective on the situation." Alice broke off as a toddler's voice squawked in the background. "Oh dear, she's finished her nap already."

The girl's cry of, "Mommy, I need you!" cut straight to Zady's heart. When she'd last seen Linda, the child had just begun stringing two words together, and now she'd spoken a whole sentence. She was growing up fast.

Without me. But that had been the arrangement, and she had no intention of trying to change that. "Will you consider having a serious discussion with Bill?" Zady asked. "Or is it too late for that?"

"No. I was just letting off steam. I haven't consulted a lawyer or anything." Alice sounded less frazzled. "You're a terrific friend. I should have remembered that sooner."

"Please stay in touch. I care about you."

"I'll call with an update when I have one."

"You can count on me."

After they said goodbye, Zady finished dressing and applied makeup, her mind whirling. Would Linda really have to grow up in a single-parent home? Surely a five-minute conversation with her hadn't resolved Alice's problems.

Zady had believed she was doing the right thing by donating her eggs and entrusting her daughter to two loving parents. Surely interfering now would be selfish, and possibly harmful. Or was she rationalizing?

It would be hard to focus on Nick's issues with his son while her thoughts were buzzing with what she'd learned. But she'd promised to be there for him and his little boy, and Zady meant to keep her word.

NICK WISHED HE'D done more than muck out the empty fast-food sacks and grocery receipts littering his blue coupe before Zady climbed in. As he steered onto the freeway with Zady belted into the seat beside him, her soft floral fragrance sensitized him to the messy accumulation of lint, fingerprints and window streaks that a bachelor took for granted.

But surely there was another cause for her remote attitude than his messy car. Since she hadn't brought it up, he risked a guess. "In case you're worried, Marshall didn't seem concerned about you and me having a friendly chat yesterday."

"Did you mention today's trip?" Zady asked.

"It never came up."

"I'll tell him tomorrow, unless you'd rather I didn't talk about your son."

"No, that's fine. I corrected his erroneous impression about my relationship with Caleb."

"How'd he take it?"

"Oddly enough, with a touch of envy."

Zady didn't respond. She continued gazing out the window at a cluster of low-rise buildings.

It wasn't an inspiring landscape. Far from the beach and harbor from which the town's name derived, the view included stretches of modest houses punctuated by big-box stores and light-industrial buildings.

Zady's silence left room for Nick to ponder what lay ahead. He'd concentrated on paying off his debts and saving for a down payment on a house, equating economic security with providing a loving home. *But I'm his father.* Having grown up largely without one, Nick, of all people, understood what a painful hole it left in a child's heart to live apart from his father.

He'd considered his cousin incredibly lucky to have a dad who stuck around. But judging by Marshall's comments yesterday, Upton Davis's occasional presence hadn't been enough.

"I've been thinking," he said aloud. "Maybe I owe it to my son to bring him to live with me."

Zady swiveled toward him. "I realize these are his grandparents, but to a little kid, they're like parents. He must have bonded with them. You can't just yank a kid out of a happy home because you love him."

What did *she* know about it? "My goal is to keep him safe and happy," Nick protested. "I'm questioning whether I've been fair about that."

She folded her arms. "You brought me along for my feedback, right?"

"Yes. And?"

"And I have the impression that you've been willing to stay on the fringes of his life if that's what's best," she returned. "If he's happy with his grandparents, why change now?"

"I haven't committed to changing anything." Nick didn't understand why she spoke with such fervor. "I'm afraid the Carrigans may plan to sue for custody, and they're building a case that I'm a neglectful dad."

"And you'll fight them for all you're worth, no matter what's best for your son?"

He was growing more confused by the minute. "I assumed you'd be objective."

"I am!"

"Then where is this coming from?"

Her mouth opened, and quickly clamped shut. Busy transitioning onto another freeway, Nick allowed her space to reflect.

"I suppose it would help if I knew more about the circumstances of Caleb's birth and your relationship with his mother," Zady said more mildly.

"Good idea." Nick recalled telling her that Bethany had died in a boating accident, but that left a lot of ground to cover. "About four years ago, I'd just finished my residency at UC Irvine and was working at a clinic in Fullerton, near where I grew up. When I met Bethany at a party, we clicked right off. Mutual attraction and all that."

"Hot sex," she summarized.

No point in dwelling on that obvious truth. "She was fun to be around." Bethany had had thick dark hair, a merry laugh and, he'd discovered, a flawed sense of responsibility. "We dated for a few months. She told me she was on the pill, and I used a condom, too. Hey, I'm a doctor, not an idiot."

"The pill failed and the condom leaked?" Zady rolled her eyes. "Yeah, right. In case you forgot, *I'm* a nurse."

"It turned out that Bethany only took the pill sporadically. But I'll admit, I got careless, too. We were both responsible."

Even on a Sunday, there was a steady stream of cars and trucks on the road, but having a passenger enabled Nick to use the carpool lane. He accelerated onto a soaring single-lane overpass, swooping above regular traffic.

"Having fun?" Zady asked.

Taking the hint, he eased off the gas. "Too fast?"

"I left my stomach back on the 55," Zady said. "However, I appreciate the illustration of how you approach relationships—full speed ahead."

"Unfair," he protested.

"Finish the story."

Blending into the carpool lane on Interstate 5, Nick dredged up more memories from that difficult period. "When Bethany told me she was pregnant, I did what I figured was the right thing. I asked her to marry me."

Zady regarded him skeptically. "A romantic proposal with flowers, a ring and so forth?"

"More of a 'we should get married' proposal," Nick admitted.

"And to your astonishment, she declined."

"She insisted on placing the baby for adoption."

"You didn't object?"

"I had no right to pressure her," he said. "How could I insist Bethany do what I wasn't prepared for—raise a child alone?"

"It's hard to face the consequences of your actions," she murmured.

About to protest this slur on his character, Nick hesitated.

There was some truth to it, he supposed. He'd reached quite a few major decisions without fully considering where they might lead. While many had worked out well, that had been due as much to luck as to his merits.

When asked why he became an obstetrician, he generally responded that nothing compared to the adrenaline rush of delivering a baby. But the real story was more complicated.

While his decision to become a doctor had sprung in part from his passion for science, Marshall's determination to study medicine had provided the crucial impetus. If his cousin could do it, so could Nick.

He'd proved that by gaining admission to medical school and excelling in his classes. As for his specialty, during his training, he'd been surprised at how many of his classmates picked a field because it offered a regular schedule. Among the most popular had been radiology, dermatology and anesthesiology. Few were willing to pursue obstetrics, with its irregular hours, stressful demands and life-and-death urgency.

As a workaholic, Nick didn't object to the hours, and he believed women deserved excellent medical care. He'd never regretted selecting this specialty.

Yet he hadn't truly fallen in love with babies until he'd held Caleb in his arms, a week after the birth when Bethany had finally allowed him to visit. The precious little guy, helpless and innocent and filled with untold possibilities, had sneaked right into Nick's heart and laid claim to it, forever.

"I'm still sorting out the consequences of becoming a father," he conceded in response to Zady's remark.

"What changed Bethany's mind about adoption?"

"Her parents," he said. "The Carrigans showered her with attention and gifts, pointing out that this might be their only grandchild. Which turned out to be true."

"Gilt and guilt. That first one was without the *u*," she noted.

"Got it."

"Tell me about the Carrigans," Zady said. "I need to be prepared."

Images sprang to mind: Benjamin Carrigan, or Bennie, was reticent and solemn except when gazing with adoration at his grandson. And Elaine had a round face that had made her appear warm and motherly until lately, when she always seemed to be scheming.

"He's a retired stockbroker. She was his office manager." Occupations didn't sum up a person, but they provided clues—in this case, important ones. "Bethany was raised with a gorgeous home, new cars and trips to Europe."

"What kind of work did she do?"

"She attended classes at Cal State Fullerton but never graduated." Nick had trouble understanding that lack of focus, but then, Bethany's parents had been quick to write checks for her when money ran short. "She held a range of jobs—waitressing, salesclerking and so on, but none of them stuck."

"Dare I guess that Caleb's growing up indulged, as well?" she queried.

Indulged. That was a kinder word than *spoiled.* Still, it would be hard to resist doting on that cute kid. "In a good way. Last Christmas, the house was full of great food, music and love, although everyone missed Bethany terribly."

The Carrigans had kindly invited Nick to join them on Christmas morning. Elaine had fixed an egg-and-cheese casserole and baked gingerbread, while Bennie had played old favorites on the piano. A glittering pine tree had spread its branches above a pile of presents.

"My parents mostly fought on Christmas," Zady said wistfully. "And just about every other day."

"Mine, too." Much as his father's desertion had hurt, it had provided a measure of relief from frequent arguments. "Did they divorce?"

"Dad stuck around, but he drank. I found out later that he cheated on my mom, too," Zady said. "Sorry for dredging this up. It's water under the bridge."

"I gather we both grew up under the same bridge, like trolls," he observed.

"And I picked a troll to have a ten-year relationship with." Her nose wrinkled. "I wish I understood more about relationships and parenting."

That was true for Nick, too. "I have to admit, I can't imagine snatching Caleb from Bennie and Elaine to live in an apartment with whatever overnight care I can scare up."

They exited the freeway and followed surface streets to the semirural community of La Habra Heights. Large lots, many used for raising horses, lay along winding roads, with scattered trees sheltering houses that varied from small adobes to Tudor-style mansions.

Rounding a corner, Nick spotted the familiar carriage-shaped mailbox that stood at the entrance to the Carrigans' property. Their long, gravel-covered driveway led through jacarandas and evergreens to a hilltop home.

Christmas lights still wreathed the front of the two-story house. The roof was missing several shingles—possibly loosened in the storm that had struck ten days ago—and a shutter hung at an odd angle.

It had been nearly a month since Nick had visited the house. Since then, Elaine and Caleb had met him at a park once, and on another occasion she'd dropped the boy off at Nick's old apartment. Then there'd been last week's puppet show.

"Does it usually look like this?" Zady asked.

"Not even close."

Something was definitely wrong.

Chapter Six

Mounting the porch steps, which creaked badly, Zady regretted pressuring Nick to drop his idea of claiming his son. She'd been overly influenced by her concern about Linda.

When Zady had donated her eggs, she'd pictured the child being raised under idyllic circumstances, but that didn't give her the right to go back on her word. By contrast, Nick had legal custody. If he chose to provide a home for his son, he could do so. Maybe that was in Caleb's best interest.

Life had a habit of zigging when you expected it to zag. They both had to deal with the unexpected as best they could.

They rang the bell and it echoed inside the house. Light footsteps pattered on the floor, and the door opened to reveal a small, dark-haired figure gazing up joyfully. "Daddy!"

Caleb flung himself into Nick's arms. The tall man swung his son around, raising a storm of giggles from the boy. The love radiating from Nick filled Zady with nostalgic yearning. She couldn't have said whether it was for her father or for the man she used to imagine someday marrying.

They stepped into a formal entrance hall lined with flowered wallpaper, while crown molding framed several interior doorways. A curving staircase rose to the second floor. The only furniture was a white Regency side table below a framed mirror.

The stooped figure of a woman moved toward them from the interior. She should be using a cane, Zady thought, and guessed that their hostess was trying to avoid showing weakness.

"Caleb, please don't answer the door until I reach it," she reproved the boy gently. "Nick, it's good to see you and your, uh, friend."

"You did get my email that Zady was accompanying me?" Nick set Caleb on the wooden floor. After receiving a nod, he introduced the two women.

"Pleased to meet you." Elaine Carrigan didn't offer to shake hands, and Zady noted that her fingers were bent with arthritis. That accounted for the cobweb in one corner of the mirror and the scuffed state of the floor. But if these people were as wealthy as Nick had indicated, why not employ a cleaning service?

"Caleb, this is my friend Zady," Nick told the three-year-old. "She's eager to meet you."

Zady smiled down at him. "I'm a nurse. I work at the Safe Harbor Medical Center with your father."

"You're a nurse?" Elaine regarded her with increased interest.

"I assist Nick's cousin Marshall," she said.

"Hi, Zady." Caleb drew out the vowels in her name. "That's funny. Zay-dee. Zay-dee."

"Don't be disersp...disrespectful, young man." His grandmother looked annoyed that she'd stumbled over the word.

"Zay-dee!" the child sang out and skipped toward the nearest doorway.

"Caleb! Not the living room. Let's join Grandpa in the den." When the boy obediently changed course, Elaine followed slowly.

Nick was frowning. Obviously, he had concerns, also.

Elaine and Caleb led them to a large room with tall windows. Against the far wall, an upright piano stood with its keyboard covered and a book of holiday songs in the music rack. Dark antiques dominated the room, brightened by a child-size table covered with crayons and paper.

From an armchair, a heavyset man rose stiffly. “I’m Bennie Carrigan.” He extended a hand to Zady, who introduced herself as she shook hands with him. “A pleasure to meet you, young lady. Nick’s new friend, I gather?”

“Colleague and neighbor,” Nick added.

While Caleb danced about, displaying toys for their admiration, Zady performed a surreptitious assessment of the boy’s grandfather. Bennie’s genial expression didn’t hide the sadness in his dark eyes. He’d undergone tragedy this past year, but the loss of his daughter hadn’t caused the puffiness in his neck or the effort it clearly took for him to remain upright.

Surely Nick hadn’t missed the signs of illness, either. This must be recent, or else the pair had disguised their problems on Christmas.

Elaine didn’t offer refreshments. That was fine with Zady, who’d rather not impose any more than necessary.

“If you’d like to take Caleb outside to play, feel free,” Elaine told them. Through the windows, Zady glimpsed a swing set and a slide on the shaggy rear lawn. Judging by the accumulation of leaves, none of it had been cleaned recently.

Nick, who’d been tussling with the boy, drew his son into a hug. “Caleb, I need to speak to your grandparents alone. Zady, would you play with Caleb in his room?”

“No! I want Daddy!” The little boy blew out cheekfuls of air. Judging by his defiant stance, he was on the verge of throwing a tantrum.

“I could read to you,” Zady offered.

His nose twitched. “Maybe.”

Nick slanted Zady a grateful look before turning to Elaine. “Can we talk?”

When the older woman didn’t respond, Zady feared she

might refuse Nick's request. Then her husband spoke. "I believe this conversation is overdue."

The grandmother pressed her lips together before relenting. "Very well."

"Will you show me your room, Caleb?" Zady asked the little boy. "You can pick your favorite book."

"Okay." With a reproachful glance at his father, he trotted ahead to the staircase.

Zady was glad she'd accompanied Nick today, if only to keep his son busy. As they mounted the steps beside a stair-lift track, she heard the rumble of voices from the den. After what she'd witnessed, it seemed inevitable that Nick would have to take physical custody of his son. Had he considered what challenges lay ahead?

Zady would never forget one weekend not long after Dwayne had left his wife and moved with her twenty-year-old self to Santa Barbara. He'd brought his three young children for a weekend at their apartment, dumping them on Zady with little notice while he worked a construction job.

The smallest had been younger than Caleb was now, and the others close in age. That tumultuous weekend, with Zady increasingly overwhelmed and the resentful youngsters running out of control, had set the tone for years of conflict.

Upstairs, landscape paintings lined the hall, off which opened four doors. She caught a medicinal smell along with the rank scent of unwashed sheets. Zady's stomach clenched, not from revulsion but from sorrow. These people must be in serious difficulty.

Caleb's room occupied a sunny corner, with a view over the woods where evergreens softened the starkness of bare winter branches. A child-size bed, its headboard painted with fairy-tale characters, sported a patchwork quilt thrown over bunched sheets.

A laundry basket atop the bureau held a pile of clean,

folded clothes. Books spilled from shelves, while an open cabinet displayed a jumble of toys and games.

Caleb plucked several books from the mess. "These are my favorites."

"Oh, I love these, too." Zady sank onto the floor, brushing aside scattered pieces from a children's game. As she did, a framed photo on the table caught her gaze.

Downstairs, several family pictures had included this same dark-haired young woman, whom she assumed was Bethany, but Zady had been reluctant to pay obvious attention. The subject of their daughter might be painful to the Carrigans.

In this portrait, Bethany glowed with personality. Those bright blue eyes were mesmerizing, and a mischievous smile invited friendship. "Is that your mommy?"

"Yeah." Caleb plopped beside her with a book. "Can you do voices?" He held out *Winnie-the-Pooh.*

"It wouldn't be a good story without voices," Zady responded, taking the well-worn book.

She jumped into the delightful tale and was pleased by Caleb's giggling responses as she altered her tone to suit each character. What a cutie! When he nestled against her, Zady slipped an arm around the little guy.

From time to time, she picked up the murmur of voices from below. What was being decided? Perhaps the Carrigans and Nick were reaching a compromise.

When Caleb's interest drifted from the story, Zady joined him in playing with teddy bears. That activity didn't last long, either.

"Tell me what you do every day," she suggested. "Do you go to preschool?"

He nodded. "The bus picks me up."

"Have you learned your colors?"

"Yes." Caleb pointed at objects to demonstrate, and was able to count to ten, too. He chattered for a while about his little friends, jumping from topic to topic until he had to use the bathroom.

"I'm potty trained," he informed her proudly.

"Great." That was one chore Nick wouldn't have to worry about. "Is there a second bathroom I can use?"

"In Grandpa's room." From the hall, he pointed it out. "I'm not 'lowed in there. Or Grandma's room, either." He didn't indicate which of the other doors led to Elaine's room.

"I'll wait till you're done." Zady didn't wish to intrude into either of the Carrigans' private spaces.

Standing in the hall, she experienced a sense of strangeness. What was she doing here, mixed up in the personal affairs of a man she barely knew?

Under other circumstances, she'd have been attracted to Nick, with his strong masculine presence and sense of humor. But in addition to his troubled relationship with Marshall, his situation as a single father marked him as off limits.

Moving to Safe Harbor had been the first step of Zady's plan to reclaim her life. She'd wasted her twenties on a selfish man, his ungrateful kids and a ridiculous feud with her twin fed by their mother's insecurity. Since changing jobs last fall, she'd begun to reestablish herself and, after a frank talk with Zora, built a closer relationship with her sister.

They'd joined forces to keep their manipulative mother at arm's length. The fact that she'd remarried and moved to Oregon simplified matters, as she could hardly expect to be included in their daily activities.

Zady's thirtieth birthday had reinforced her determination to proceed with the next step: establishing a family of her own. No more secondhand men or secondhand children, either. So, although her heart went out to Caleb, she had no desire to take on someone else's problems.

Then again, no one had asked her to. She was helping a friend today, nothing more.

Fidgeting in the hall as Caleb lingered in the bathroom, she studied another photo of Bethany, basking in sunlight. Why had the young woman rejected Nick's proposal? Granted, a pregnancy alone wasn't a good enough reason to marry, yet with his warmth and love for his son, he had husband potential. And Bethany must have recognized the guy's sexy appeal. What *was* he like in bed?

Get a grip! That might be easier if she weren't standing here growing antsier by the minute. Urgent need overtaking her qualms, Zady gritted her teeth and darted through Bennie's bedroom, trying to ignore the unmade bed…*whoa.* An oxygen tank? She'd have to think about the implications of that later.

Bursting into the bathroom, she used the facilities quickly. While washing her hands, she reached for a towel and knocked over a couple of the prescription bottles cramming the counter. Why so many? she wondered as she straightened them. And although Caleb seemed to respect his grandparents' order to stay out of here, surely medications like these should be kept in a locked cabinet.

The names of the medications jumped into focus. ACE inhibitors. Beta blockers. Diuretics…

Now she understood what was ailing Bennie. And why any halfway measures for Caleb's care would be at most a stopgap.

VISITING THE CARRIGANS' mansion brought back Nick's childhood sense of inadequacy. His grandparents' spacious home, as well as his aunt and uncle's, had stood in stark contrast to the series of low-rent apartments in which he and his parents—and later his single mom—had lived.

This grand room and its magnificent antiques dwarfed the efficiency unit he presently occupied. And despite their frailties, the elder Carrigans exuded the confidence of wealth and success. Most of all, they loved Caleb and offered him stability. How could Nick remove his son from them?

Yet, clearly, keeping up with a three-year-old and a large house was straining their capabilities. Regardless of his worries about day care, finances and Caleb's emotional state, he couldn't allow matters to continue on their current course.

As usual, Elaine seized control of the conversation before he could. "We won't let you take our little boy away. He's all we have." She lowered herself stiffly onto a formal sofa like a queen assuming her throne. "We've suffered a few health setbacks, and our housekeeper quit right after the holidays. But we'll soon have matters under control. In the meantime, Caleb is flourishing. You can see that for yourself."

The boy did look healthy and cheerful. Nick kept track of his progress in preschool and reviewed reports from his medical checkups, so he had no reason to believe Caleb suffered from neglect. But if the housekeeper had simply quit, why hadn't they hired an interim cleaning service?

Nick took a diplomatic approach. "You mentioned health problems. As a physician, I believe you should concentrate on regaining your health and reducing unnecessary stress."

"Our grandson is not 'unnecessary stress'!" The older woman's anger flared. She possessed the same temperamental fire as her daughter had. Unfortunately, Bethany had lacked her mother's sense of duty. Growing up without boundaries had translated into reckless behavior that had led to her death.

Over her parents' objections, Bethany had spent the Fourth of July weekend with heavy-drinking friends at a lakeside cabin. She'd planned to take Caleb along until

Elaine informed Nick of the plan. They'd joined forces, threatening to report her for child endangerment.

After angrily accusing them of trying to control her, she'd gone without her son. Boating and alcohol had proved a deadly combination when one of the men sped around the lake, lost control of the motorboat and smashed into a larger vessel. There'd been injuries on both boats, and Bethany had been thrown overboard. Authorities had found her body later with a major head injury and indications that she had drowned. The tragedy had devastated her family.

But in the aftermath, Elaine and Bennie had played a vital role in providing a stable home for his son. "I'm grateful that you've been here for Caleb," Nick said. "You're right—he is flourishing. But he's growing fast, and you aren't getting any younger."

"We're hardly at death's door," Elaine snapped. Bennie, who'd sunk onto his chair, winced at her tone. "I'm only sixty-four and Bennie's sixty-three. That's young!"

Younger than Nick had realized—not quite old enough for Medicare, which meant they must be fielding heavy medical bills. While he contributed child support, Nick presumed his money went for food, clothes, utilities and the boy's doctor visits. He didn't send enough to underwrite the expenses of such a large household, nor could he afford to.

Above them, the floor shifted in Caleb's bedroom. Nick appreciated Zady's willingness to entertain his son. She'd been a good sport about everything he'd dropped on her today.

Deep breath. Hold on to your patience and proceed to the point. "I'm not proposing to yank Caleb out of here today," Nick said. "But I'd like your help in transitioning him to my home."

Bennie drooped but didn't argue. His wife, however, went into full fighting mode.

"Your home?" Elaine repeated. "You live in a residential motel, don't you?"

"I've been researching apartments," he said. *And I'll do that in earnest now.*

She gestured around the room. "You'd drag a little boy from this beautiful house and cram him into an apartment?"

"Lots of children grow up just fine in apartments." *Including me.* Well, he'd not always been fine, Nick amended silently.

"You're a playboy bachelor who works nights." Elaine must have stewed over this topic beforehand, assembling her arguments. "On advice of our attorney, we didn't fight you for custody when Bethany died, but if you try to take Caleb, we'll fight and we'll win!"

"Elaine!" A fierce note in Bennie's voice halted her flow of words. "You know we've been discussing moving into assisted living."

She glared as if her husband had committed an act of treason. Reassured that Bennie agreed with him, Nick hastened to defuse the situation.

"You should preserve your savings, not waste them on lawyers." A custody battle would be a drain on his resources and theirs. "Of course, I'll rely on your advice and continuing involvement with Caleb."

"Any chance of your renting a house?" Bennie inquired. Nick appreciated the suggestion, which might counter Elaine's argument on that score.

While a house would cost extra, it should provide a more comfortable environment. Nick had been sending larger-than-required monthly payments to retire his student loans faster. If he cut those payments to the minimum, he could free up money for rent.

"No reason why not," he said. "Safe Harbor's a family community with plenty of residential areas."

"But what about your schedule? You can't just farm

the boy out to sitters," Elaine grumbled, switching tactics. "What will you do, hire a teenager to sleep over, or park Caleb at a stranger's home every night?"

If only Nick still worked days…but he'd signed a year-long contract. Moreover, he'd committed to his patients and to relieving the other doctors, and the extra money would be more necessary than ever if he rented a house.

However, Caleb was top priority. "I'm willing to investigate what it would take to transfer to a position with better hours."

"Even if you succeed, obstetricians always have to be available on weekends and evenings," Elaine parried. "You said so yourself after Bethany died. How will you find a sitter at a moment's notice? What about the impact on Caleb?"

"Other doctors manage." Nick flashed on a conversation with Adrienne Cavill-Hunter, who'd held the overnight shift before him while raising her small nephew, now her adopted son. She'd spoken highly of a licensed sitter who had looked after Reggie while she worked nights. "I have a colleague who's recommended a licensed home."

"A licensed home!" Elaine scoffed. "He deserves his own home."

Despite his frustration, Nick kept a firm hold on his temper. "We'd all prefer perfect circumstances, but we don't have that option."

"What about your friend?" Bennie asked unexpectedly. "She's a nurse and your neighbor, right?"

"At the motel," his wife said acidly. "What's the point of renting a house and then dumping him in a trashy place like that every night?"

"It isn't trashy." Nick doubted his statement would carry much weight, nor would a tour of the place impress her. "But as Bennie points out, we've only begun to explore possibilities."

Elaine's hands tightened, but instead of forming fists,

she jerked from the pain. Nick felt a twist of sympathy. She must be suffering daily while she prepared meals for Caleb, assisted her husband and struggled to keep this big house in shape.

In any event, she had to yield to reality. And perhaps she *was* weakening—they'd progressed from threats of a court battle to hashing out details. For Elaine's sake, as well as everyone else's, Nick decided to seal the deal while he could. "I'll tell you what. Let me see about renting a house and finding suitable overnight care. If I do that, will you—"

His proposal was cut off by the scamper of little feet in the hall, followed by Zady's steps.

"Look what I learned!" the boy cried as he ran in, his face alight. "Come on, Auntie Zee!"

"Auntie Zee?" Elaine's forehead furrowed.

"That's what my goddaughter calls me," Zady explained apologetically. "I'm sorry. He got bored upstairs."

"That's all right," Nick said.

Eager to show off his new game, Caleb began to sing, "'You put your right foot in…'"

"'You put your right foot out.'" Singing along, Zady took his hand and joined in demonstrating the hokeypokey.

Bennie started singing, too, and Elaine cracked a smile.

"Whee!" Waving his hands in the air, Caleb twirled around beside Zady.

Caleb and Zady might as well both be kids, Nick reflected. Then inspiration struck.

He had a potential solution to their problems. Now he just had to sell it to the Carrigans…and Zady.

Chapter Seven

"I'll grant you this," Zady said as they cruised along the freeway, Nick keeping the car a shade below the posted speed limit of sixty-five so he could prolong the conversation. "It isn't the worst idea I've ever heard."

Her ironic tone didn't bode well. "But?" he prompted.

"It's right up there near the top." Her mouth twisted and, although he didn't tear his gaze from traffic, Nick was sure she'd rolled her eyes, too.

"Maybe I didn't explain well enough." He considered the advantages to be obvious. However, experience had taught him that what one person said and what the other person heard weren't always the same.

She thunked the back of her head against the seat rest, which he gathered was the equivalent of banging one's head on the wall. "Allow me to sum up. You rent house. I move into house. I become house slave."

"You mean like the elf in Harry Potter?" he asked to lighten the tone. "You are much cuter than Dobby."

"How reassuring."

Shifting into a slower lane to avoid ticking off the driver of the truck behind them, he imagined his very feminine companion living with him in his house. In his kitchen, on his couch, in his shower…

Nick yanked his thoughts away from dangerous territory. *Focus on strategy.* Should he use guilt or practicality?

Zady had done him a major favor today and it would be wrong to push her too hard. After the demonstration of the hokeypokey, she'd accompanied Caleb outside for another quarter of an hour at his request. During that precious interval, he'd presented his proposition to the Carrigans: If he rented a house and arranged for suitable overnight supervision—possibly Zady—would they cooperate with him on transitioning Caleb into Nick's home?

Bennie had agreed at once. Although Elaine had been sullen, she'd eventually yielded, as well.

He decided to use logic. "Consider the financial aspect," he said in a reasonable tone. "You can't afford an apartment unless you share with other people. Instead, you'll have a room rent-free in a house with a..." With a what? What were the advantages of living in a house? He had no idea. "A private yard and a garage." That sounded right.

"How could any woman resist?"

"I'll throw in utilities and food." Nick would add a stipend if finances allowed, but he couldn't promise that. "I'll mostly be away when you and Caleb are both sleeping, and that's only four nights a week."

"Plus four evenings, bedtimes and breakfasts." The late-afternoon light brought out the reddish cast to her brown hair. "Nick, I hate waiting on people. Personal care is *not* my strong point."

"You're a nurse."

"I deal primarily with adults," she said. "You're great with Caleb."

It was apparent to him that she had the maternal instinct that Caleb needed during this difficult period. If only Nick could circumvent her knee-jerk rejection. "It doesn't have to be permanent. In a year, I'm sure I can switch to the day shift."

"A year's a long time. And you'd still be on call for off-hours deliveries."

He had no easy answer. Reluctantly, Nick conceded that his colleagues had had good reason to choose specialties with regular hours, not that he regretted his choice. "It'll be my responsibility to figure out how to handle that."

"And my leaving will upset Caleb all over again," she reminded him. "I'm sure there must be others who would leap at an opportunity like this."

He wasn't about to trust his son to a stranger. Well, perhaps the licensed sitter Adrienne had recommended, but only if he had to.

Nick longed for stability, for his son *and* himself. To establish a routine with a sense of permanence. As for what he'd do when Zady departed, he couldn't worry about that now. At least, with her initial help, he and Caleb could begin to put down roots and adjust to sharing a home.

"The Carrigans trust you. That's a huge compliment." The miles were passing too fast, and his window of opportunity was slipping away. "Zady, think of the money you'll save."

"Think of me turning thirty-one in another year," she said. "I already wasted a decade. Living with you and Caleb will throw me off my plan."

"What plan?" Even if the answer didn't advance Nick's cause, this topic sparked his curiosity.

"Never mind."

"You have a plan?" he prompted again.

"I have a pain in the neck sitting next to me, whom I do *not* intend to room with," she snapped. "That's another issue—boundaries. You're pushy. I hate pushy men."

"I'm not pushy. I'm driven by my convictions." Before she could attack his shaky logic, Nick said, "Consider security, then. You'll be a lot safer sharing a house with a man."

"Who's gone four nights a week?" she countered. "And the crime rate in Safe Harbor is, what, in the negative range?"

"How can a crime rate be in the negative range?"

"When people bend over backward to help each other,"

she responded quickly. "Admit defeat, Nick. Though I agree Caleb can't stay with his grandparents. Mr. Carrigan suffers from congestive heart failure."

He'd noticed the signs. "I guessed that from his puffiness and shortness of breath. But why are you so certain?"

"The medications on his bathroom counter." She shrugged. "Assisted living is the right place for him. He and his wife can't fight you. Their health won't allow it."

In congestive heart failure, the organ still pumped blood but with diminished power. Without proper treatment, fluid could build up, with potentially catastrophic results.

Medications and lifestyle changes might mitigate the problems, and surgery was an option in extreme cases. But bottom line, Bennie required more care than his wife could provide, especially while supervising a child and with her own health problems. He remembered her stumbling over a few words, and wondered if she might benefit from adjusting the dosage of whatever she was taking, too.

Still, even though Nick could claim his son without the Carrigans' approval, he wanted to spare the boy the kind of scars he bore from a turbulent home filled with conflict. "It's in Caleb's best interest for us all to work together for a smooth transition."

Moving on to another potential reservation she might have, he asked, "You aren't concerned about sharing a house with me, are you? Despite what my cousin thinks, I'm not a playboy."

"Don't tell me you're trying to blame Marshall for my refusing to double as your nanny!"

"No such thing." However, her comment reminded him of her association with his cousin. Did he really want his personal details laid out for Marshall to pass judgment on? Not that Nick believed she'd spy on him, but doctors and nurses tended to let down their hair during breaks. Plus they might overhear conversations with fellow staffers. "You *will* be seeing him every day. I hadn't considered that."

"You hadn't considered a lot of things."

She was right; he might have been a bit impulsive back there at the Carrigans' house. The fact that he enjoyed Zady's company had influenced him, as well. It could be fun, sharing a house with her and Caleb, fixing meals, playing games and goofing around. And Nick would benefit from having someone to consult with and share observations of his son's behavior. But he couldn't shoehorn Zady into that role.

Ahead, a freeway sign announced they were approaching the Safe Harbor off-ramp. Reluctantly, Nick accepted that he'd have to move to plan B.

"You're right," he said.

"I am?"

"I'll find someone else."

"What changed your mind?"

"Caleb deserves a sitter who wants to be with him." Nick shifted his coupe into the exit lane. "I'm sure a licensed care provider will warm to him."

"Of course she will. He's a cutie." Her wistfulness signaled regret—unless he was imagining that.

"He's adorable. And, like all kids, a handful." Nick supposed he was about to receive a crash course in hands-on parenthood. Just as well that he'd have an experienced sitter as a guide.

He'd contact Adrienne for the phone number of the woman she'd recommended and start vetting available houses. He would work this out, for his son's sake.

THE START OF THE WEEK was especially busy for Zady because Marshall didn't usually schedule surgeries then. While he was operating, she had time to follow up with patients, prepare for his afternoon appointments and assist the other urologists with whom he shared office space. On Mondays, however, she proceeded at a dead run.

During her training as a registered nurse, Zady had been encouraged by an enthusiastic teacher to consider focusing on urology. After earning her RN degree, she'd landed a position in a large clinic in Santa Barbara. The doctor she'd assisted had treated men, women and children diagnosed with everything from congenital abnormalities and incontinence to prostate disorders and cancer.

At Safe Harbor, although Dr. Davis also treated a range of patients, his client list reflected the center's emphasis on fertility as well as his skill as a reconstructive microsurgeon. Many patients sought vasectomy reversals or help for erectile dysfunction.

While any medical disorder affected people's emotions, Zady observed that men were particularly sensitive about issues they thought reflected on their masculinity. A cool, restrained physician like Marshall Davis suited this specialty well, as many men appreciated his businesslike approach.

In her opinion, women responded better to a show of caring, and she wondered how Nick interacted with his patients. It would be interesting to watch him deliver babies. Did having a son influence his practice?

Stop thinking about them. Neither the boy nor the father was her concern.

At midmorning, she received a text from her friend Alice Madison.

Can we talk?

As a nurse, Alice knew better than to call while Zady was on duty, although that didn't explain why she hadn't simply waited until the evening.

Will call in a few minutes. After assisting the last patient of the morning, Zady retreated to the snack room. Sometimes she preferred to eat there in relative privacy, like today, so she could return Alice's call.

Her friend answered on the second buzz. "Oh, Zady!" She spoke breathlessly, as if she'd been jogging, which she probably had. Alice had always been a fitness advocate. "I have a huge favor to ask. Please don't say no till you hear me out."

"A favor?" There seemed to be a lot of such requests these days, Zady thought. Did she have a sticky note pasted to her forehead reading, "Universal volunteer"?

"You know Bill and I are having problems. *Were* having problems, hopefully in the past tense." Alice's voice had regained its usual confidence. "He swears he loves me more than anything, and begged me to bring Linda and help him to run the seminars. I told him it's ridiculous to drag a toddler around while we're working, and then it hit me. You've been wishing to spend more time with her, right?"

Uh-oh. Zady was reminded of a time when she'd promised to accompany her sister on a daredevil roller-coaster ride, and discovered, too late, that her stomach had stayed behind. "I do recall uttering those words, but…"

"She can spend the month with you!" Alice crowed. "It'll be perfect. Linda adores you, and you can introduce her to your hometown. Plus, your sister is there to help, right?"

"Zora has twin babies," Zady said.

"Oh." Her friend paused only briefly before barreling ahead. "I checked the website and there's day care at your hospital."

That had been presumptuous—or simply practical. Zady wasn't always sure how to interpret Alice's actions. Tall and blonde, she'd initially struck Zady as too gorgeous to befriend a freckled kid who couldn't walk straight in heels higher than three inches. Zady had always felt a little starstruck with Alice, and therefore vulnerable to her influence.

But she did long to stay close to Linda, and if she rejected her friend's request, that might put a wedge between them. Also, Zady cared about the state of her friends' marriage. If Alice and Bill could renew their relationship on this trip, the benefit to their little girl would be huge.

"It'll be a tight squeeze in my unit," she said. "I'm living in a residential motel."

"It's only for a month," Alice repeated. "There's no one else I trust. Bill's folks live on the East Coast and his mom's in poor health." Alice's parents had died years earlier, Zady recalled. "Please say yes!"

Despite reservations and an awareness that she hadn't examined all the angles, Zady couldn't refuse. "Okay. When do you leave?"

"Next Sunday," her friend said. "Thank you thank you thank you! I'll email you with more details. Keep track of whatever you spend on her food and stuff and we'll reimburse you."

"Fine. I'll see you Sunday. And congratulations on talking things over with Bill."

"You're an angel!"

Zady clicked off in a daze. What had she just agreed to?

"Are you all right?" The masculine voice startled her. She hadn't noticed Marshall entering the break room.

"Yes." While she'd rather keep her private business out of the office, the situation might affect him, Zady reflected. "I promised to take care of my goddaughter for a month, starting next week. It's a family emergency."

At a vending machine, Marshall selected a sandwich. He often ate at his desk, catching up on medical news and reviewing plans for surgeries. "Won't that be difficult?"

"Yes. I feel like I just volunteered to climb Mount Everest." Zady braced for him to object. Not that he had the right to rule her personal decisions, but during their initial interview, he'd emphasized that he was a perfectionist who expected the best from his staff.

"How old is your goddaughter?" Marshall asked.

"Two and a half." Which was, Zady conceded silently, a turbulent age. "It's only for a month, and I'll do everything in my power to make sure this doesn't affect my work." Surely he wouldn't fire her when she'd done nothing wrong—yet.

"Your friend must place a great deal of trust in you." Marshall seemed to be searching for words. "To ask you to be a godmother, then leave her child in your care. That's quite a responsibility."

"I love Linda," Zady said. "I'm willing to take on the challenge." An urge to babble welled up, about how she would possibly cope with a toddler and adapt her sparsely furnished apartment to the child's needs. But Marshall never invited confidences, and Zady suspected she'd regret exposing any more of her concerns.

Never a man to chitchat, he said, "She's a lucky little girl," and departed.

Grabbing her salad from the refrigerator, Zady ate it while walking next door to the hospital, where she consulted the day care center's staff. Yes, they had room for a toddler starting next week. That was a relief.

The rest of the day, Zady focused on her duties. She owed her full attention to her patients and her doctor. If anything, Marshall's sympathetic response to her situation had reaffirmed her dedication to him.

Only when she arrived home in the early winter darkness did the doubts creep back in. The term *seedy* didn't exactly apply to the Harbor Suites, but it was far from welcoming. How strange and disorienting this would be for Linda, removed from her parents' care for a whole month, and dropped into an unfamiliar environment.

She supposed they could hang out at Zora's house. At

ages eleven and thirteen, the Adams girls would dote on Linda, and the place was always full of activity. But Zady didn't dare. Too much contact was likely to raise questions she didn't want to answer.

Linda bore a strong resemblance to Zady. Fortunately, no one here knew Alice, who was not only tall and blonde but also had markedly different bone structure. But there'd be frequent video chats, and sooner or later, her sister or brother-in-law was bound to notice that the little girl didn't look like her mother.

Zady and the Madisons had agreed to keep the egg donation secret until Linda was old enough to understand. Even then, it would remain confidential, to share only if Linda wished.

Best to limit exposure to Zora's household. Too bad, Zady mused as she approached her doorstep.

She halted in surprise at the sight of a large bouquet of lilies and roses on her stoop. The scent lifted her spirits, and when she carried the vase inside, she discovered that their freshness transformed the room.

The card read, "Thanks for yesterday. Nick."

What a sweet gesture. And how considerate not to have them delivered to her at the office, where they'd have piqued her coworkers' curiosity.

After setting the flowers on a place mat atop the coffee table, Zady fixed a light meal. As she polished it off, she decided that, despite the beautiful bouquet, the longer she stared at the décor in her living room, the more depressing it seemed for a little girl.

The Gently Used and Useful thrift shop had evening hours and affordable prices. What a great place to pick up indoor play equipment and a cheap toy chest. After Linda left, Zady could donate her purchases to charity.

She threw on a light jacket. Outside, the night air had a crisp edge, while the darkness intensified sounds and smells: hamburgers grilling, a video game squawking, a child laughing.

Once Linda arrived, they'd be sharing strolls together. What a great opportunity to develop a closer bond and create memories with her goddaughter.

Approaching the parking lot in the patchy glare of the streetlamps, Zady had an idea. She and Linda could make a video log, or a digital photo scrapbook, so this sojourn would never fade from their memories. Then Alice and Bill could share it, too. And when Linda was older and learned the truth about their biological connection, she'd have no reason to feel neglected or abandoned.

She's my child. Maybe the only one I'll ever have.

At the thought, Zady missed her step on the sidewalk. Struggling to regain her balance, she staggered a second time, unable to reach out both hands because she'd instinctively clutched her purse. Footsteps rushed toward her, and someone caught her arm.

"Are you okay?" asked a man's voice nearly identical to Marshall's, the words almost the same as the ones her doctor had used earlier, too.

Great. She'd bumbled around like an idiot in front of Nick. "I'm fine. Just embarrassed at my clumsiness." As Zady straightened, his warmth cocooned her against the cool breeze.

His cheek brushed across the top of her head. "I've missed you," he murmured.

She nearly shot back that it had been only twenty-four hours, but the truth was, she'd missed his playfulness and spontaneity, too. How could Nick be so much like Marshall yet so utterly different? "So have I." Hastily, she added, "Don't take that personally."

"How else could I take it?" His chuckle vibrated through her.

"What I meant was, thank you for the flowers." His gift

showed him to be considerate. "You were kind to think of it."

"You went out of your way for me yesterday," Nick responded. "I don't know how I'd have coped at the Carrigans' without you."

The glare of headlights swinging into the parking lot reminded her of their surroundings. Easing out of Nick's arms, Zady recalled that it was past six. "Aren't you late for work?"

"I have Mondays off." His dark jacket emphasized the ruggedness of his shoulders, stronger and broader than his cousin's. "Matter of fact, I'm about to check out a house for rent. I'd appreciate a second opinion, if you aren't busy."

"The last time I agreed to help you, it turned into a major expedition," she returned.

"How about if I throw in hot chocolate afterward?" He raised an eyebrow teasingly. "Plus, dessert at Waffle Heaven, if you're in the mood."

"If I eat that, you won't have to rent a house because I'll be as big as one." However, she couldn't deny that she enjoyed being with him. Not only that, but it occurred to her that it might entertain Linda to play with Caleb once in a while, and this house could provide the setting. She should check it out. "Okay, I'll go. But that was hot chocolate *and* dessert, right?"

"Plus a second one to take home," he promised.

"That would be a bad idea." So was this trip. But Zady didn't care.

She really *had* missed him.

Chapter Eight

Ordinarily, Nick had no trouble tracking multiple subjects simultaneously. In high school, a counselor had suggested he become an air traffic controller. He'd have considered that career had his cousin not chosen medicine and presented Nick with a different challenge.

Today, however, his usually well-ordered mental tracks threatened to smash into each other. In addition to reading about the development of three-year-olds, he'd checked out housing rentals, discovering issues he hadn't considered, such as the cost of furniture, the required background check, the significant security deposit and the possibility of hazards to small children.

On top of that, his Friday-night shift posed a problem for Adrienne's recommended care provider, who reserved weekends for her family. If he hired her, Nick would have to juggle a second sitter for Fridays. Adrienne had suggested a high school or college student, but the same person might not be available every week. That struck him as too disruptive for Caleb.

Nick assumed he'd figure it all out eventually. Meanwhile, his problems loomed like the immense cliffs along the river in one of his favorite movies, *The Fellowship of the Ring.*

Running into Zady this evening had calmed him. Her cute face and whiplash retorts yanked Nick out of his absorption with his problems.

Not only did he value her opinion on the house, he had an ulterior motive. In retrospect, he'd reevaluated his qualms about trusting her with the job. She'd babysat her ex's kids for years. And as for revealing his secrets to Marshall, which secrets were those, anyway? She was still his—and Caleb's—best option.

As he drove north through Safe Harbor toward the house, Nick wondered how low he dared stoop in trying to enlist her aid. No outright fabrications, but might she be susceptible to bribery? Assuming he could afford it, of course. Which he couldn't. Scrap that idea.

"Quit calculating," Zady commanded.

He halted at a red light on Safe Harbor Boulevard. "I beg your pardon?"

"You keep shooting glances at me like you're measuring me for something. I half expect ropes to drop from the ceiling and bind me to my seat." Beneath the streetlights, her frown took on a harsh quality. "A second opinion is all I'm offering."

"That's all I expect."

"You lie."

"Then why'd you come?" he demanded, despite the risk that she'd hop out while still within walking distance of home.

Zady heaved an exaggerated sigh. "For the distraction. Don't ask from what. It's none of your business."

"My cousin isn't hassling you about visiting Caleb with me, is he?" Although Nick didn't believe he'd mentioned it to Marshall, Zady might have.

"Your cousin is a kind, decent human being," Zady retorted. "You should give him more credit. And no, we didn't discuss Caleb. Although Marshall *is* a good listener."

That statement aroused Nick's competitive instincts. He'd decided to accept a certain division of loyalties due to Zady and Marshall's professional connection, but he didn't expect to compete with his cousin in any other sense.

Swinging onto a side street bordered by apartment clusters and small houses, Nick tempered his response by saying, "You bring out the best in him. Marshall isn't famous for his bonhomie."

"His what?"

"His easy friendliness." A side effect of an excellent memory was the acquisition of an extensive vocabulary. Sometimes that proved useful; other times, people found it off-putting. Like now, judging by Zady's dubious expression. "I'm a good listener, too. Try me."

"Tell me about the house," she countered.

"It was just posted today on a rental website," Nick said. "It's empty and available for immediate occupancy."

"More," she said.

"Such as?"

"Number of bedrooms."

"Three." More than he required—unless she was willing to live in. "The rent's on the high side, but it includes furnishings. Mr. Tran, the owner, inherited it from his parents and takes pride in its upkeep. He supervised the painting and upgrades personally."

"Speaking of bonhomie, it sounds like you had quite a conversation with him," Zady observed.

"It turns out he works at Rose's Posies, which supplies bouquets to the hospital gift shop," Nick explained. "He advised me which flowers to send to you."

"I like him already. And thank you for those again. They're beautiful."

"My pleasure."

When he spotted the one-story, ranch-style house on their right, Nick scored a parking spot on the street right in front. Yard lights showed eggshell-blue paint on the stucco exterior, with dark gray trim around the windows. As if to defy the concept of winter, roses bloomed alongside the walkway.

A danger of thorns, Nick thought. But they weren't likely

to cause serious injury, and if Caleb hadn't already learned caution around rosebushes, Nick would warn him.

"It's pretty." Zady spoke wistfully.

"No comparison to the Carrigans' house." Nick emerged from the car. "But I'd have loved a place like this when I was a kid."

"Me, too." She joined him on the sidewalk. "Mr. Tran must be inside." She indicated the windows, where a glow filtered through the woven curtains.

"Let's not keep him waiting." Eagerness propelled his footsteps. Although he hadn't yet viewed the interior, Nick felt as if he was coming home.

The man who answered the bell was older than he'd expected, possibly in his seventies, which meant his recently deceased parents must have been in their nineties. Short and thin, he had neatly brushed gray hair and a warm smile. "Dr. Davis!"

"Mr. Tran." Nick shook hands with him. "This is my friend, Zady Moore."

Mr. Tran shook her hand. "You work at the medical center also?"

"Yes, I'm a nurse."

"Good, good." He ushered them into a spotless living room that held an entertainment stand, couch, bookshelf and coffee table. Although in fine condition, none of the furnishings had much personality, and Nick guessed that the elder Trans' special belongings had been replaced with items geared for renters.

That suited him fine. Less risk of damaging costly antiques.

"I won't be living here," Zady noted. "I'm along merely as an observer."

"Where do you rent now?" Mr. Tran asked.

"The Harbor Suites."

"Dreary!" he exclaimed. "This is much nicer. And

cheaper if you split the rent. Let me show you the kitchen. I've installed many new appliances."

How odd that the older man seemed intent on having Zady join Nick. Perhaps he believed women kept a cleaner house than men. The Carrigans had reacted similarly, Nick recalled. She certainly had an appealing personality—more approachable than his.

In the kitchen, the shiny gas range impressed him, and the refrigerator was a recent model with an excellent energy rating.

"Too bad it's dark outside." Mr. Tran opened a sliding door from the kitchen to the patio, where the porch light revealed only dark shapes. "The yard is beautiful, very private, with high hedges. By the way, if you have a pet, there is an extra security deposit."

"We don't," Nick assured him. "I do have a three-year-old son, as I said on the phone. Is there space for play equipment?"

"Yes, for sure." Their host kept up a line of encouraging patter as he shut the door and escorted them around the rest of the house, showing off the utility room with an up-to-date washer and dryer, the pantry, two bathrooms and three bedrooms, one of which lay on the opposite side of the living room from the others. "Privacy for the lady," he noted.

"Why are you so encouraging?" Zady asked. "There must be lots of renters interested in such a lovely house."

"But they are not a doctor from the medical center! And a nurse." Mr. Tran's head bobbed with approval. "No one will be better than that." To Nick, he added, "I can offer a five percent reduction in the rent if you handle routine repairs. I'll pay for materials."

Routine repairs—how hard could that be? A mental calculation reassured Nick that, if necessary, he could hire the occasional repairman with what he'd save. Better yet, he'd figure out how to do the work himself.

"Sounds great." But if Zady didn't accept his offer, he didn't need three bedrooms. He'd save more by renting a smaller place. "Can you allow me—us—twenty-four hours to decide?"

Mr. Tran weighed the question for a split second before addressing Zady. "Do you have children also, Mrs. Nurse?"

To Nick's surprise, a no didn't immediately spring from her lips. "I have a goddaughter." After a beat, Zady added, "I just arranged for her to stay with me for a month while her parents are traveling."

She'd mentioned her goddaughter during their visit to the Carrigans, he recalled.

A houseful of children might be fun. Or drive them crazy. But it was only for a month, and if this little girl turned the tide with Zady, he'd be grateful to her.

"In a tiny unit at the motel?" the landlord inquired. Mentally, Nick awarded the man points for persistence, and additional credit for manipulating Zady more baldly than he himself would have dared.

"She's two and a half," Zady responded. "I doubt she'll mind."

"Let me show you something." Mr. Tran led them to a large, isolated bedroom and opened the double closet to reveal a cot. "An extra bed." A wave of the hand indicated a folded wood-and-rice-paper screen with three panels. "You can divide the room for privacy."

"There's plenty of space." Nick swallowed the urge to lobby more strongly.

"It *would* be convenient." A tremulous note in Zady's voice indicated she might be weakening.

Nick was already sold. How could she resist this charming house? Well, Mr. Tran had done his best. Now the ball was in Nick's court. "May Mrs. Nurse and I have a moment to talk?"

"Of course!" The landlord regarded them thoughtfully. "I will step outside onto the patio. I will hear nothing."

"You don't have to wait in the cold," Zady replied. "We'll talk out there. Seriously, I could use the fresh air."

"You are a kind person," Mr. Tran said with evident relief.

He *was* elderly, despite his vigor, Nick reflected. "Thank you. We won't be long."

Surely if Zady was set on refusing, she'd have already turned him down, he mused as he followed her outside. He longed to live here. And after seeing Zady light up the rooms tonight, he couldn't picture doing so without her.

HOW COULD A HOUSE cast a spell over her? Zady had dreamed of living in a place like this all her life.

Aware that she'd never be able to afford one on just her income, she associated having a house with finding Mr. Right, followed by Baby Right. Now Nick dangled the lure of living in this minipalace rent-free.

Nevertheless, the psychic price was too high. No sane woman would agree to a second job as nanny to Mr. So-Wrong-She-Couldn't-Imagine-Anyone-Wronger-Unless-It-Was-Dwayne. Yet here Zady stood in the cold air of an early-February night feeling utterly enchanted, the scent of jasmine and the twitter of night birds only enhancing the effect.

She kept picturing Linda toddling happily about with Caleb in the cheerful kitchen, clouting each other over the head with blocks, screaming and then cuddling with her while muffins in the oven perfumed the air. Exactly who would be baking those muffins, she had no idea. Perhaps Mr. Tran would be willing to drop by occasionally. A man who knew about flowers might also bake for his tenants.

She must be delirious. Or under a spell.

Standing close enough to shelter her against the chill breeze, Nick radiated persuasion without speaking. If he pressured her, she'd stomp inside. *Please do that. Save me from this insanity.*

"Do you suppose it's fate?" he asked.

"Do I suppose *what* is fate?" She prepared to march away, any second.

"You said this business with your goddaughter just happened." He paused, but she couldn't contradict him. "And Mr. Tran is eager to have us."

"Are you casting him in the role of heavenly messenger?"

"You didn't see the faint outline of wings?" he replied lightly. Before she could muster a sarcastic reply, he changed the subject. "Tell me about your goddaughter."

"Her name is Linda," she said.

"That's Spanish for 'pretty.'"

"What's Spanish for 'I didn't just take stupid pills, so don't try to con me into living here'?"

"But this place is perfect." Nick's smile gleamed in the moonlight.

Zady refused to succumb. "In a month, Linda will be home with her parents."

"And you could stay in this home with its brand-new kitchen…"

Thank goodness, he'd provided the ammunition she sought. "Are you under the impression that you'd be getting a free maid, cook and laundress?"

A slight widening of the eyes indicated she'd caught him off guard. So he *had* assumed that.

Nick rallied fast, however. "Actually, *you'll* be scoring a free maid, cook and launder…laundry…whatever the male equivalent is. I'll clean. I'll, uh, fix food when I'm home. And I already wash clothes. You've seen me do it."

"You touch my underwear, you die."

"I promise to launder judiciously," he responded. "Only what's mine and Caleb's. How's that?"

Oh, heavens, they were negotiating. How had she slipped

into this? "I refuse to commit to a long-term arrangement. Think how upsetting it will be for your little boy when I move out. It's better to establish him on a consistent schedule with a regular sitter."

Nick scuffed his shoe against the concrete. "As it happens, the licensed sitter I had in mind isn't available on Friday nights. I'd be juggling substitutes one night a week. Plus, Caleb would have to stay over at her place the other three. Having someone live-in would be far preferable."

"Can't the hospital change your overnight schedule to Monday through Thursday?" she asked, ignoring the second part of his statement. "That would solve the problem with the sitter." Not the part about having to sleep in someone else's bed, but she couldn't help that.

"I doubt it. My fellow doctors aren't any more eager to work Friday nights than babysitters are." He regarded her sadly. Milking it a little.

If Zady hadn't gone with him to the Carrigans' house and met Caleb, she'd have simply walked away. But that little boy was in a nest where he felt safe, and now he had to be yanked out of it. The poor kid deserved a break.

What was wrong with her? Why was she providing exactly the arguments that she'd have rejected ferociously had Nick voiced them?

"Six months," he said.

"Excuse me?"

"I committed to my shift for a year," Nick said. "But I'm only asking you for six months. If you'll move in for that long, it will give me a chance to make other arrangements for Caleb or negotiate a schedule change at the hospital. Free rent *and* food, remember. That includes laundry detergent."

Leave while you have the strength. "I'd be working for you *and* your cousin. Ever think of that?"

His mouth snapped shut. Then it reopened. "Granted,

I expect you to honor my privacy. Loyalty matters, especially in such close quarters. But I wouldn't expect you to tell me about what goes on in his practice, either. Surely that shouldn't pose a problem."

"I'm not sure— What's that?" From the bushes poked a pointy nose. "It isn't a skunk, is it?"

"Hold still."

She had no trouble obeying.

A cat-size white rat with black markings advanced onto the patio. Zady tried to scream but nothing emerged. All she could do was cling to Nick's arm, registering his strength and the odd fact that he didn't seem alarmed.

"Wow," he said.

"Wow, what?"

"It's a possum. Technically, an opossum."

"Seriously?" She'd heard of the nocturnal creatures, marsupials that raised their young in pouches, like kangaroos. No one had mentioned how ugly they were, with that long naked tail.

"Do you suppose they're endangered?"

"That's hard to believe," Zady said. "Who would get close enough to harm one?"

To her embarrassment, she uttered a squeak as the creature skittered across the patio. At the far side, it paused and regarded them with beady eyes, as if asking, *"Who are you and what are you doing in my territory?"*

"We won't hurt you." She hadn't meant to speak aloud.

In a flash, it vanished into the darkness. "You can't let him down now," Nick said. "He's counting on us to respect his territory."

"This isn't his territory, it's Mr. Tran's," Zady said. "Besides, he might endanger the children."

"Possums are harmless," Nick assured her. "I've read that they eat insects and other small pests. And how fascinating for the kids to experience nature at close range."

"You could do a sales job on a cockroach in the kitchen," she muttered.

"Which we're more likely to find at the Harbor Suites than in this house." Nick ran his hand along her arm. "You sure you're all right?"

Zady refused to be laid low by an encounter with a possum. "I'm fine." She withdrew, and immediately missed the sturdy bulge of his muscles.

"Shall we go in and tell Mr. Tran we'll take the place?" he murmured.

Through the glass doors, she gazed into the glow of the kitchen. Everything appeared shiny and up-to-date, in contrast to the weary decor of her motel unit. Here, Linda could play in an enclosed yard with a small companion, who badly needed the stability of a live-in sitter. Moreover, six months of free rent and meals would refresh Zady's depleted bank account.

The place came with a dangerously attractive man. She'd be sharing meals with Nick, inhaling his masculine pheromones, becoming vulnerable to him when she ought to be seeking the man of her dreams.

For heaven's sake, her experience with Dwayne had armored her against falling for the wrong guy. Surely she'd be impervious to the allure of bossy Dr. Single Dad.

Almost impervious.

"Six months," Zady said.

"Done." He high-fived her.

Only after they'd gone inside, made arrangements with a beaming Mr. Tran and headed home did she realize that tomorrow she'd have to tell Marshall what she'd agreed to. Well, as Nick had said, she ought to be able to keep her jobs separate—if only the two men in her life could stay on good terms.

Chapter Nine

On Tuesday morning, while Marshall was in surgery, Zady restocked supplies, set up for afternoon office procedures and phoned to remind patients of appointments. In the age of the electronic calendar with its beeping alarms, she didn't understand why people often lost track of scheduled events—but perhaps they experienced such apprehension that they forgot to list doctor visits on their calendars.

In person or on voice mail, she kept her tone pleasant, even though she had better things to do this morning than nag. Yesterday's pact with Nick had kept her awake half the night, drawing up to-do lists. By late morning, she was grateful to be able to start work on them. True, these weren't part of her duties, she mused with a touch of guilt, but she wasn't cheating her employer, since she often skipped breaks and cut short her meals to attend to her duties.

Zady emailed Alice about the move on Sunday and provided both her old and new addresses, for good measure. She also posed questions that had piled up in her mind: What did Linda like to eat? How far had she progressed with potty training? What toys was she bringing?

She informed Zora of the new situation, also via email, which prompted a visit from Lucky. He popped into Marshall's office shortly before the lunch hour, moving at near-lightning speed, and at first Zady assumed that her brother-in-law had come for something related to his new duties.

His promotion to director of nursing for the men's fertility program had been officially announced the previous day. He'd circulated a "We're a team!" memo expressing appreciation for the staff and promising regular reports on the progress of the expansion. In keeping with the theme of teamwork, he still wore his navy nurse's uniform rather than a suit, she noticed when he barreled up to the nurses' station.

After chatting briefly with the other two RNs, Lucky caught Zady's arm and steered her into the break room. "My wife called about your new living arrangements."

"You can release my elbow," she said.

"Sorry." With a self-conscious grin, her brother-in-law obeyed. "I just… What were you thinking?"

"Are you speaking as my nursing supervisor or as Zora's husband?"

"I'm speaking as a man with common sense."

"Well, quit doing that." Leaning against a table, Zady tried to ignore the vending machines that loomed over them as if glowering. Did they disapprove of her choices, too? "I explained to Zora that I'm supervising my goddaughter for a month. She'll be happier in a house with a playmate."

"Yes, but you signed on as a live-in nanny for six months." Concern darkened Lucky's brown eyes. "If you're having financial problems, you could have asked Zora and me. We're family."

That was all Zady needed—another male interfering in her life. "You're my sister's husband, not my father." Seeing his hurt expression, she added, "I'm sure you mean well. And since you're eager to be involved, I'm sure Nick could use your help moving in his son's furniture. Shall I let him know you're available on Sunday?"

That brought Lucky up short. After a bit of throat-clearing, he nodded. "I'll contact him directly. And listen, Zady, call whenever you need a spot of emergency babysitting. You're welcome to join us for the occasional meal, too."

"Much appreciated."

Lucky paused as if weighing whether to continue scolding. Then, with a shrug, he left.

The two other nurses scurried in. "You'll be living with the other Dr. Davis and two toddlers?" asked Jeanine, a tall, whip-thin nurse in her fifties who'd raised six children. "Do you have a masochistic streak?"

The acoustics in this building were much too good, Zady reflected. "I'm the sitter, not the girlfriend."

"A nanny for a hottie like Nick Davis. Interesting." In her late forties, Ines had a short, rotund body that provided dramatic contrast to Jeanine's bony build. "I sense a budding romance."

Zady groaned. During her middle-of-the-night list-making mania, she'd recognized that a subversive part of her longed to cast Nick in the role of dream guy. Since this same weakness had manipulated her into sticking with Dwayne long after any rational woman would have hit the road, she rejected it. That didn't mean she'd obliterated the temptation. Yet.

"In a word, I have no romantic intentions," she said.

"That's more than a word," Ines noted.

"The word is no. It's a purely practical arrangement. He's the dad and I'm the nanny."

"We've seen movies about nannies." Ines removed her lunch box from the refrigerator. "They land in bed with the dad."

"Mary Poppins didn't do that," Jeanine objected.

"Yes, but she had Bert the chimney sweep. Did you see the size of his broom?"

If this comedy team was eating here, Zady would flee to the hospital cafeteria. She needed solitude to review her messages and edit her lists.

To her relief, Ines pointed disapprovingly at her friend's lunch box. "The special today is fettuccine Alfredo. You promised to join me!"

Jeanine wavered. "It's fattening."

"It's your favorite, and mine, too." Ines never worried about calories, which explained her round shape and also her upbeat moods.

Jeanine sighed. "Do you like tuna, Zady? You can have my sandwich."

She'd brought a small green salad that offered no competition to a tuna sandwich. "I'd love it. Thanks." Gratefully, she accepted her colleague's lunch box.

"Enjoy it while you can," Ines advised. "Soon you'll be fixing peanut butter and jelly on an assembly line." She had a couple of children with her husband and a pair of stepchildren, who actually liked her, from what Zady had heard.

"No, I won't. The day care center serves lunch." Zady pointed out. "Go enjoy your fettuccine."

"We intend to," Ines responded, and tugged Jeanine from the break room. She paused in the doorway to say, "Well, hi, Dr. Davis. Your nurse has news for you."

It was fortunate that they made a quick getaway, because Zady was ready to fling the lunch box at them. There went her carefully phrased explanation to Marshall, the timing of which had accounted for a good part of last night's wakefulness.

As she searched for words, he saved her the trouble. "I got the gist from the hall. Something about working as my cousin's nanny." Impossible to read his reaction from his tone. "During his overnight shifts, I presume."

"It started with my goddaughter, Linda." She explained about agreeing to take the child for a month. "And Caleb's grandparents have health problems. Nick's renting a house."

"A house? That should be a new experience for him."

Did she detect a sarcastic note? "It's new for me, too."

"I didn't mean to sound negative."

"Neither did I. It should be fun." She hurried on, to smooth over the awkwardness. "When we were touring the place, a possum wandered onto the patio and nearly gave me a heart attack. That doesn't usually happen in apartments."

"I've run into raccoons in my yard." Marshall had bought a house in town, Zady had learned when she fielded a few calls from his real estate agent during last month's escrow. "Just keep the possums from nesting in the attic or under the house and you'll be fine."

Good advice, Zady supposed, but unnecessary. "That'll be the landlord's problem, or Nick's. I'll strictly be handling the overnight supervision of both kids and, well, related stuff. *Not* cooking and cleaning. I already have a job. With you."

"I'm not sure how you can avoid cooking for the kids, but Nick should hire a cleaning service," Marshall said.

"That's a brilliant idea." Marshall's childhood in a privileged environment had its positive side, such as his awareness that people didn't have to do all the dirty work themselves, Zady mused.

"Don't tell him it came from me. He won't appreciate it."

That was an unusually personal remark from her reticent boss. "I gather you guys rub each other the wrong way."

"Only for the past thirty-four years."

"Since Nick was born?"

"Correct. I have no memories from when I was that young, but I'm sure we loathed each other from the day he entered my world. Sorry. I didn't mean to speak so bluntly," Marshall said. "How old are these children?"

"Caleb's three and Linda's two and a half." Zady hoped he didn't hear her stomach growling, responding to the siren call of the tuna sandwich.

"They'll be in day care here?"

"Linda will. I'm not sure of Nick's plans for Caleb. He

attends preschool, but I'm assuming he'll switch to someplace local." Zady wondered if Nick had thought of that yet, and decided to message him about it.

"Regarding a preschool, you might ask our new staff psychologist for a recommendation," Marshall said. "Dr. Brightman is a child and family counselor. I presume she's familiar with facilities in the area."

The man was full of helpful ideas. "I'll pass the word along. And I promise never to reveal a source."

A rare smile transformed his face. "Once your goddaughter's settled, feel free to bring her to the office for a visit."

"Thanks. I will."

Nick ought to listen to his cousin as she did, Zady mused as she tore into her lunch. He might be surprised.

Or perhaps, like her and Zora for too many years, they'd simply find new issues to fight about.

She remembered Nick's worries about divided loyalties. She was already agreeing to hide information. It might be harder than she'd believed to keep her jobs separate.

IN HIS TEENS, when Nick used to read for fun, he'd been fascinated by the green light on Daisy's dock and the allure it held for the hero of *The Great Gatsby.* Ah, the magnetic appeal of a woman. The draw of the unattainable dream. The…

For heaven's sake, he thought as he paced his motel suite on Saturday night. The light from Zady's unit across the way was merely yellow-beige filtered through cheap curtains. Tomorrow they'd be sharing a house. Why did he keep staring over there?

No doubt because, despite their proximity, they might as well be on different continents. Although messages had flown between them all week, Nick had only glimpsed her in passing, yet he'd felt her influence in a thousand ways.

At her insistence, he'd hired a twice-a-month cleaning service recommended by the landlord. Also thanks to her, he'd obtained a recommendation from Dr. Brightman and enrolled Caleb at the Starbright Lane Preschool near the Safe Harbor Civic Center. The school's van would pick up his son at home each morning at eight-thirty—before Zady left for work—and deliver him to the hospital day care center at lunchtime.

Nick had never realized that having a child involved such complicated scheduling. Luckily, there were high-quality facilities in the area, and he'd managed to stretch his budget—barely—to accommodate all this.

Would Sunday ever arrive? Adrenaline pumping, Nick paced through his rooms, double-checking that he'd packed all but tomorrow's absolute essentials. That hadn't been difficult, since most of his belongings remained in boxes from his previous move. Nor had he bought many groceries. In the kitchen, a small cooler stood open to receive the refrigerator's meager contents in the morning.

He had a full day planned, transporting his stuff to the house and then, with Lucky's assistance, driving to La Habra Heights to collect Caleb and his furniture. Elaine had promised to have everything ready, although she'd delayed the hour from 2:00 p.m. to 3:00 p.m. and then 4:00 p.m.

Thank goodness Nick wouldn't have to put up with her unpredictable ways much longer. That wasn't entirely true, since she and Bennie had promised to visit Caleb at his new home next weekend, but Nick would have more control over the circumstances. And surely Elaine's eagerness to see her grandson would discourage her game-playing.

From the corner of his eye, he glimpsed a flash of light in Zady's unit. Or so he believed, since for once he hadn't been staring out the window. Yes, she'd opened her door. Who could be visiting at seven o'clock on a Saturday night?

It was none of Nick's business. His relationship with

Zady was purely that of colleagues. But what if she was in danger? Even a town with a low crime rate might be the scene of an unpredictable outrage.

Like you sticking your nose where it doesn't belong?

"ALICE!" ZADY STARED in surprise at her blonde friend. "I thought you were arriving tomorrow, at the house."

"Things changed and we figured it might be easier to explain in person than on the phone." Alice ducked her head apologetically. "I hope it's okay."

"Auntie Zee!" Behind Alice, a small fireball wiggled loose from her father's hand and shot forward. Zady grabbed her goddaughter and staggered backward, the hug turning into a near-wrestling match.

"You *are* excited. Me, too." As she cuddled the eager girl, Zady reflected how utterly unprepared she was to play sitter tonight, with her possessions jammed into suitcases and her larder nearly empty.

"We brought gear." Following his wife into the apartment, Bill Madison shrugged a duffel bag and a backpack off his rugged frame. "There's food in the car and I'm not sure what-all else. As usual, my wife couldn't resist buying out the store."

With his short beard and neatly trimmed brown hair, the big man could pass for a therapist. Which he was—a physical therapist trained to assist patients during rehabilitation from orthopedic surgery and sports injuries. He'd brought that expertise into establishing their health-seminars business, dubbed the Best Madison for Living Well. Zady found the pun on "medicine" a stretch, but Alice said clients enjoyed it.

"We realized we'd miscalculated how long it will take to travel and set up for Monday's seminar in San Francisco." Alice laid a large envelope on the table. "Here's the information about our medical insurance and Linda's health history, and a letter authorizing you to get treatment. Hang on while we fetch the rest of the stuff."

"Sure." As the couple headed back to the parking lot, Zady reflected that she and Linda would have to share her queen-size bed tonight. Well, that should be fine.

"Where do I sleep?" Linda trotted into the next room.

"In here with me." Following, Zady noticed how much her goddaughter's coordination had improved in the past few months. "We'll go to our new house tomorrow."

"Let's go tonight!" The child regarded her imperiously.

"Tonight I have to tickle you like this." Dodging forward, Zady suited words to actions and was rewarded with a gale of giggles. "And swing you around like this." Gripping Linda under the arms, she swung her in a circle, careful to avoid the furniture.

"Whee!"

Setting her goddaughter on the carpet, Zady caught her breath. "Do you remember how to do the hokeypokey?"

"Hokey! Pokey!" Short, reddish-brown hair haloing her head, the toddler tried to sing and kick simultaneously, and succeeded mostly in flailing her arms.

"Watch the lamp!" Zady moved it aside. "Good job, Linda."

From the front room came the stomp of footsteps and the rumble of male voices. What on earth? She'd expected a few shopping bags, not a moving crew.

In the living room, Bill and Nick were lowering a toy chest to the floor. "Your neighbor was kind enough to help," Bill explained, dusting off his hands.

"He's the doctor I'll be working for," Zady explained as Alice appeared with two grocery sacks.

"You mean Dr. Davis?" Alice asked.

"That's me." Nick stretched his shoulders.

"I thought she already worked for you."

"That's Marshall, Nick's cousin. I emailed you about the

two of them." Zady frowned at Nick, who was grinning at the confusion. He hadn't been amused by it when they'd first met and she'd slammed the door in his face, she recalled tartly. "I'll be working for Marshall during the day and babysitting for Nick during his overnights."

"It was in her email," Bill assured his wife.

Alice set the sacks on the kitchen counter. "Sorry for the temporary brain fog. You wouldn't believe how much we have to organize for our trip."

"I can see that." From the sacks, Zady put a half gallon of ice cream in the freezer.

"Nice to meet you, Nick." Bill shook his hand and thanked Zady for taking their daughter. After a hug for Linda, he and his wife turned to exit.

"Mommy?" Braced with legs apart in the middle of the living room, Linda stared at her parents in dismay. "Don't go."

"Oh, sweetie!" Hurrying over, Alice scooped her up. "Remember what I told you? You're staying with Auntie Zee for a few weeks while we're gone."

"For a month," Bill corrected, stroking his daughter's hair.

"She doesn't understand how long a month is," his wife grumbled. In a sweeter tone, to Linda, she said, "Honey bear, we'll video chat every night."

"Or as often as we can." Her husband regarded Zady as if expecting commiseration. "I don't believe in promising more than might be possible."

"We'll have fun." Zady hoped her friends weren't always this touchy with each other. Their complicated work and travel plans must be putting them under pressure.

The goal was to save their marriage. She hoped that would be easier to accomplish once their trip got under way.

Nick stayed behind after they left. To her raised eyebrows, he responded, "I thought a little entertainment might distract Linda."

Talk about an offer she couldn't refuse. "Why don't you play with her for a few minutes. I'll scoop us some ice cream."

"Ice cream!" Linda cheered.

"While Auntie Zee is doing that, let me show you something." Nick guided Linda to the couch. "I loaded a few kids' games on my phone. How about this one?"

"Yay!" Beeps and whistles filled the room as her tiny finger poked randomly at the screen.

"Uh, that's not exactly how you play it."

More beeps. More whistles.

"But obviously, those game designers don't know everything," Nick said.

Chuckling, Zady dug disposable bowls from a sack. With the ice cream conveniently squishy, she scraped hunks into the bowls.

Preparing to summon the others to the table, Zady paused to watch them poking at the phone side by side, Nick almost as gleeful as Linda. What a cute scene, and what a great dad he'd make. Or already was.

She'd been apprehensive about supervising his child. It hadn't occurred to her that he might help with Linda.

At her summons, the pair scrambled to the table. Nick fetched a booster seat for the little girl while Zady tucked a paper towel into Linda's collar.

"You're good with her," she told Nick.

"She's adorable." After adjusting the little girl's chair, Nick took a seat. "You know, she bears a strong resemblance to you. And she doesn't look anything like Alice." After dipping his spoon into his dessert, he halted abruptly. "Zady, is she…?"

Could he have guessed? "Is she what?"

Nick glanced at the child. She was too busy eating to pay attention. In a low voice, he said, "Adopted?"

He wondered if Zady had given birth and relinquished her daughter? Relief washed through her that he'd missed the more complicated truth. "I can assure you, Alice had her by C-section. While I doubt she'll ever show you the scar, it's there." She forced herself to stop talking before she could rattle on nervously.

"Sorry. Just a thought."

When they were done eating, she declared it was bedtime for Linda *and* for her. It might be early, but they had a big day ahead.

"I'm glad I met Linda tonight." Nick studied the little one wistfully. "You guys make the cutest picture."

Linda yawned, showing baby teeth, gums and a mouth colored brown from the chocolate ice cream.

"Well, not quite picture-perfect," Nick joked.

"Nothing a little tooth-brushing won't fix."

"That's true." With a salute, Nick ambled out. Linda scampered to the window, pushed aside the curtain and waved at his departing figure. Zady was pleased that Nick glanced back, spotted her and returned the wave.

"Nice man," Linda said.

"Yes. You're right." Things might change once they lived under the same roof—Nick's roof. But even if he turned into Dwayne's clone, Zady wasn't the naive girl she'd been ten years ago. Nor, despite an undeniable attraction, did she harbor delusions about Nick becoming her boyfriend.

Too demanding. Too unforgiving toward his cousin. Too already a father. After her miserable experience with more-or-less stepkids, she refused to go down that road again.

Six months, that was her maximum. "One day at a time," Zady said out loud, and rummaged through Linda's duffel for a nightgown and a toothbrush.

Chapter Ten

On Sunday, despite his earlier frustration, Nick was relieved that Caleb's grandparents had delayed the pickup until 4:00 p.m. That allowed them plenty of time to get the house in shape.

In the morning, he drove his belongings to the new house. There, he discovered a glitch: Mr. Tran had overlooked his instructions to remove the bed and bureau from Caleb's bedroom. He couldn't reach the landlord on a Sunday, and the furniture was too heavy for Nick to shift to the garage by himself. He texted Lucky, who promised to arrive early.

It was important to Nick that Caleb go to sleep tonight surrounded by his familiar possessions. *And he will.*

Nick returned to the Harbor Suites to assist Zady and Linda in packing her car and putting their excess items in his. At the new house, they ate sandwiches and spent the early afternoon unpacking, rearranging the living room and making up the little girl's cot. An easygoing child, Linda ran about enthusiastically, then played with her toys.

Unbelievable—he'd scored a house! Nick reflected when he took a moment to catch his breath. And a live-in friend and a delightful little girl who seemed remarkably even-tempered for a toddler. Linda curled on the couch poking at the games on his phone while the grown-ups planned meals for the next few nights.

The fridge and pantry were well stocked with their combined supplies. The pots and pans, plates and tableware filled the drawers and cabinets.

To his relief, Zady relaxed her insistence on avoiding the kitchen. "I'll cook dinner for the kids Tuesdays through Fridays, on your work nights. You're responsible for Saturdays through Mondays."

"No problem."

"You *can* cook, right?" she pressed.

"I have a few specialties." And what Nick didn't know, he could learn.

She nodded, although he detected a trace of skepticism in her expression. "I'm going to take a nap with Linda."

"Need any help?"

"Putting her to bed or sleeping?"

Nick grinned. "How about both?"

She poked him in the ribs. "Snoozing with my boss? No, thanks."

Her boss. He'd almost forgotten that part, Nick conceded as he watched her stroll out of the kitchen, curly hair floating and softly rounded derriere swaying with natural sensuality.

Zady didn't belong to him, and the four of them weren't a family. But after the difficult adjustments since Bethany's death and Nick's change to the night shift, he finally felt as if he was regaining his balance.

Lucky arrived around 2:00 p.m. with a borrowed van. "Nice place," he announced when Nick admitted him. "Pretty much what I have in mind for me and Zora when we can afford a house of our own."

"We like it."

After Nick showed him Caleb's bedroom, the nursing supervisor pushed up the sleeves of his jersey. "We can do this in an hour. Let's dig in."

They dismantled the bed and lugged it to the garage, then returned for the dresser. It took more angling and heaving than Nick had anticipated, but they moved that without damaging it, too.

"I really appreciate you doing this." Nick felt good about what they'd accomplished.

"No problem."

After leaving a note for Zady, who remained napping in her bedroom with Linda, they headed out. Traffic flowed well until they hit a jam halfway to La Habra Heights. The van lacked an onboard computer, but Nick's phone showed an accident a couple of miles ahead.

"How bad is it?" Lucky's fingers drummed the steering wheel.

"They're moving the damaged cars to the shoulder." It appeared the lanes would be clear soon. Taking an alternate route would waste more time than it saved, Nick calculated.

All the same, he gritted his teeth as they inched along. He'd hate to be late, but in view of his experiences with Elaine, calling to warn her wouldn't accomplish anything. He might as well use the opportunity to get better acquainted with Zady's brother-in-law. "Your new position keeping you busy?"

"Sure is," Lucky said cheerfully. "I've been planning in-service training, reviewing patient-care standards and screening office nurses for Dr. Rattigan, since I won't be able to assist him as much as I used to."

"I'm surprised you can do it at all. Surely he doesn't expect you to perform double duty."

"I plan to keep an eye on things for him." Lucky tapped the accelerator, increasing their speed from a 15 mph creep to a 20 mph crawl. "I owe it to him. A few years ago, when the doctor I worked for retired, nobody would hire me. One look at my tattoos and they dismissed me as a ruffian. I would have removed the tats, but the process is painful and expensive."

"And I hear it leaves scars." Zady had mentioned that Lucky hailed from a rough neighborhood in LA. To Nick, his achievements seemed all the more impressive that he'd come so far. "How'd you manage while you were out of work?"

Lucky accelerated as the traffic opened up ahead. "I spent a year temping for a nursing service. When Cole joined the staff at Safe Harbor, I didn't believe my application to be his nurse had a chance, but I figured I'd try."

Obviously, Cole had hired him. "He didn't mind the body art?"

"The only thing that mattered to him was how I regarded patient care and whether we could deal comfortably with each other."

It struck Nick that he, too, had grown up in a rough area, and neither of his parents had graduated from college. But unlike Lucky's parents, neither of them had showed a strong work ethic. How had *he* become a high achiever?

The answer was partly his inner drive, and partly his reaction to Marshall's side of the family. While a few teachers had encouraged Nick to aim high, it was primarily the disdain of his aunt, uncle and cousin that had spurred him to prove himself. How strange.

"I nearly got a tattoo once," he recalled. "As a teenager. But I didn't figure it was worth the grief. Marshall's folks sneered at me enough already."

"Some guys would have done it to spite them," Lucky observed.

"I defied them by succeeding in medical school." Also, Nick had figured body art might put off future employers. "I can understand your devotion to Cole."

"He's an amazing man." Lucky glanced at the faster-moving lane to their left but apparently decided not to risk a sudden move. "We just heard Friday that he received a grant to establish two new surgical fellowships. It hasn't been announced, so I'd appreciate your keeping mum, but we're excited."

"Congratulations." A grant meant his cousin would probably be successful in his bid to secure offices for the urology fellows. That wasn't likely to go down well with Nick's colleagues, but betraying a confidence would be a poor repayment for Lucky's kindness.

Finally they left the freeway, wound through the heights and approached the Carrigans' address. Next to the carriage-shaped mailbox, a for sale sign had been stuck into the ground.

"They're selling their house?" Lucky said.

"No one told me."

True, the Carrigans had said they planned to move into assisted living, but what other surprises awaited him? Nick wondered with a twist of uneasiness. He hoped he hadn't been a fool to assume Elaine was losing her power to manipulate him.

ZADY AWOKE IN the dim late-afternoon light with a sense of dislocation. Where was she? The bed didn't feel familiar and a night-light cast an eerie shadow through the wood-and-paper screen closing off part of the room.

She turned toward the window. A small gap in the curtains revealed rosebushes and, across the street, a ranch-style house illuminated from within.

A house much like this one. Now she remembered where she was.

Zady groped onto the bedside table for her phone. It read 4:34 p.m. She must have slept over an hour, but there were no sounds from the rest of the house, only Linda's soft breathing from behind the screen.

Rising, she peeked at her goddaughter. The girl lay curled beneath the covers, her arms around her favorite doll.

A glow of pure love spread through Zady. How adorable this child was. If she'd given birth to Linda as Nick had suspected, she'd never have been able to part with her. Would she ever have another child and a man to shelter them?

Don't you dare fantasize about Nick.

She ought to freshen up before he and Lucky returned—but entering her bathroom would force her to sneak past Linda and risk waking her. Instead, Zady crossed the living room. She saw no reason not to use the main bathroom, which opened both into the hall and, through a side door, into Nick's room.

A splash of water didn't do much to restore her appearance, the merciless mirror informed Zady. Her hair was a mess, but she'd left her purse in her bathroom, and she wasn't about to borrow Nick's brush.

It lay on the counter beside his electric razor, next to a bottle of aftershave lotion that exuded a spicy scent. When Zady reopened the door to Nick's room as a courtesy, the air that flowed around her felt infused with his maleness. Since leaving Dwayne behind, she'd missed that humming awareness of a masculine presence.

When another inspection showed Linda still sleeping, Zady dared retrieve her brush. After achieving little more than rearranging the tangles in her hair, she retreated to the kitchen. Earlier, she'd brewed a pot of coffee, and now she poured a cup and sat down with her phone to write a memo to herself.

Essential qualities in a man, she tapped out.

No sense listing obvious stuff like sex appeal, hygiene or the absence of a criminal record. In fact, anything that applied to Nick could be omitted. The goal was to provide reinforcement should she weaken.

Number 1. Fresh start—no stepkids or ex-wives! Excellent.

Staring at the tiny keypad, Zady wondered what idiot had put the exclamation point on the number pad, requiring an extra step to reach it. To her, that punctuation mark was as important as a comma or a period.

Moving right along…

Number 2. He has never mistreated or abandoned a girlfriend. Maybe she should add, *Or delivered a halfhearted proposal after she got pregnant.* But it was important to her psyche that she maintain the appearance of objectivity.

Number 3. Financially stable. Although Nick earned a good income, he had student loans. And a guy who could only afford to pay his nanny room and board was barely hanging on.

Number 4. There ought to be a number 4. What was it? Unfair to list working a day job, since that would rule out too many otherwise-eligible guys. Instead, she typed, *Doesn't put me in the middle of family feuds, especially involving my doctor.*

That was too specific. She deleted everything after "feuds."

Zady sat back, pleased to have covered the necessary ground. She'd have to remember to keep looking at her list until being around Nick wore so thin that she no longer, even at the most insidious level, considered him boyfriend material.

The doorbell rang. Who was that? With her hair frizzing and her makeup worn off, she was in no state to greet anyone. Then it occurred to her that Mr. Tran might be stopping by to welcome them. She'd better hurry, because if he rang again, he'd wake Linda.

She should have peered outside first, Zady realized, too late. She opened the door to reveal the last person she'd expected.

Her boss. Her *real* boss. Dr. Marshall Davis.

THE INTERIOR OF the Carrigan house had undergone a thorough cleaning since last weekend, Nick noted when Elaine insisted on escorting him and Lucky on a tour of the premises. "Our real estate agent recommended this cleaning company. Didn't they do a marvelous job?" She indicated the spotless kitchen with a stove and refrigerator so old they qualified as fashionably retro.

Nick mumbled his agreement and reached for Caleb's hand. The little boy peeked apprehensively at his grandmother. She nodded, bathing them in an overly bright smile, and Caleb took his father's hand gingerly.

What was her angle? Surely Elaine and Bennie, who remained resting in the den, didn't imagine that cleaning up the property and listing it for sale would make any difference to his plans.

"We should start moving Caleb's furniture," Nick said. "I'm sure Lucky has other plans for this evening." *As do I.*

"His furniture?" Elaine repeated as if he'd sprung this idea out of the blue. "Oh, dear."

"Surely you don't plan to take it with you to assisted living." Nick doubted their new apartment would have any extra room.

"No, but the agent says it's important to keep the house fully furnished. Prospective buyers have to be able to visualize themselves living here."

"Wouldn't that be easier *without* someone else's furniture?" Lucky asked. Astutely, in Nick's opinion.

Elaine shrugged. "She says to keep it furnished, and she's the expert. But his clothes and toys are packed." Turning, she led them toward the stairs.

Nick and Lucky exchanged glances. Clearly they both found her behavior peculiar. But although Nick's child support had no doubt paid part of the cost of the furniture, he couldn't insist she surrender it.

This meant he and Lucky would be stuck carting the bed and bureau back from the garage. More important, Caleb faced an unnecessarily difficult transition.

With luck, he'd be distracted by his new playmate. Nick was glad he hadn't mentioned Linda to the Carrigans. Heaven knew how Elaine would have used Linda's presence against him, but he suspected she'd have figured out a way.

In the bedroom, they found some of Caleb's toys and games still scattered on the floor. "Pick those up and bring them along, okay?" Nick asked his son.

"Okay, Dad."

No fussing or arguing. Was that disappointment on Elaine's face, or was he reading too much into her expression?

With Lucky and Nick hefting the boxes and Caleb carrying loose items, it didn't take long to stuff his possessions into the van. After the last trip downstairs and through the entry hall, Lucky stayed outside while Nick went to take leave of the Carrigans.

After apologizing for not rising from his armchair, Bennie thanked Nick for his cooperation. "You were right. We'll be better off in assisted living."

"I hope you can visit us." Nick meant that sincerely. Maintaining continuity with the boy's loved ones mattered a great deal. "If you can't, I'll bring Caleb to see you. Let's make plans for next weekend."

"That will depend on the real estate agent."

"Elaine!" warned her husband.

"It's not as if we're going to vanish from his life," she said. "Although Nick might wish we would."

"Not in the least. That would be horrible for him." Nick hadn't forgotten his disorientation and anger as a ten-year-old when his father had left abruptly. He'd never forgiven his dad for disappearing.

While Nick had a measure of sympathy for the man due to his bipolar disorder, the pain of his father's rejection had been deep and long-lasting. Years later, Quentin Davis had made a few feeble attempts to restore contact, but Nick had rebuffed him. And his father hadn't tried very hard to persuade him otherwise.

Caleb had already lost his mother. Nick didn't intend for his son to lose any more family.

"So you'll come visit us next weekend?" he asked.

"Of course." Elaine's attitude appeared to have undergone a rapid change. "We'd love to see your house. And that sweet nurse." To Caleb, she said, "Without Zady, none of this would be possible. You'd have to limp along with your sick old grandparents."

That was hardly the case. "His home is with me now," Nick corrected. "With or without Zady."

"I think she deserves more credit than that, but let's not argue." Stiffly, Elaine bent to hug her grandson. "You'll forget all about us the minute you're with her."

"No, I won't." Caleb clung to her. "Grandma! Grandpa! Don't send me away!"

In the boy's shrill voice, Nick heard heartbreak, along with exhaustion and hunger. Understandable, since it was almost dinnertime.

"I'll tell you what." He eased Caleb away from Elaine. "Let's order pizza while we drive home so it'll be ready when we get there."

"Okay." Despite his assent, Caleb's pace dragged as they went out.

Lucky didn't say much until they were on the freeway. Caleb remained silent, too, strapped into his booster seat behind them.

Keeping his eyes on the well-lit freeway, Lucky asked quietly, "Is she always like that?"

"Elaine? Like what?" Nick was curious how the other man had interpreted her puzzling behavior.

"Saying one thing and meaning another."

That was the exact quality he'd been struggling to identify. Now the appropriate word sprang to mind. "You mean passive-aggressive? I suppose she is, somewhat."

"More than somewhat. She defines the term." Lucky

frowned as a car with ultrabright headlights zoomed up behind. He slowed, and the inconsiderate driver swerved past.

"She's always been strong-willed and a bit overbearing, but never this erratic," Nick said. "I have no idea what she expects to gain."

"Neither do I, but I'd watch out for that dame."

From the rear seat, a little voice cried, "My grandma's not a dame!"

"Little pitchers have big ears," Lucky muttered. Nick hadn't heard that phrase in years.

He turned to face his small, defiant son. "Caleb, what do you think a dame is?"

"I don't know."

"It's a lady."

"Oh."

The kid's obvious tension reminded Nick of his earlier offer. "What's your favorite pizza topping?"

"Uh, cheese."

"What else?"

"More cheese?"

"Most people love pepperoni, too," he prompted.

"Not me," Lucky put in. "I'm a vegetarian."

They spent the next few miles considering ideas for toppings, ranging from the practical—onions, mushrooms and tomatoes—to the improbable, including licorice bits and strawberries.

With Caleb giggling, Nick called Krazy Kids Pizza in Safe Harbor. He ordered two pizzas, one vegetarian with strawberries and one pepperoni with licorice.

"We don't have licorice, sir," the woman said.

"Okay, hold the licorice," Nick told her. "Are you telling me you have strawberries?"

"Yes. Frozen, not fresh."

"That won't do," he responded. "Hold the frozen strawberries, too."

Beside him, Lucky snorted with laughter. Caleb joined in.

Everyone sighed wearily but happily when they exited in Safe Harbor. Before moving here last month, Nick had driven Caleb on a tour of the town, including a stroll on the quay that bordered the harbor. Now the boy peered out the side window as they left the main boulevard. "Where are the boats?"

"The ocean's farther south," Nick told him. "We're almost to our house."

"Oh." He sounded disappointed.

Lucky drove slowly down their block and halted in the driveway. "I nearly clipped that silver sedan. Parked close to the curb, isn't it?"

Nick studied the expensive vehicle. "People who drive luxury cars think they own the world."

"Whoever it is, he has a doctor's parking sticker," Lucky observed.

The last thing Nick needed in his current mood was to deal with an uninvited visitor, he reflected dourly as he unstrapped Caleb. His shoulders and arms ached, and the tasks of unloading the van and hauling the furniture from the garage remained to be done.

Was there any chance their unexpected guest would pitch in? That slight hope faded when he opened the door to find Zady curled on the couch, Linda in her lap, while a lanky man lounged beside them, holding a book so they could all see the pictures.

What a cozy image. It should be Nick there, sharing a happy moment with his family, not his look-alike. What the hell did Marshall think he was doing, horning in on Nick's territory?

Chapter Eleven

Recalling her intention of creating a video log, Zady used her camera to capture Linda's squeal of joy on meeting her new playmate. Caleb's initial shyness melted into a grin as the little girl hugged him. Zady also caught the wonder on Marshall's face as he observed the children's interaction.

The only sour note—which she avoided recording—was Nick's scowl. That might be partly due to the grandparents' refusal to part with Caleb's furniture, she supposed after Lucky related the story, but why did Nick greet Marshall with such a curt nod?

Her boss had been a lifesaver when Linda had awoken crying for her parents, and Zady was unable to reach them by phone. Inspired by her account of the possum, Marshall had brought a children's book about exploring nature in the backyard, written and illustrated by a nurse at the hospital and her biologist husband. Although darkness was descending, they'd taken Linda on an exploration of the yard, an activity that had short-circuited her tantrum.

They'd just settled down to read when Nick had arrived, followed minutes later by a pizza delivery. To Zady's disappointment, Marshall declined to join them, no doubt in response to his cousin's obvious antagonism.

"I'm not really a pizza kind of guy," Marshall said.

"More the caviar type," Nick remarked as he paid the Krazy Kids driver.

Zady had an inappropriate urge to slap him. Mercifully, Lucky broke the awkwardness. "All we got were pepperoni and vegetarian. We tried to order licorice, but they were out."

"And strawberries, too," Caleb said.

"Have fun." Marshall started for the door.

"Don't go, Dr. Marsh!" That was what Linda had started calling him, to his and Zady's amusement.

"If I stay, I'll be a nuisance," he said.

Nick glanced thoughtfully at the little girl, who was hanging on to his cousin's belt. "We *could* use another set of arms."

Another set of arms? That was how he referred to one of the country's most gifted reconstructive surgeons? Zady narrowed her eyes at him. Ignoring her, Nick carried the pizza boxes toward the kitchen.

"We'll be maneuvering heavy stuff. You shouldn't risk injuring your hands," Lucky said.

"I'm not made of glass," Marshall replied. "I'd be happy to pitch in. And that pizza smells great."

"Sit with me," Linda commanded.

"So young and already bossing men around," Lucky said. "I like this girl."

After washing up, they gathered at the table, a tight fit with three tall men, Zady and two wiggly toddlers. But it was fun, she thought.

Marshall regarded his plate uncertainly. "No silverware?"

"No nothingware," Nick responded.

"The goal of eating pizza," Lucky said, "is to beat everybody else to the slice with the most good stuff on it, cram it into your mouth and snatch the next-best slice."

"Like this?" asked Caleb, and, missing his mouth entirely, smacked himself in the face with a slice.

"Me, too!" Linda sang out, and plunged her hands into the pizza. Thank goodness Zady had made sure the girl had washed her hands.

"Kids, try to remember you're at the dining table, not in a zoo." Zady's remark aroused giggles. "Marshall, if you'd like silverware, I'd be happy to fetch it." She hoped she remembered which drawer it was in. The spacious kitchen around them had several storage areas, including overhead cabinets, drawers and a pantry.

He shook his head, his cheeks touched with red. "I'm game. In many places in the world, no one uses silverware."

"Because they're starving?" Nick asked.

"No, because it's customary. Ever try Ethiopian cuisine?" Marshall asked. "You use a big round slice of flatbread as both your plate and your utensils. You tear off a piece, scoop up the food from the serving dish and do what Caleb's doing now, preferably without the mess. It's delicious."

"You've been to Africa?" Lucky asked, coming up for air.

"More like Anaheim." Marshall chose a slice of pepperoni. The rest of them had nearly finished their first serving. "They have a couple of great Ethiopian restaurants."

"I'd like to try one of those places," Lucky said.

"I'll send you the addresses."

"Thanks." Lucky regarded Nick. "So, how should we handle unloading and unpacking?"

While the men sorted out their plans, Zady supervised the kids. A little spillage didn't bother her, but when it migrated beyond their bibs, it threatened to stain their clothes.

She tuned back to the conversation when Marshall said, "I'm not sure if you know, Caleb, but you're named after our grandfather."

"Your grandfather?" Caleb asked.

"Marshall and I are cousins, so we have the same grandfather," Nick explained. "He'd be your great-grandfather if he were alive."

"You must have fond memories of him," Zady said. "I presume that's why you chose the name."

"He was a smart guy, if a little rigid." He polished off his third slice. "Who's ready for action?"

The men pushed back their chairs and left. While they worked, Zady and the kids opened Caleb's boxes to retrieve his pajamas. To her annoyance, Elaine had piled games and an old scrapbook on top of his clothing, and if there was a toothbrush, it had disappeared into the depths.

"Never mind. I have an extra one," she told him.

To background noises of scraping and thumping, she helped the children brush their teeth and change. On the couch, with Linda on her lap and Caleb beside her, she read to them from the book Marshall had brought.

Afterward, in her bedroom, the three of them sang "Twinkle Twinkle Little Star," and Caleb helped her tuck in Linda with her favorite doll.

In the front room, Zady remembered that she hadn't heard from Alice and Bill. A check of her phone showed no messages or missed calls. Well, they'd been driving all day and must be exhausted.

"Can I stay up late?" Caleb asked.

"Just till the guys get your room ready."

She was debating what to do with him next, when Nick came in to announce they'd finished. Lucky and Marshall both took their leave.

"See you in the morning," her doctor said to her, flexing his shoulders. "Fortunately, I don't have surgery. I might be a little stiff."

"Thanks, both of you." Nick met his cousin's gaze straight on. "You and Lucky have been troopers."

"Glad to help." Approaching the couch, Marshall reached down to shake Caleb's hand. "I enjoyed meeting you. You remind me of Grandpa, in the best way."

"Me, too," the boy said, then looked confused when the grown-ups chuckled.

After the guests left, he went to bed without protest. As Zady watched Nick say a prayer with him, she was pleased by how neatly the men had arranged his furniture, with a few stuffed animals on the bureau. While much remained to unpack, they'd done the hard part.

The room was smaller than Caleb's former one, and the sounds, including the occasional murmur of a passing car, reminded her that he'd lived until now in a rural setting. But tonight, regular breathing signaled that he'd fallen asleep almost instantly.

"Having Linda here is good for him," Nick observed when they were alone in the living room. Lint and dust flecked his brown hair and his usual clean, spicy scent was laced with honest sweat.

"And Caleb's a morale booster for her." Zady perched on the arm of the sofa. "How will you handle his schedule tomorrow?"

"Even though I have Mondays off, I plan to let him ride in the preschool van to help him get accustomed to the routine," Nick said. "I'll follow in my car."

"That's a good idea," Zady acknowledged. "What about at noon?"

"They'll send him to the hospital at lunchtime. Around one, I'll stop by the day care center to reassure him that everything's okay and make sure he eats lunch as planned."

"You're a great dad." Zady intended to pop in to visit Linda during her breaks, too.

Still on his feet, Nick regarded her warmly. "I can't imagine how I'd have handled this without you. Elaine was right. You're essential."

"I don't understand why she sings my praises." Zady had barely met the woman, after all. "And some of her behavior is weird." She described how the boxes had been packed.

"Lucky and I both think she's passive-aggressive. I guess I'm not devious enough to get ahead of her."

"She's expressing hostility indirectly?" Zady hated sneaky people who smiled to her face while stabbing her in the back. Dwayne's older daughter, Randi, had developed that unfortunate tendency when she'd reached her teen years, creating trouble by telling her father and mother lies about Zady after each visit.

Zady wished she could have established a friendship with the girl. As a nurse, she'd taken the lead in explaining the facts of life to the children when their parents had neglected to do it. But Zady had been troubled to see Randi acting out as a young teen, getting involved with a boyfriend several years older. The girl had resented Zady's concern, and Dwayne had dismissed her suggestion that he and his ex-wife seek counseling with their daughter.

"That would explain why she jerks me around," Nick reflected.

Oh, right, they were discussing Elaine being passive-aggressive. "That's too bad. I'm still not sure how I fit into the picture, though."

"Let's hope this will all die down now that Caleb lives here. Especially since she and Bennie are moving into assisted living." Nick strolled to a position behind Zady. "You did a lot of hauling today, too. Aching muscles?"

"You bet."

He reached down, his fingers probing her neck muscles. Slowly, he kneaded them until the knots eased, then progressed to her spine. It was heavenly.

The tension in Zady's body yielded to a tingling awareness of how much she enjoyed Nick's touch. His strength *and* his gentleness.

She rested her head against his chest. *Just let the warmth flow through you.* It seeped into the lonely spaces of her heart, releasing old hurts, rejections, failures. The warmth cocooned her, *Nick's* warmth.

Her breasts tightened and a melting sensation spread through her. A longing to yield, to trust.

But Nick wasn't a fantasy guy. They were only beginning to get to know each other, and the challenges of sharing a house and child care meant having to be realistic. *And on your guard.*

"Your muscles just tightened." Nick's hands stilled. "Is something wrong?"

"Not exactly."

"Not exactly in what way?"

When he sank onto the couch beside her, Zady searched for an answer that would be honest but not too revealing. "I'm still figuring out where the boundaries are."

"Between us?" He stretched his shoulders. "Of course between us. Stupid question."

"The massage was great." Although he deserved one in return, that would be too intimate, Zady decided.

"You're welcome." Nick plopped his feet on the coffee table.

"Shoes off."

"Hmm? Oh." He kicked off his shoes before putting his sock-covered feet back on the table. "Have to get in the habit of setting a good example, don't I?"

"We're parents now, in a sense," Zady agreed.

"This is like being married without the fun part," Nick teased.

"If I had more energy, I'd slap you."

"If I had more energy, you'd miss."

Her glance fell on the book, which she'd left on the coffee table. "Did you see this? A nurse and her husband wrote it, about exploring the backyard. Their little girl shot some of the photos."

Nick flipped it open. "Terrific. And already slightly smudged."

"After Marshall brought it over, he and Linda and I toured the yard with it." It had been impossible to avoid a few fingerprints on the pages.

"A gift from my cousin. Interesting." Nick set the book down. "You admire him, don't you?"

"He's been supportive about this whole move," she responded. "And he picked out that book after I mentioned our close encounter with a possum."

"You bring out the best in him."

"There's a lot of best to bring out."

If Nick had an answer, he must have been too tired to mention it. All he said was, "I'm going to collapse in my room now."

"Me, too." Recalling the sleeping girl, Zady added, "Very quietly."

"I'll lock up and switch off the lights. Now that I'm the man of the house."

"Okay, boss."

They'd survived moving in and sorting out the kids and their stuff, Zady reflected as she strolled wearily to her room. But she suspected there'd be many more hurdles ahead.

WAS IT POSSIBLE that for once in their lives, his cousin envied him? Nick wondered the next morning as he flipped pancakes, one of his few culinary specialties.

Last night, he'd caught a hint of longing in Marshall's gaze as they set up Caleb's room with stuffed animals and cartoon-character sheets. And the man had gone out of his way to find a book that would please the children.

If Marshall wished to get married and have kids, surely he'd have little trouble finding the right woman. The guy owned a house larger than this one and owed no med-school debts, plus he'd inherited a significant amount five years ago when his father died. Nor was he bad-looking. He could be charming, too, when he stopped passing judgment on everyone around him.

In college, Nick recalled his cousin dating a lively girl named Belle. For several years, she'd joined family celebrations and given the impression they were all but engaged. After graduation, for reasons Nick never learned, they'd broken up.

All day, curiosity about his cousin's unexpected reaction to Caleb and off-duty friendship with Zady teased at Nick. He wasn't sure why it bothered him, especially when matters were progressing smoothly in his new home. Zady had appreciated the breakfast he'd cooked, and, as he'd hoped, having Linda around kept Caleb on course during preparations for the day.

After following his son's van to preschool, Nick had observed the first half hour of activities before concluding it was okay for him to leave. He had plenty of unpacking and organizing to do at home.

Home. That's what was troubling him—the possibility that Marshall not only envied him having a son, but coveted his closeness to Zady. The man had established a relationship with her outside the office, nothing inappropriate, but there were plenty of instances at Safe Harbor of doctors marrying nurses. The eminent Cole Rattigan had wed his surgical nurse. Come to think of it, Nick's office mate, Jack Ryder, was married to his surgical nurse, too.

Why should Nick care? Zady wasn't his girlfriend, and she'd only promised to stay on as nanny for six months. Also, he refused to compete with his cousin in the romance department. A woman ought to be able to figure out which man she truly cared about.

The problem was that, so far, Zady hadn't shown any indications of falling for either of them. Since she was, in a sense, his employee, Nick supposed he should keep his distance. But did she have to be so much fun to hang out with? And did she have to have freckles that tempted him to play connect the dots all the way down her chest until he unbuttoned her blouse?

Well, Nick had domestic duties. He headed for the supermarket.

That night, he prepared vegetable lasagna from an internet recipe. It emerged runny, but everyone claimed to love it.

After dinner, they took turns shooting videos of the kids romping around and performing a hilariously clumsy version of the hokeypokey. As a bedtime story, Nick found a website on his phone about the disputed history of the song and dance, which had been around since the early 1800s. There'd been versions known as the Hokey Cokey and the Hoey Oka.

"This has nothing to do with karaoke, where people sing along with recordings," he informed the children as the four of them curled on his queen-size bed. "That's a Japanese term."

"You're confusing them," Zady said.

"If children aren't confused occasionally, their parents are oversimplifying things," Nick replied, although he suspected she was right.

"I'm tired." Linda yawned.

"Me, too." Caleb folded his arms. "I want to say goodnight to Grandma and Grandpa."

"I miss my mommy," Linda said.

"Not your daddy?" Nick teased.

Zady scowled at him above the children's heads. He supposed he deserved that for inviting trouble.

"Auntie Zee made a funny face!" Caleb cried.

"Funny face." Linda twisted her mouth. Caleb responded with a similarly grotesque expression.

Nick joined in, welcoming the change of subject, since he had no desire to phone the Carrigans. He had no patience to spare for Elaine's shenanigans.

"I wish I'd grown up with parents like us," Zady said after they'd put the kids to bed and retreated to the kitchen. She was fixing a cup of herbal tea, while Nick took out a few odds and ends for a snack.

"Hilarious and brilliant?" he asked.

"Able to play without arguing or..." She shook her head.

"Finish the sentence," Nick instructed.

"Or drinking too much, or spinning wild stories, like my dad used to do," Zady said wistfully.

"I'll bet my dad told crazier stories than yours." He dropped a handful of walnuts into a bowl, adding a dozen bite-size pieces of shredded wheat.

"My dad promised we'd move to Hawaii, ride plumes of lava and have dolphins for friends," Zady responded. "He was just kidding, but when we were little, we believed him."

"How did your mom react?"

"She told him to get stuffed," Zady said. "That's putting it mildly. But somehow they stayed married until..."

"Enough of the unfinished sentences," he reminded her.

"Until he died of a heart attack in bed with someone else," she finished sharply.

"I'm sorry." That must have been a shock. "How old were you?"

"Twenty-two." She shook off the memory. "What kind of tales did your dad tell?"

Nick chose from an assortment of disturbing examples. "Most often, that he had movie stars and directors following him around, offering him film contracts."

"Was he joking?"

"Afraid not."

"That *is* crazy," she conceded.

"He was bipolar, and in his manic phase, he confused the

faces of strangers with those of famous people." The truth had dawned on Nick gradually. "By the time I understood how seriously ill he was, he'd abandoned us."

"How awful for you *and* your mom."

"She handled it in her unique fashion," he recalled with a mixture of sadness and affection. "Mom was given to magical thinking. She seemed to believe she was starring in a Cinderella story and that if she kept sticking her foot out, one day someone would place a glass slipper on it."

"You're exaggerating."

"Not by much." He missed his mom's reality-defying optimism, but not the gullibility that had led her into foolish relationships and overspending. Money had vanished as quickly as she obtained it—often faster. "She was a nursing assistant in a convalescent home. I gather her patients found her entertaining."

"Is she still alive?" Zady asked.

"She died of cancer two years ago," he said. "How about your mother?"

"Remarried, living in Oregon and stirring up trouble whenever possible between Zora and me," she told him. "She was jealous of our closeness, we discovered later. Sad, huh?"

"It's always a jolt when kids learn that their parents are human." He chose not to point out the parallel to Elaine's behavior. No sense bringing up the Carrigans while he and Zady were getting closer. "I wish I'd made a better start with Caleb, that I'd fought harder for time with my son."

"Is that realistic?" she asked. "I mean, considering the circumstances."

"Maybe not, but I could have tried." Finding his bowl empty, he debated refilling it, but he'd consumed more than enough calories today.

Zady carried her cup to the sink. "Good night, other Dr. Davis."

"For Linda's sake, I hope you don't snore."

"Me, too." She sauntered away.

Arranging his bowl and her cup in the dishwasher, Nick hummed softly until he recognized the tune as the hokey-pokey. Heavens, that woman was nothing if not memorable.

They'd also just shared the most revealing, intimate conversation he'd ever had with a woman. Or with anyone.

Chapter Twelve

Heading for the break room on Tuesday evening, Nick couldn't wait for a cup of coffee and a few minutes of peace before beginning his shift in Labor and Delivery. As usual during the evenings, he'd spent the past two hours meeting new patients, coming quickly up to speed on their medical histories and gently probing subjects that they hesitated to verbalize.

These days, a woman's obstetrician-gynecologist often functioned as her primary medical provider. Today he once again wished for the wisdom of TV's Marcus Welby as he listened to his patients' marital problems, personal insecurities and symptoms that might or might not be important.

Opening the door to the break room, Nick barely had a chance to wonder why it had been shut before he discovered the reason: four faces fixed on him as he entered, all displaying wariness.

His suitemates, Jack Ryder and Adrienne Cavill-Hunter, along with nurse Lori Sellers, had been joined at a table by a dark-haired man with a short mustache. Their tension reminded him about the dispute over future office space.

"Nick, I'm not sure if you've met my husband, Jared." Tucking a strand of brown hair behind her ear, Lori gestured toward the newcomer. "He's a neonatologist."

"Pleased to meet you." Nick shook hands with the fellow. In truth, though, he wasn't pleased to make anyone's acquaintance at this hour, even though he shared their concern. "Please excuse me if I don't linger. I'm due over at the hospital."

"You haven't heard?" demanded Jack, who, instead of sitting with the others, was leaning against the counter within easy reach of a box of doughnuts.

"Don't play Twenty Questions with him." Adrienne had the impressive knack of always appearing fresh and neat, her blond hair pulled into a bun and her suit unwrinkled beneath her white coat. "The hospital announced that a couple of surgical fellows will be joining the staff."

As he poured a cup of coffee, Nick recalled Lucky mentioning a grant. He'd had no difficulty complying with the other man's request for discretion, since he'd been off duty until tonight. "Well, we expected more staff in the men's program, right?"

"Yes, but they don't intend to stop there," Jared said. "A few minutes ago, I was leaving my office on the sixth floor—"

"Where he's crammed in with another neonatologist and two pediatricians on what's supposed to be the orthopedics floor," Lori put in.

"And I happened to pass the conference room," her husband continued. "Cole and Marshall Davis were in there reviewing applicants. Your cousin—I got the relationship correctly, didn't I?—was suggesting other foundations that might sponsor fellowships."

"A veritable conspiracy of evil," Nick murmured, only half kidding.

"Those guys have the administration's ear," Jack complained. "Dr. Tartikoff ought to stick up for us, since he's the fertility chief, but he's more concerned about the opinions of the other superspecialists."

"Plus, who would dare pressure him? He's intimidating," Lori said.

"Ultimately, allocating office space falls to Dr. Rayburn, doesn't it?" As administrator, Mark Rayburn struck Nick as much more approachable than Owen Tartikoff, an internationally renowned fertility expert notorious for his abrasiveness.

"Yes, but we aren't party to their backroom conversations," Jack said. "We've voiced our concern at staff meetings, but as far as we can tell, those concerns were not heard."

"The more people who show solidarity with our cause, the stronger our case," said Lori's husband.

"Good point." Nick resented his cousin's high-handed approach. A major decision like allocation of office space should be conducted with input from the entire medical staff, not just the urology department. "What's next?"

"We intend to act soon," Jack said. "Beyond that, I'm not at liberty to say."

Figuring he deserved a reward for having his peaceful break stolen from him, Nick took a doughnut. "Keep me posted."

As he hurried down the stairs—it was faster than taking the elevator, and better exercise—Nick tamped down his qualms about leaping into a controversy. He might be the new guy, but he intended to stay at Safe Harbor, and his future ability to accommodate a practice might be at stake.

His cell rang as he emerged into the lobby. Could it be an emergency in Labor and Delivery? In the split second before he brought the screen into clear view, he had a more alarming thought, that something had happened to Caleb.

His caller ID read, Unknown. "Dr. Davis," he answered.

"Nick Davis?" a man asked gruffly.

Despite the passage of years, despite the distance physically and emotionally, Nick instantly recognized the voice.

It was his father's.

ZADY WAS LOADING the dishwasher when she received a call, a very welcome one. And several days overdue.

"I'm sorry we haven't been in touch sooner." Alice's contrite face appeared on Zady's screen. "Bill was out with clients last night and again tonight."

"Is he with you now?" Zady asked.

Her friend shook her head. "No. He asked me not to call until he came back, but honestly, I'm dying to talk to my baby. I figured if we wait too long, she'll be asleep. How is she?"

Zady glanced into the living room, which doubled as a playroom, since the house had no den. "She and Caleb are playing with his toddler train set."

"Sounds like fun. Is she upset about not hearing from us?"

"She asks about you, but I try to keep her busy." Zady filled in her friend about the past few days. Linda seemed to enjoy the day care center and the other children, was eating and sleeping well, and only fussed when tired. "She's almost *too* easygoing," Zady admitted. "Eager to please." *As if she's afraid I'll leave her, too.* But she didn't want to imply a criticism.

"You have a gift with her," Alice said. "I suppose it's natural you're on the same wavelength."

"I love her, but I'm no substitute for you and Bill," Zady hurried to reassure her friend. "You look great, by the way."

Alice touched her smoothly curled mane of blond hair. "I had it done at the hotel beauty shop. Picked up a new suit, too. I mean, why are we earning all this money if we can't enjoy it?"

Something didn't feel right to Zady. Her friend appeared to prefer going shopping to confronting Bill about spending more time together. Hadn't recapturing the magic in their relationship been part of the reason for traveling without their daughter?

Reminding herself it was none of her business, Zady

carried the phone into the living room. "Linda, it's your mom."

The girl bounced to her feet, scattering blocks. "Mommy!" She ran over to grab the phone. "Mommy, Mommy! Hug me!"

Alice's laughter warmed the air. "Wish I could, sweetie pie."

As the pair chatted, Caleb grabbed a block and threw it at Linda. Zady batted it aside. She didn't blame him for his jealousy, but he had to learn better ways to express it.

"Let's go punch a pillow, okay?" she told Caleb.

He scowled. "No."

On the phone's speaker, she heard another voice—Bill's. "Daddy!" Linda jumped up and down, nearly dropping the device. How fortunate that he had come home early enough to join the conversation.

Caleb's jaw fixed angrily. "It's my turn."

"To talk on the phone?" Zady asked.

He nodded fiercely. "I miss Grandma and Grandpa, too."

"Of course you do." However, Nick hadn't given Zady permission to call the Carrigans except in a dire emergency. "Hang in there till Linda's call is finished, and I'll see if I can reach your dad. To be sure it's okay."

He folded his arms and hunkered down.

A few minutes later, the Madisons said good-night to their daughter and thanked Zady again for taking care of her. "My pleasure," she responded. "I just hope this trip is accomplishing its mission, or should I say, missions."

"Our sales are exceeding expectations." Bill's bearded face dominated the small screen. "Plus, I've lined up a couple more seminars that should expand our business's reach."

"I meant…" *Stop there. You aren't a marriage counselor.* "Connecting with you tonight was good for Linda. Call again soon, okay?"

"We will," the Madisons chorused.

The instant the call ended, Caleb sprang up. "Now me!"

"Let's make sure it's okay with your father." She pressed his number.

It went directly to voice mail. He must either be delivering a baby, with a patient or on another call.

Zady left a brief message. "I can't reach him," she told Caleb. "Let's wait a few minutes in case we hear back."

"It's not fair!" His voice rose to a shriek. "I want my grandma and grandpa! I want them now!"

While Linda stared, Zady registered that the boy was approaching meltdown. And, in a sense, he was justified. How could a child this young be expected to watch a companion bask in her parents' love while he remained shut off from his grandparents?

She made an executive decision. If Nick didn't like it, he could chew her out later.

Last night, they'd opened up to each other, revealing sensitive memories that until now Zady had shared only with her sister. Afterward, she'd nestled into her sheets and fallen asleep imagining Nick's arms around her and his body infusing hers with its heat. Having him yell at her and remind her that she was little more than paid help ought to remedy her weakness for him in a hurry.

"Okay," she said. "Let's call them."

"WHAT DO YOU WANT, QUENTIN?" Nick demanded curtly into his cell. Being forced to linger in the lobby to talk to his father rather than risk having others overhear added to his annoyance.

"I understand I have a grandson."

"Don't tell me it took you three years to figure that out." His dad could have learned about Caleb from Nick's mother, had he bothered to talk to her while she was alive. Or by doing a search for Nick's résumé online.

Quentin Davis coughed. Nothing about the sound was

severe or indicative of disease, Nick registered automatically; it was just a dry cough, the kind that implied uneasiness. "I mean, I hear he's living with you now."

"So?" Nick disliked being churlish, but he owed his father nothing.

"I was hoping I could meet him."

"Why? To build up his expectations before you abandon him? He's already lost his mother. He doesn't need your brand of parenting."

The silence on the other end lengthened until Nick wondered if his father was still there. "Dad? I have patients waiting."

A long breath resonated from wherever Quentin was. Bakersfield, California, working the night shift in a warehouse, he'd said when they'd spoken a few years ago. "The truth is, I want to see you."

Nick strained for patience. "Is something wrong, Dad? How's your health?"

"It's fine." Quentin sounded mildly amused at the suggestion. "You expecting the cliché where I show up and tell you I'm dying? No such luck. But there *are* matters I should have disclosed to you before, and I can't do it over the phone. Let's arrange a get-together."

"There's a lot going on in my life right now," Nick said. "If whatever it is has waited this long, it can wait a while longer."

"I'm not getting any younger," his father observed—speaking of clichés. "Besides, Marshall seemed to think…"

"What does Marshall have to do with this?"

"I didn't have your current number and I wasn't sure where you were working," his father said. "I saw online that Marshall was at Safe Harbor, so I called him."

Marshall had joined the staff several months earlier, which explained why his profile was on the hospital's website, but Nick's wasn't. "And he provided my personal information."

"He was very pleasant," Quentin said. "You could learn from him."

"How charming that you had a fun chat with my cousin and he filled you in on my private business."

"You may not understand an old man's longing to come clean about his youthful mistakes." Typical. Quentin often dismissed the severity of his wrongdoing by terming them "youthful mistakes."

"You're right. I don't."

"Everybody deserves a second chance."

"Not everyone." Nick was surprised at the amount of anger he still felt toward his father. "Dad, I'm clicking off now. Whatever you have to say, put it in a letter and mail it to me here at the hospital. Be sure you remember my first name is Nick. As for Marshall, feel free to call him whenever you like." Grimly, Nick ended the call.

What colossal nerve his father had. He was probably attending a self-help group that urged participants to apologize for past mistakes. Well, Nick had longed for his dad to be there during his adolescence, but Quentin hadn't bothered to reach out to him then. Now, even had he been willing to see his father, he refused to let the man near Caleb. The boy had more than enough on his plate.

With spot-on timing, the elevator doors opened to reveal his cousin. Nick had almost forgotten that, according to Jared, Marshall was still in the building.

Too agitated to guard his words, Nick blurted, "I just had an unexpected call from Dad. I guess it wasn't unexpected to you, though."

Marshall's eyes narrowed. "Some of us would be over the moon if we could talk to our fathers."

"There's a reason he didn't have my phone number," Nick returned. "He chose to walk out of my life. Once

I survived adolescence, I decided it was best he stay out of it."

Weariness put an edge on Marshall's voice. "Why not give him a break?"

This, from Dr. Arrogance? "After you and your parents considered him the world's biggest loser? You made no secret of your opinion."

"That was a long time ago." In the dimly lit lobby, his cousin's face appeared shadowed. "And speaking of old issues, whatever crap is afoot with the staff about the new office building, I hope you're not taking sides just to get back at me."

So word of the mini rebellion had reached the powers that be. "I'll do what I believe is best."

The creak of the elevator indicated they were about to be interrupted. "I don't care to argue the point," Marshall said. "But Uncle Quentin has a right to meet his grandson."

"A right?" Nick scoffed. "If you were a parent, you'd think differently."

"Maybe." When the doors parted, revealing Jack, Lori and her husband, Marshall broke off. "Good night."

"Night."

The arrivals watched the tall man stride out of the medical building. "Tell me this doesn't mean you're throwing your support behind your cousin," Jack said.

"Of course not." A check of Nick's watch showed he was ten minutes late. "I agree with you."

"Great!" Jack clapped him on the shoulder. "I'm glad you're on our side."

"Me, too." The camaraderie felt good. This man, and the others he'd met with tonight, were rapidly becoming friends as well as colleagues. "See you tomorrow."

Nick strode out, determined to stand up for what was right, regardless of the consequences.

BY THURSDAY, ZADY was mad. Hopping mad. Boiling mad. The most frustrating part was that she wasn't sure whom she was angry at, or rather, at whom she was *most* angry.

She didn't lack for candidates. Elaine figured high among these. On the phone Tuesday, after Caleb had described his new preschool and how much fun he was having with Linda, his grandmother had said that since he was getting along so well with Zady, she and Grandpa didn't need to visit the next weekend.

Shocked, Zady had said, "There's no substitute for you." Elaine's smug response over the phone's speaker had been, "We'll see."

Was she trying to make Caleb act out? If so, she'd succeeded. Caleb had thrown a full-out tantrum, screaming and pitching his toys.

Perceiving the anguish and resentment beneath the outburst, Zady had ached for the little guy. However, when he failed to respond to gentle persuasion and one of his toys hit Zady in the forehead, rage had flashed through her. Struggling not to overreact, she'd ordered him straight to bed.

Next on her list of people she was angry with came Nick. When he'd belatedly returned her call Tuesday night and learned of the evening's events, he'd told Zady she should act more nurturing toward his son and implied she was favoring her goddaughter. Furious, she'd replied that she'd had enough of domineering, self-centered males in her life and that he should back off or find another sitter.

Last but not least among those she was mad at was… herself, for lashing out at him. He'd had a rough evening, Nick had explained apologetically the next morning. He'd described an unwelcome call from his father and an argument with his cousin.

Impulsively, Zady had hugged his strong frame. And he'd drawn her closer and rested his cheek against her hair. For a moment, she'd been lost in his arms, her heart twisting as he admitted how much he depended on her and regretted his unfair accusation about favoring Linda. She'd longed to protect him from all these stresses, as she wished she could protect the children.

Remembering that, she was angrier at herself than ever for nearly falling for the guy. What was she, an emotional basket case? Taking the plunge and ignoring the consequences smacked of the old, reckless Zady. Had she forgotten how high the price could be the instant a sexy man held her close?

She was older now. Smarter. Supposedly more sensible. And grinding her teeth at night as she tried to figure out what inherent susceptibility kept bypassing her common sense about Nick.

Meanwhile, she'd tried to be patient all week with Caleb, who grew more and more sulky each time Linda's parents called. There was so much of Nick in the cute boy. At bedtime, when he snuggled close, she felt a swell of tenderness. Then he'd pull away again. Was Zady somehow alienating him? She'd never managed to win over Dwayne's kids despite years of trying.

Well, Linda seemed fine. Zady hadn't messed up that relationship.

On Thursday afternoon, she put a damper on her turbulent thoughts and paid extra attention to her duties at work. Nevertheless, Marshall was unusually dour and impatient with her, although he never outright snapped at her. She didn't believe she'd done anything wrong, but these days, Zady wasn't sure of her assessment of other people.

About five-thirty, after their suitemates had left, her boss stopped by the nurses' station, where Zady sat alone, double-checking information in the computer. "Aren't you due to pick up the kids?"

How odd that he kept track of such a thing. "I called the

day care and they said it's okay if I'm late. I want to be sure the records are in order."

"If I was tough on you today, I apologize." Despite his pleasant words, Marshall stood glowering into space, his hands balled into fists. "There are some ridiculous politics going on among the doctors, but I don't mean to let it affect me *or* you."

Zady had heard the rumors, thanks to her brother-in-law. "Lucky's mentioned it, too. If you're talking about the allocation of new space in the Porvamm."

"The what?" Obviously, he didn't spend much time listening to the hospital gossip mill.

"That stands for..." Zady took a deep breath and let fly. "The Portia and Vincent Adams Memorial Medical Building."

"Porvamm?" he repeated. "But there's an extra B at the end."

"Must be silent."

His lips twitched. "Must be."

Thank goodness, she'd sparked a smile. "I've been busy trying to teach a pair of toddlers how to compromise," Zady went on. "Too bad some of our staff missed that lesson. Not you!" she added, alarmed that he might misinterpret.

That drew an open laugh. "Don't worry, I'm not offended," Marshall said. "But I am worried. Mark Rayburn believes this conflict will work itself out by the time modifications to the building are complete. I respect his experience as an administrator, but we're at a point where doctors are barely civil to each other."

"Someone ought to sit down and work out the logistics," Zady ventured. "Surely some offices in this building will be vacated, so that will open up space. Then, how many new doctors are likely to join the men's program in the next few years? Crunch the numbers."

"It sounds sensible when you put it that way," Marshall said. "I'll run it by Cole."

"Don't say it came from me," Zady pleaded.

"Why not?"

"Who am I to lecture anyone about using common sense when my life is such a mess?" She sighed.

"It doesn't appear that messy to me," Marshall said.

"Caleb practically hates me and I don't know why," she admitted. "His behavior dredges up old wounds from my ex-boyfriend's kids, who were little monsters. I'm still not sure where I went wrong with them."

"You might talk to the new staff psychologist, Franca Brightman," Marshall said. "She's available to staff as well as patients."

The woman had provided an excellent preschool recommendation. But that was different from entrusting her with personal secrets. "You're saying I should see a shrink?"

He lifted his hands in a pacifying gesture. "She might provide useful insights."

If Marshall held Dr. Brightman in high esteem, perhaps Zady should consult her. But she'd always considered therapy a sign of weakness, as if it indicated that she couldn't handle her own problems.

"I appreciate the suggestion." Since she'd lost her concentration anyway, she logged off the terminal. "I'd better pick up the kids. See you tomorrow."

"You bet. Thanks for your help today."

"You're welcome." She'd only done her job, Zady mused as she went to fetch her purse and sweater. However, she was glad to hear that she'd done it well.

Now she had to tackle her other problems. While a counselor might be perfect for patients, Zady would prefer to figure out her own solutions. But she tucked the idea away, just in case.

Chapter Thirteen

That evening, Zady was tense while Nick broke the news to Caleb that he'd been unable to set up a visit with his grandparents for the weekend. "They're too busy, what with selling their house, packing and moving into assisted living. We have to bear with them, Caleb. They're old folks, and they're confident you're doing well here. So am I."

His nod toward Zady was intended, she presumed, to be reassuring. Perhaps he considered it a good sign that Caleb didn't argue, but she noticed how grimly the boy sat staring at his food, hardly eating.

Off Nick went to see patients. At home, Zady braced for the worst. Sure enough, the squabbling between the children intensified as she was clearing the dishes, climaxing in a scream from Linda. Running into the living room, Zady found her goddaughter holding a doll with its arm torn off.

"He did it!" A trembling finger pointed at Caleb.

"So what?" The boy folded his arms defiantly.

"Go to your room," Zady ordered.

"I don't have to!" He planted his legs apart and glared. "You're nobody."

Any second, she might swat his bottom, the way her father used to do to her. "Go to your room now or you'll regret it."

He must have recognized the determination in her voice, because he obeyed. Uneasily, Zady listened for crashes or other indications that he was venting his fury on his surroundings, but when she peeked in, he was working on a puzzle.

"My dolly!" Linda wailed when Zady returned to the living room.

"I'm sorry, sweetie." She sank to the floor to hug her distraught goddaughter. "Maybe we can fix it."

"She's broke." Tears ran down the little girl's cheeks.

Before Zady could calm her, the phone rang. It was Alice, from Seattle. The sight of Linda's tear-streaked face wrenched at her mother, as Zady had feared.

"Caleb broke her doll. He's upset about not seeing his grandparents," Zady explained. "Things are a little tense around here, but they'll be fine."

"Bill's out with a client again, and I can't stand being away from my daughter." On the tiny screen, Alice's face creased with worry. "I'm coming home."

"Yes!" Linda shouted. "Come home, Mommy."

What about Alice and Bill's plan to revitalize their marriage? "I thought you were working on…you-know-what," Zady said.

"We've been traveling nearly a week and haven't spent a single evening focusing on each other." Tonight, Alice's blond hair hung limply around her face, as if she'd given up on both her grooming and her marriage.

"Don't quit yet." Surely Bill wasn't such an idiot that he'd lose his wife rather than cut back on his hours. "Talk to him. He's lost sight of the issues."

"It's like talking to a blank computer screen," Alice said. "Okay, enough about me. Linda, cutie, tell me about day care. Are you making new friends?"

The little girl responded eagerly, and the conversation ended on a positive note. There were no further references to Alice abandoning her trip.

Zady held Linda in her lap while they searched online and found that the Bear and Doll Boutique in town performed repairs. "We'll tuck Dolly and her arm in a drawer and get them fixed later," she promised. "Okay?"

"Okay."

Linda prepared for bed without protest. As she was settling the little girl under the covers, Zady spotted Caleb in the doorway. He'd played quietly in his room longer than she'd expected.

"I'm sorry, Linda," he said. "I don't hate you. I hate Auntie Zee."

Pain squeezed her. She'd grown accustomed to him lashing out in anger, but this calm declaration cut deeply. Surely an experienced sitter wouldn't arouse this level of antagonism. If he'd grown to loathe her, maybe Zady shouldn't be supervising him.

Yet the prospect of losing him tore at her. Inside the little boy, she saw sweetness and longing, and she treasured the moments when he ran to her.

Also, leaving meant breaking contact with Nick, possibly forever, aside from the occasional casual encounter at the hospital. They could hardly remain friends if she upset his son to this degree.

She didn't believe they'd reached that point. But later, when Caleb refused to let her read him a good-night story, she wondered if she truly had blown any chance of winning his love. She'd hoped to ease his transition; instead, she might be adding to his problems.

Still brooding on Friday morning, Zady was grateful that Marshall's busy surgery schedule meant she didn't have to face questions about her downbeat mood. At lunch, she decamped to the hospital cafeteria.

She spotted her brother-in-law dining with the hospital's nursing supervisor. Lucky and Betsy appeared to be discussing business, which meant she had a good reason to avoid them.

Scanning the tables, Zady noticed a mane of strawberry-blond hair on a woman sitting alone. Why didn't Franca Brightman join the other doctors? Zady wondered. Was it because the psychologist had a PhD rather than an MD, or didn't she care for company?

The other tables were occupied either by strangers or by people Zady would rather avoid. Tray in hand, she approached the counselor. "Hi. Mind if I join you?"

Franca set down the computer tablet she'd been reading. "Not at all. You're Marshall's nurse, aren't you?"

"That's right." Zady introduced herself, and Franca did likewise. Declining to be called Dr. Brightman, she insisted on first names. In her early thirties, wearing a light green pantsuit, Franca seemed friendly, a good quality in a therapist.

However, Zady could hardly launch into a litany of her problems. Nor did she want to. "I was admiring your hair color. That's a pretty shade."

"You think so?" Franca twisted a lock to examine it. "My natural color is Little Orphan Annie red and I'm sick of it. Plus, there are so many redheads on staff here, I was getting lost in the crowd. That's unusual for me."

"It suits you. And I'm a big fan of freckles."

"You have an excellent crop, yourself."

"Thanks." Okay, they'd broken the ice, Zady mused, unwrapping her sandwich. Now what? By chance, the other woman provided the answer when she gazed out the glass door at Marshall. "Do you know Dr. Davis well?" Zady asked.

Franca snapped her attention away from the patio. "We both did our undergraduate work at UC Berkeley. He dated a friend of mine."

"Ah," Zady said, as if that explained their connection, although it didn't. Well, Marshall's relationships were none of her business. "Actually, he recommended I talk to you about a problem I'm having, but I don't feel comfortable talking to a…a…"

"Shrink?"

"Yeah."

"I'm happy to provide a free consult," the other woman said. "Or we can chat now, if you'd prefer."

"It's your lunch break."

"Listening to people isn't work," Franca corrected. "Especially…" She paused.

Especially Marshall's nurse? Nope, Zady was reading too much into this. "A fellow freckled person?"

"Exactly."

Curiosity propelled her to ask, "Do you find you're always analyzing people's behavior? I mean, subconsciously?"

"I try not to." Franca ducked her head. "But since you asked, feel free to tell me about your situation. Or not."

"I really could use your feedback," Zady admitted. Where to begin? "I don't know if you heard, but I'm the overnight sitter for Nick Davis's little boy, in exchange for room and board." She outlined the situation with Caleb, his deceased mother and his grandparents. She explained about Linda receiving calls from her parents and Caleb's outbursts afterward. "He keeps saying he hates me and I don't understand why."

"How do you feel about him?" Having finished her pasta primavera, Franca sipped a cup of tea.

"He's adorable," Zady said. "He's so much like, well, Nick and Marshall both. I'd love to be there for him if he'd let me, but he rejects me more and more. I can't figure out what I've done wrong."

"From what you've said, I'm not sure you've done anything wrong," Franca responded. "Caleb is grieving for his mother *and* for the home he just left. As for his grandmother, even though she claims to appreciate you, clearly she's not helping the situation."

"Caleb's fine when Nick's around," Zady pointed out. "It's just me he dislikes."

"He can't direct his anger at his father. Nick is the only stable person in his life." Franca rested her chin on her palm, a position that emphasized the heart shape of her face. "Of course, without observing Nick or Caleb directly, I can only speculate."

"I guess the kid does have good reason to consider me temporary," Zady conceded. "I keep hoping we'll bond, but things are deteriorating. And I still think it could be partly my fault."

"Why?"

"When he attacks me, it reminds me of the bad relationship I had with my ex-boyfriend's three kids." She checked the wall clock. Twenty minutes left, and for once, she had no desire to hurry back to the office.

"Whatever you're feeling, Caleb's probably picking it up," Franca agreed. "What happened with the boyfriend's kids?"

"They were horrible to me." Memories darkened Zady's mood. "They used to call me names and refuse to eat my cooking. They even threw my clothes on the floor and stomped on them. Every visit was a battle. Dwayne didn't support me at all. He was usually out working. Or, in retrospect, cheating on me."

"And the children took it out on you," Franca murmured.

"Yes. Their hateful behavior went on for years," Zady said. "I could understand it when they were toddlers, but by the time I broke up with Dwayne, they were in their teens. The kids should have been old enough to see I was trying to be their friend, trying to please them."

"How old were they when you and their father got involved?"

She searched her memory. "Two, four and six."

"Did he leave his wife for you?"

"Yes. He was unhappy," Zady hastened to add. "His wife treated him like a meal ticket. Of course, she resented me. Maybe she put them up to it."

There was a pause while Franca mulled over this information. Outside the cafeteria, Zady saw Marshall in conversation with Cole and the administrator. She could afford to stay a few more minutes.

"How did you meet Dwayne?" Franca asked.

"I was working in a toy store during Christmas," Zady said. "To help pay for college. He came in to buy presents for his kids. He seemed kind and nurturing, not at all like my dad."

"A sympathetic father figure."

"Yeah. What a joke that turned out to be."

"How old were you?"

"Twenty," Zady said. "Vulnerable and stupid." A picture sprang to mind, of Dwayne's penetrating blue eyes and the sympathetic tilt of his head as he'd flirted with her. The children he was shopping for had hardly seemed real to her…and evidently to him, either.

"But he wasn't much of a father, was he?"

"No." Then it hit her, the piece of the puzzle she'd been looking for. "What a jerk! His wife was struggling with three little kids and he dumped them to run off with a wide-eyed admirer. No wonder they hated me! I wrecked their home." Guilt swept over her. "I must be an awful person."

"You're responsible for your own actions," Franca said. "But you didn't betray their mother's trust or run out on them. Their father did that."

"All the same, it makes sense now," Zady said. "I never had any chance of winning them over, no matter what I did. And I don't have a chance with Caleb, either."

"But you aren't responsible for Caleb losing his mother or his grandparents," Franca put in.

"In his eyes, I might be. Perhaps you're right, and Caleb unloads on me because he can't aim his anger at his dad, and that's what Dwayne's kids were doing," Zady reflected.

Oh dear, she'd lingered too long, Zady thought as Marshall entered the main cafeteria room from the patio. "Gotta go. Franca, you've been a great help."

"Please call if you have questions." The psychologist handed her a business card. "And you might, after you've had a chance to consider all this."

"Okay." Lifting her tray, Zady glimpsed an unfamiliar expression on Marshall's face as he regarded the two of them. Wistfulness? And it wasn't for her, she felt certain.

If he liked Franca, Zady seconded that emotion. Much as it hurt to confront her guilt toward Dwayne's children, the insight had opened a window of understanding for her.

Now she had to figure out what the new vista meant and how it affected her current relationships.

ON SATURDAY MORNING, at the end of a long shift, Nick was retrieving his belongings from a locker in the doctors' lounge when Jack Ryder, green eyes shining with fervor, waylaid him. The other obstetrician had been called in to assist with a spate of extra deliveries and C-sections.

"Monday afternoon, five o'clock, our break room. Be there," Jack commanded.

"Is this about our rebellion?" Receiving a nod, Nick noted guiltily, "It's my day off. I should spend the time with my son."

"It's an important strategy session. Thanks to your relationship with Marshall, you're a key player for us." Enthusiasm vibrated through the other doctor.

"Is there some kind of hurry? The Porvamm won't be ready for occupancy until next fall."

"Next summer," Jack corrected. "They've moved up the target date. So they'll be handing out the offices any day now."

Nick peeled off his soiled white coat and stuffed it in a laundry bin. "That does sound ominous. What kind of strategy are we devising, short of marching around with signs?"

"That shouldn't be necessary now that we have a secret weapon." As if unable to contain his news any longer, Jack burst out, "We've enlisted Fightin' Sam!"

"Who?" If Nick didn't get out of here soon, he'd drape himself over the other doctor and fall asleep.

"Dr. Samantha Forrest, pediatrician." Jack spoke the name reverently. "She's famous for going to bat for her patients and standing up to the hospital's powers that be."

Nick remembered meeting Samantha Forrest. The blonde had a forceful personality, as well as another distinction. "Isn't she married to Dr. Rayburn?"

"Which makes her the one person at the hospital who isn't afraid to face off with the administrator!"

The situation worried Nick. Was it really fair to pit husband against wife? "Personally, I like Dr. Rayburn, and I have the impression he's a good listener. Also, plenty of people aren't afraid to stand up to him. Dr. Tartikoff, for instance."

"Dr. Tartikoff's not in our group," Jack reminded him.

"True." And once the new office space was assigned, there'd be little to no chance of changing things. "I'll rearrange my schedule for Monday."

"Till then!" With a wave, Jack sauntered out.

Nick was curious to hear what Dr. Sam and their colleagues had in mind, and the office space was important to him, too. Plus, he wouldn't mind one-upping his cousin.

Not that he viewed the controversy as a personal conflict between him and Marshall, but the man's arrogance reminded him of the put-downs and brush-offs he'd doled out during their teen years. Nick had always had shabbier clothes, less approval from their strict grandfather and more character flaws, as Marshall had been quick to point out.

This time, the guy had overstepped. Marshall wielded a lot of influence, thanks to his growing reputation and the possibility that he could help secure surgical fellowships.

But he ought to respect the doctors in other specialties rather than dismissing their request.

During the short drive to his house, Nick's thoughts flew ahead to Zady. She'd taken on far more responsibility than she'd signed up for, and he'd have to ask her for yet another favor in order to attend Monday's meeting. He wondered if it would cause more problems with Caleb. Why couldn't Zady get along better with Caleb? His son was a sweetheart. If only Nick weren't so tired and distracted, maybe he could figure out what she was doing to provoke the boy.

Grateful to be home, he turned into his driveway, pressed the remote and rolled into the garage. Wait a minute. Why was there water on the floor?

The door from the house flew open. Caleb, his body quivering with eagerness, bolted toward the car.

"Hang on!" Nick's voice finally stopped him. "Hey, little guy. What happened here?"

Caleb studied the small pool of water. "It's Auntie Zee's fault."

Here she came, her mouth twisting as she heard the accusation. "Seriously, did you do this?" Nick got out carefully.

Her gaze traced the source of the puddle. "The water heater must be leaking. Caleb! Come back here. And take your shoes off before you go inside."

Pouting, the boy obeyed. Nick returned his attention to Zady. "Well?"

"Well, what?" she demanded. "You think I broke the water heater?"

His tired brain churned into action. The water heater, housed in a small closet within the garage, must have sprung a leak, as she'd said. Caleb's accusation had been knee-jerk. "No. I'm sorry."

"I'll call the landlord," Zady said.

"Please don't." A shiver of dismay ran through Nick as he recalled his rash offer. "I promised to take care of small problems in exchange for a break in the rent." Honesty won out. "I don't have a clue how to fix a water heater."

"Neither do I," Zady said.

"Maybe I could figure it out, but I'm too exhausted to function," he said, aware of Caleb watching wide-eyed from the doorway.

She nodded. "I can see that. I'll handle it. But would you back the car out and clear the garage?"

"I can manage that."

When he entered the house, he found Zady on the phone. "Thanks, Lucky," she said. "We'll call him."

"Who?" Nick asked after she hung up.

"A plumber. Lucky says you don't fix water heaters, you replace them." She regarded him with what appeared to be a slim margin of sympathy. "Go to bed. I'll take care of it. You get to pay, though."

"Mr. Tran said he'd reimburse me for materials." Thank goodness Nick had retained enough working brain cells to remember that.

"I'll save the receipt."

"You can pay with this." He handed over his credit card, then addressed their small audience of two. "Hi, munchkins. I'm sorry I'm too tired to do anything but collapse. Zady is a magician. She will magically fix everything."

"Zady will have a few words with you later," she said. "Once you've rested."

"Absolutely," Nick mumbled, and staggered into his room. He barely managed to pull off his shoes before he fell, fully clothed, onto the bed. Sleep took him instantly.

Chapter Fourteen

The exhaustion on Nick's face eased Zady's irritation. Adrenaline might have powered him into action if another baby had to be delivered, but otherwise he'd reached the limits of his endurance.

Summoning plumbers wasn't among her duties, but they both had to pitch in and function as a team, for the children's sake. However, she wished his first instinct hadn't been to assume she was at fault.

Throughout the morning, Zady remained aware of the guy sprawled on his bed. She'd glimpsed him there after he'd accidentally left the door ajar. His long, lean body had tempted her to loosen his clothes and settle him comfortably. She might also wipe a washcloth gently across his face and stroke the hair from his forehead.

Or not. Definitely not. Instead, she closed the door.

The plumber Lucky recommended proved a cooperative soul. After asking her to provide information posted on the heater, he picked up a replacement en route to the house. He worked quickly, and as quietly as he could. From Nick's bedroom, Zady heard no signs of stirring.

Since she had to stay on the premises and entertain the kids, she turned the occasion into a teaching moment. On the internet, she found an article about how water heaters work. Fortunately, the devices were simple enough for a child to understand—just a tub and a heating apparatus connected to pipes. The toddlers seemed fascinated to learn how hot water arrived in their faucets.

"Here, show Linda what it looks like." On the couch,

Zady let Caleb hold her tablet, tracing the picture with his finger.

He peered at the page. "Is it as big as ours?"

"Yes." It hadn't occurred to her before, but to a child, a tiny picture might as easily represent a toy-size apparatus as a life-size one.

"Big water." At Linda's insistence, Zady had carried her into the garage when she went to jot down the specifics for the plumber. Caleb had accompanied them, carefully avoiding the puddle, which had expanded slightly.

"Enough water for us all to take hot showers," she said.

"Cool." Linda had picked up that word at day care.

"You mean *warm*." Caleb grinned.

"Very clever." Zady fist-bumped him.

After the plumber left and they ate lunch, she drove the kids to the Bear and Doll Boutique. The owner, a sixtyish woman with champagne-colored hair, introduced herself as Ada Humphreys and assured them she could repair the doll.

"I broke it," Caleb admitted.

"It'll be good as new," Ada assured the children. "By the way, I teach craft classes here. When you guys are older, you might enjoy making your own teddy bears and doll clothes." To Zady, she added, "They're a little too young yet."

"Caleb is advanced for his age." While not certain that was true, Zady wanted to praise him, since he'd been cooperative this morning.

"I'm sure he is," Ada said. "Your children are both darling."

My children. Zady could hardly speak through the lump in her throat. "Actually, I'm the care provider. But thanks."

The funny part, she reflected as she watched the children trot about examining the bears and dolls, was that she felt as attached to Caleb as she did to Linda. With her goddaughter, the bond had been instantaneous. Until a few weeks ago, Caleb had been a stranger. Yet today, she experienced a rush of tenderness toward the little boy.

Was it because he reminded her of Nick? But the attachment was more personal than that. She treasured Caleb's inquisitive personality and spark of intelligence. What fun it would be, and what a challenge, to help him grow and develop.

Don't forget, he isn't yours.

Her cell jingled. She'd been experimenting with ringtones and hesitated for a second, at first believing it might be the store's piped-in music. Oh, wait, she'd chosen that sound for Nick.

"It's all taken care of," Zady said to him when she answered. "I left you two receipts, one for the heater and one for the labor. They're on the kitchen table."

"I miss you." The ragged edge to his voice cut right through her defenses.

Surely he meant he missed the children. "We're at the toy store."

"Let's spend the afternoon at the harbor. I've been promising to take Caleb." He didn't refer to his initial remark or her evasion, so she must have been correct.

"What fun!" Zady signaled the children. "Come on, little people." Then, cautiously, she asked, "Did you just mean your son?" She'd hate to promise Linda a trip that didn't materialize.

"Won't you join us?" There it was, a note of yearning. Her foolish, gullible heart gave a leap, to which any sensible woman would have responded by smashing it with the nearest baseball bat.

"We'd love to," Zady said.

For Linda's sake, of course.

WHEN NICK WAS growing up, family had meant parents who quarreled and couldn't be relied upon. It had also meant stern grandparents at whose house he'd gathered on holidays. There, his aunt and uncle could be counted on to criticize him and praise their supposedly perfect son.

He'd longed for an ideal family like those he'd seen on classic TV shows: wise fathers and resourceful mothers with mischievous, adorable children. After his experience with Bethany and a few other brief, failed relationships, though, Nick had doubted such a thing existed in the real world.

Until today. Now he understood how a couple could function as a team, exchanging a few words that resolved differences without conflict, and share the same special moments. How had this happened?

He'd awakened to a silent house. Everything had been in order, except for a scattering of toys in the living room. The plumber had done his deed, the water in the garage had vanished, the beds were made except for his own, and after a hard night's work, he should have luxuriated in the solitude and peace. Instead, he'd missed Zady with an intensity that rocked him.

He'd feared she might insist on handing over his son and spending a free day with her goddaughter. Or demand that he babysit both tykes, considering how much extra effort she'd put in this week.

Instead, she'd joined in the fun with all four of them. Or, rather, she'd created the fun. It was Zady who invented a simplified scavenger hunt along the wooden quay, girls versus boys. They competed to spot a boat with a red sail, a surfboard in a shop window and a fisherman on the pier with a bucket by his side. No one worried about winners or losers. Both children were winners, in Nick's opinion, learning colors and words while moving so fast they stayed warm despite the crisp sea breeze.

"What does the air smell like?" she asked the kids when the game wore thin.

"Salt," Linda said.

"Fish," Caleb added.

"Both right," Nick said. "And coffee."

Zady grinned, her freckles standing out in the thin February sunshine. "That's our cue to have a snack."

He bought them muffins and hot chocolate—plus coffee for him—at the harborside Sea Star Café, where they chose an outdoor table with an overhead warmer. As an elderly couple passed, Nick heard the woman observe, "What a lovely family."

He looked at Zady. Busy assisting Caleb in buttering his crumbly muffin, she merely smiled. Had she heard the comment above the murmur of the ocean? If so, how did she feel about it?

Nick knew better than to assume anything about the long term. Zady's loyalties naturally lay with her goddaughter, her boss and whatever future she had in mind.

But even if that didn't include him, at least now he had a sense of what it would mean to be part of a family, if he ever found the right woman. But how could anyone else match Zady? With unruffled assurance, she soothed Caleb's embarrassment when he dropped his spoon and reassured her goddaughter when a nearby leashed terrier burst into a volley of barking.

When Linda scrambled onto her lap, Nick noticed again what a matched set those two were. No wonder people assumed they were mother and daughter. Just for today, why not pretend they all belonged together?

After the snack, they took a walk on the beach that lay west of the harbor. The children were restless, so Nick figured it was his turn to hatch a game. "Let's pretend we're pirates and hunt for buried treasure."

"Treasure?" Linda's eyes widened.

"Gold!" Caleb said, swinging Nick's hand eagerly.

He hadn't meant to raise unrealistic expectations. "More like stuff people lose in the sand."

"Or pretty rocks and shells and sea glass," Zady said.

"What's sea glass?" Nick asked.

"You don't know, Dad?" His son regarded him sternly.

"I don't know everything," he admitted.

"My sister mentioned that her obstetrician comes here to collect sea glass," Zady explained. "It's pieces of old bottles, jars, plates and so on that have been lost in shipwrecks or thrown away. Over the centuries, the waves buff and smooth them. In ancient times, the pieces were called mermaid tears."

"I want mermaid tears!" Linda cried.

"I'll find you one," Caleb offered, and darted ahead.

Amazingly, he scored a thumb-size amber piece, gemlike and glowing in the sunshine. Soon the kids were scampering about, sand sticking to their shoes and pants, picking up all manner of glittering objects. Nick and Zady scurried to supervise and ensure they didn't cut themselves.

They tucked the treasures into a couple of plastic bags Zady produced from her purse. "It's good to have them handy," she explained to Nick.

At home, with the kids cleaned up and napping, he hoped for an hour or so alone to talk with Zady. To his disappointment, she retreated into her room with Linda, claiming weariness.

Nick's attempts to concentrate on medical journals proved fruitless. He pictured Zady sleeping curled, or possibly sprawled, in the other room. How cute she was. And how much cuter if she came out here to keep him company.

Retreating to the kitchen, he checked his phone for messages and then replayed one he'd received earlier and ignored. It was from his father.

"Nick, it's, uh, Quentin." Mercifully, he refrained from using "Dad," a title he didn't deserve. "I wasn't entirely honest with you when we talked." What a shock, Nick thought sarcastically. "You probably guessed I'm in a 12-step program. It's important to my progress that I apologize for past wrongs. To you and others. Call me and I'll drive down whenever you say. One visit, that's all. After that, you can cross me off your list. Although it would mean a lot if I could meet Caleb. But that's not the main point. Call me."

What did he mean, "to you and others"? Nick's mother was no longer alive to receive an apology. If the man had offended other people, he ought to apologize to them separately or explain further. Instead, this felt like a way of maneuvering himself into Caleb's life.

Irritated, Nick placed a call, not to his father but to the Carrigans. Elaine spoke sharply at first, repeating that they had back-to-back buyers touring the house tomorrow and couldn't possibly see Caleb. However, she softened when he told her how upset her grandson was about the canceled plans.

"A week from tomorrow, you bring Caleb and we'll have a reunion," she promised. "Come hell or high water."

"Done."

After setting a time, he thanked her and ended the call. Only then did it occur to him that she hadn't invited Zady. Just as well, he supposed.

Still too restless to read, Nick phoned to thank Lucky for recommending the plumber. "Glad to do it," the man said. "Listen, why don't you folks join us at our house tonight for pizza."

Great idea—socializing would be fun, and with others around, he and Lucky weren't likely to engage in a debate about work. "I'm buying," Nick replied. "How many pizzas and what toppings? Oh, vegetarian for you, I remember."

Lucky filled him in on his housemates' preferences. This promised to be a cheery end to a cozy day, Nick mused as he clicked off. Being around a family like Lucky and Zora's, as well as Rod and Karen and the girls, used to make him uncomfortable. Today, he was in the right spirit.

Not that he deluded himself about the permanence of his living arrangements. But for now, it was what he and his son needed.

MUCH AS SHE appreciated Nick's generosity and thoughtfulness in arranging dinner with Lucky's household, Zady didn't believe her sister was the right person for her to hang out with. In fact, right now Zora was the worst-possible role model to dangle in front of her.

Not just because her twin had failed in her first marriage or done stupid and even immoral things on a par with Zady's embarrassing history. The dangerous part was that Zora had made every mistake in the book and triumphed anyway. She'd had an affair with a married man—her former high school sweetheart—and, after he'd dumped his wife, Zora had married him. Even after Andrew cheated on her, she'd slept with the guy while they were on the eve of divorcing, and gotten pregnant with twins. He'd responded by signing the divorce papers that he'd sworn he meant to cancel.

In the old, moralistic stories of the Victorian era, Zora would have ended up a homeless wreck, abandoned by her children and everyone else. Instead, Zady's twin had married a wonderful guy who was a doting father to adorable babies Orlando and Elizabeth. Her ex-husband even sent the occasional child support payment after he'd moved out of state.

That happy outcome explained, but did not excuse, the fantasies that crept into Zady's thoughts as she sat at the large dining room table in Karen Vintner's house, watching Nick and the kids show off their sea glass treasures. Tiffany and Amber vowed to start a collection of their own, while the older nurse, Keely, added snippets of information she'd learned from the doctor she assisted, Paige Brennan, about her extensive sea glass collection.

In Zady's imagination, she and Nick furnished their house with a display case for these and future finds. On her finger, a ring like Zora's flashed in the light of the chandelier. Caleb called her Mom instead of Auntie Zee, while Linda—oh, heavens, seeing Linda close to Zora emphasized their resemblance, the little girl's ginger hair and animated face testament to their genetic connection. *Our* genetic connection.

One more daydream: Alice calling to say she'd decided motherhood didn't suit her and Zady could keep their daughter. No, no, no, Zady didn't wish that. She'd been glad to donate eggs to her friend, and the bond between Alice and Linda was far more powerful than anything the little girl felt for Zady. But tonight, the yearning to be a mom and beloved wife raged through her.

You idiot.

Realizing that her silence was drawing curious glances, Zady put forth an effort to join the conversation. Yet all the while, she noticed how Nick's expression brightened when he regarded her, as if…

Stop that.

After dinner, Tiff and Amber organized a game called Freeze Dancing. In the den, they played catchy music, then halted it midbeat. Everyone had to freeze in the most ridiculous position possible, while Keely snapped pictures. After fifteen minutes of this, they reviewed the pictures and voted on who looked the silliest. The winner was Rod, but they disqualified the anesthesiologist because he used props: a Mickey Mouse hat plus reading glasses that he put on upside down and crooked.

Caleb was declared the winner and Linda the first runner-up. Everyone cheered.

Riding home with the children bobbing sleepily in their

booster seats, Zady wished she knew what Nick was thinking. All day, he'd seemed light-spirited. Did he, too, wish they were more to each other than comrades in arms?

At home, they took turns reading aloud to the kids on the couch before she escorted Linda in one direction and he accompanied Caleb in the other. To Zady's delight, the little boy ran to her for a hug. "Good night, Auntie Zee!"

"Good night, you wonderful little guy," she said.

The angles of Nick's face softened as he watched them. Then he picked up his son and carried the gleeful child piggyback into the boy's room.

No doubt Caleb's mood sprang in part from Nick's earlier announcement that they'd be visiting the Carrigans on Sunday. But perhaps it meant he was finally putting behind him his irrational—or so she hoped—dislike of Zady.

When they both returned to the living room, she thanked Nick for a terrific day.

"Why thank me?" he asked.

"You organized it," she said.

"You were its heart and soul."

Happiness bubbled up. "Welcome to the Davis-Moore mutual-admiration society."

"I like that." Nick grinned. "Whoa! I hear rustling outside. Shall we sneak out there and catch Mr. Possum in action?"

"I hate for the kids to miss it." But she had no desire to wake them.

"Here's a better idea. Hold on." Nick ducked into his room and retrieved a camera and a jacket. "This does better at night than my cell. We can share the pictures with them in the morning."

"Let me fetch a sweater." The night temperatures had dipped into the forties lately.

"Don't disturb Linda. I brought this for you." When he held out the flannel jacket, Zady took it gratefully. His spicy male essence infused the fabric and surrounded her, raising excited tingles along her skin.

They slipped onto the patio. Sitting side by side in resin chairs, with the door ajar so they could hear the kids, they gazed into the starry night.

The high bushes around the yard admitted only a few flickers of light from nearby houses. The scent of barbecue from a neighbor's yard mingled with the rich smells of plants, while the background murmur of cars and TVs faded as Zady registered night sounds: the breeze in the leaves, the whisper of unseen creatures stirring.

In the cool air, Nick's hand sheltered hers. He didn't have to speak; they simply connected. A rush of heat enveloped Zady, and she leaned toward him instinctively.

Nick touched her shoulder and shifted closer. Such dark eyes, yet they picked up a hint of moonlight. Or stardust. Zady wasn't sure which, only that his mouth belonged on hers, and she opened to him.

Her body reverberated with the joy of kissing him, of his knee brushing hers and his tongue flicking against her teeth. His rough cheek fit into the curve of her palm; his breathing speeded up.

Then he stiffened. "What?" she whispered.

"It's the possum. We can't miss this." He drew away, quietly lifting the camera into place.

Zady's frustration vanished when she caught sight of the marsupial venturing across the patio with a row of babies clinging to her back. Three or four inches long, not counting the tails, the little creatures hung on as their mother paused to stare in Nick and Zady's direction.

The camera lens whirred and a light flashed. Mrs. Possum stood motionless, as if transfixed. When the light went off again, she hesitated for a minute, then scurried into the bushes.

"How're the pictures?" Zady asked. "Did you get that?"

"We'll find out." Heaving a satisfied breath, Nick added, "We sure had a clear view, didn't we?"

"I can't believe she trotted out here with her babies. Oh, I think the kids' book said baby possums are called joeys." To Zady, it felt as if fate was telling them that they, like the possum, had found a safe place. The breeze picked up, chilling her, and she shivered.

"We should go inside," Nick said, rising. He reached for her hand.

IF YOU DIDN'T SEIZE the moment, it would vanish. Vaguely, Nick recalled that sometimes impatience had led him to push too hard, too fast. But tonight he wanted the whole experience, to unite with Zady in every sense. Once they made love, surely there'd be no more question of divided loyalties.

In the coziness of the kitchen, he touched her hair, enjoying its springiness. "Better now?"

At his elbow, she peered at the camera. "How did the pictures come out?"

Nick's arm encircled her while he switched the camera to viewing mode. The first image showed the possum in profile, the babies barely discernible. In the second, she faced the camera, eyes glowing, as did the pups. The third proved disappointing, with only her hindquarters in view.

"The second one's the best," Zady said. "Can you share it with me?"

"Of course." After sending the pictures to her email and his own, Nick switched off the camera. "That was fun."

"More than fun." She rested her cheek against his arm. "Special."

A delicious quiver ran through him. "This was an almost perfect day." He swallowed before adding, "We could make it perfect."

Zady reached up and looped her arms around him. "Do you think the children are asleep?"

"By now, surely…"

The doorbell rang. Nick swore softly. Despite the desire to ignore their uninvited caller, he couldn't allow the person to ruin everything by waking the kids. "Just let me get rid of whoever that is."

"No argument here."

Gritting his teeth, Nick paced through the living room, flicked on the porch light and opened the door.

The woman standing there was tall, blonde and familiar. With a jolt, he registered that there was no way he could simply dismiss Linda's mother.

Chapter Fifteen

"It's useless." Her long legs stretched beneath the kitchen table, Alice fiddled with her teacup. "Bill keeps saying our marriage is important, but then he schedules another business appointment. And he orders me around like the hired help."

"Did you tell him you were leaving?" As soon as she'd seen her old friend in the doorway, Zady had figured the news couldn't be good. Tactfully, Nick had retreated to his room, allowing the two of them privacy.

The other woman shrugged. In the less-than-flattering overhead light, her fair skin showed more creases than Zady remembered. Although Alice was only in her early forties, her light complexion made her vulnerable to wrinkles, which she fought with expensive moisturizing creams. "What's the point? I suppose it's kind of late in the evening to swoop in here and take my daughter, but I miss her so much."

Earlier, they'd peeked in at Linda. The girl slept soundly, arms around her second-favorite doll. Some of the tension had seeped from Alice's face at the reassuring sight.

"I understand," Zady said. "It might be wise to get a good night's rest and pick her up tomorrow."

"I *am* tired after my flight." Alice ran a hand through her untidy hair. "My mind keeps listing things to do. Find a divorce lawyer. Rent an apartment—I won't be able to afford a house."

"It kills me to think of you guys breaking up," Zady said. "When you started dating Bill, I was impressed by how perfectly in sync you were. It was obvious you belonged together."

"People change," Alice said sadly.

"I realize I'm a lousy person to offer advice, but even the best relationships require adjustments." Zady sipped from her cup before continuing. "Bill loves you. Even though he wanted biological children, he offered to adopt a child when you couldn't conceive, remember?"

"His parents longed to pass on their genes," Alice reminisced. "His mother's a concert pianist—have you noticed how musical Linda is?"

The little girl did keep rhythm well, in Zady's opinion. During the Freeze Dancing game, she'd always stopped right on the beat. "Absolutely."

"If you hadn't donated eggs, I'm not sure what I'd have done," her friend said. "So you've earned the right to give advice, not that I'm promising to take it."

"There's a new counselor at the hospital named Franca Brightman." Zady recognized the irony of recommending therapy when she'd resisted it for herself. Nevertheless, Alice and Bill obviously couldn't resolve their problems on their own. "I talked to her last week and it's amazing how much insight I gained from just one…meeting." She skipped over the fact that it hadn't been a formal session. "I understand now why Dwayne's kids hated me, and why my efforts to get close to them failed. Professional help can be a real eye-opener."

"Counseling is expensive. Maybe not for you at the hospital, but it would be for us." Alice tapped the rim of her cup. She'd drained her tea. Ordinarily Zady would have offered a refill, but it was more important to pursue her point than to play hostess.

"More expensive than divorce lawyers?" she countered. "Or breaking up your business partnership?"

"I suppose that's true." Alice's lips pressed together as she weighed the idea.

"Hold on." Zady darted across the room to her purse. Usually, objects disappeared into the bag's clutter with maddening elusiveness, but she found Franca's card in the zipper pocket. A sign from fate, no doubt. "Here. Give her a call. She's new, so she might not be fully booked."

"Does she counsel people who aren't staff or patients?" Alice asked.

"It can't hurt to ask."

Her friend's fingers drummed the table. Her usually pristine nail polish was chipped, Zady noted.

"Okay." Alice rose abruptly. "I'll call Bill and propose it. One last chance. Either he cancels the seminars and hightails it home, no matter how much money we lose, or I'm moving out."

An ultimatum might backfire, Zady reflected, but it beat having Alice file for divorce without warning. "If you decide it's easier for Linda to stay here a few more days, I'm happy to watch her."

Her friend sighed. "That depends on how Bill responds. Zady, you're the best friend I ever had. Thank you."

"You know I care about you and Linda." Quickly Zady added, "And Bill."

After hugging her and checking once more on her sleeping daughter, Alice departed. Clearing away the teapot and cups, Zady hoped her advice would accomplish what the couple's traveling hadn't.

A rustling noise revealed Nick's entrance. He lounged in the doorway, arms folded. "You never told me you were Linda's biological mother."

"Why should I have? Besides, you had no business eavesdropping," Zady snapped.

"The walls are thin," Nick replied in a level tone. "Not that I'm surprised. She's a carbon copy of you."

"Her eyes are green, like Bill's," Zady protested—weakly.

"You also didn't tell me that you consulted with the new therapist. Let me guess—my cousin referred you? I gather they're old friends."

"Yes, no, yes." She clunked a saucer into the sink with more force than she'd intended. Luckily, it didn't break.

"What does that mean?"

"Yes, I talked to her at lunch. No, I didn't officially consult her, and yes, Marshall suggested it," Zady said. "It isn't a requirement of my nanny job that I tell you everything I do, is it?"

"No," he conceded. "But I had the impression we were being open with each other."

That didn't require spilling all her secrets, such as the egg donation, Zady thought tartly. Furthermore, she didn't believe he was telling *her* everything, either.

"There's nothing you've failed to bring up?" she prodded. "I'm one hundred percent current on your life?"

Exasperation fleeted across Nick's face, followed by sheepishness. "I did get a voice mail from my father. It's the same old same old—he feels a compulsion to unload on me, which I'm ignoring."

"There you go." After rinsing the china and putting it in the dishwasher, Zady dried her hands.

"There I go where?"

"Keeping secrets."

His lip curled in an expression halfway between a snarl and a laugh. "You're deliberately provoking me."

"Provoking or arousing?" The remark reminded Zady that they'd been about to scoot off to the bedroom and make love. At the memory, her knees grew weak and her prickliness threatened to dissolve into a puddle of goo.

She'd been saved by the bell, literally. Now she had to hang tough. "I know your dad let you down, but would it harm Caleb to hear about his other grandfather? Stop!" Spotting the storm clouds forming in Nick's expression, she clarified, "I mean, would it hurt to confront the guy and assess whether or not he's changed?"

"You described what he did as 'letting me down.'" Standing there, Nick loomed large, but he didn't seem angry, just stern. "He did more than that. He betrayed my trust and my mother's."

"Didn't you say he was mentally ill?" Zady stopped puttering around the kitchen, despite the urge to keep her hands busy, and focused on Nick.

"He's bipolar," Nick confirmed. "I can make allowances to an extent, but my grandparents offered to pay for treatment and Dad refused. And that was during his relatively healthy periods."

"He wasn't always—" Zady wasn't sure how to describe it "—confused?"

"He had stable periods between episodes of depression and hyperactivity," Nick said. "But he chose to abandon us rather than undergo treatment that might be uncomfortable for him. When you bring a child into the world, you have to be willing to put them first, and he never did."

Much as she wished Nick and his father could reconcile, Zady couldn't argue with his logic. And, she reminded herself, it was none of her business. "You have to do what you believe is best for Caleb."

"As you did for Linda." His manner softened. "You love her a lot, don't you?"

A lump forming in her throat, Zady nodded.

"And now you have to say goodbye again."

How annoying that tears clouded her vision. "Not exactly. I'll still be involved in her life. I hope." Unless Alice chose to move out of the area, to be farther from Bill. Zady would rather not dwell on that possibility.

"As long as I'm being nosy," Nick said, "you mentioned

once that living with Caleb and me would interfere with your plan. You never explained what you meant."

She'd nearly slipped up badly by jumping into bed with this man. Might as well tell him the truth and widen the gap between them.

"My plan is to find the right guy and have kids of my own," she said. "A guy who doesn't have a lot of old baggage. A guy I can trust and who trusts me. Who doesn't keep demanding I prove myself."

"Ouch." He ducked his head like a boy caught in a prank.

Zady's traitorous hand was tempted to reach out and rumple his hair. To brush the stubble on his cheeks while her body pressed against his.

Damn, damn, damn. Not twice in one night. "I'm off to bed," she said. "Alone."

Disappointment darkened Nick's eyes. "Just when we were having such fun sticking pins in each other."

"See you in the morning." She hurried past him, nearly breaking into a run like a coward—but a coward who would live to fight another day.

ZADY HAD SAVED them both from a mistake, Nick reflected later. They'd moved into this house for the children's sake, not to indulge their desires.

Yet he wondered about the imaginary Mr. Right. What might the guy offer Zady that Nick couldn't? A future full of kids? As far as he knew, he was capable of becoming a father again, and she'd grown attached to Caleb. A house that he owned outright, like Marshall? She hadn't mentioned that as a qualification.

On Sunday, after viewing the possum photos, the kids spent an hour prowling around the yard, trying to find the little family. They succeeded only in rousting a few lizards. Later, they drew pictures of possums and read about the marsupials in their picture book.

After dinner, Nick was in the mood for romantic comedy, although his usual taste in movies ran to action films and science fiction. The four of them gathered in the living room with a bowl of popcorn, and ended up laughing and calling encouragement to the characters of a madcap story of love lost and found. Although much of the film was above the kids' heads, they enjoyed it.

When the hero knelt to propose to the heroine, Caleb asked, "What's he doing?"

"Asking her to marry him," Zady said.

"He loves her." Linda clasped her hands to her heart.

The little boy peered up at Nick. "Did you do that with Mom?"

Zady's sympathetic gaze met Nick's. He decided to rise to the occasion by telling the truth.

"No," he said. "Maybe if I had, she'd have accepted my proposal." Not that he believed he and Bethany would have been happy if they'd gotten married, but they could have tried, for their son's sake.

He caught the sparkle of tears on Zady's lashes. Why? Because he'd expressed affection for the woman he'd once had a child with? Or because she wished for a man to open a ring box and make her dreams come true?

It was unrealistic. Yet that week, Nick felt as if things were changing between them. He'd begun to depend on her, to trust that he could count on her loyalty.

Late Sunday night, when Alice reported that Bill was headed home, he noted Zady's mixed reaction. Pleasure that her friends planned to work on their marriage, and perhaps also that Linda could stay in this house another few days to allow the couple to concentrate on each other. Also, though, sadness that her little girl would soon be departing.

Nick held her sympathetically but released her quickly. When the time came to make love, and he believed it would, he didn't want to take advantage of her in a vulnerable moment.

On Monday, Nick was glad he'd made the extra effort to meet with Jack's group of rebels, newly joined by Samantha Forrest. The fiery, sharp-featured pediatrician wasn't afraid to be confrontational, and her ferocity energized the others.

She proposed an ambush for the following Monday. Samantha planned to visit her husband in his office, ostensibly to take him to lunch. Instead, she'd arrive with their group and demand he allocate a floor in the new building to obstetricians, pediatricians and others outside the urology program.

It was a strong tactic, and rather devious, Nick supposed. However, if the leaders of the men's fertility program hadn't been so bigheaded, this wouldn't be necessary.

"It's going to be brutal," he told Zady that evening. They were fixing dinner while the kids played in the living room.

"Mark Rayburn strikes me as a man who can handle situations like that," she responded.

"It bothers me that Samantha's working against her husband," Nick admitted. "Ambushing him seems disloyal on her part."

"That's her choice," she said. "She must believe she's justified."

"Even if it means betraying his trust?" That reminded Nick of another point. "Maybe I shouldn't have shared this information, considering that you work for the enemy."

"The enemy?" Zady paused by the pasta pot, a spaghetti fork in her hand. "I thought you realized that it is possible for me to respect your privacy *and* Marshall's."

"Of course." Nick hadn't meant to question her integrity. "Let's change the subject. Have you heard from the Madisons?"

"Franca agreed to meet with them tonight at her old office." The counselor had retained the space to accommodate her longtime patients. "I'm hoping they'll make real progress. But being around Linda has been special."

After turning off the burners on the stove, Nick hugged her. "I know how hard this must be."

"I'm happy for them." She sniffled. "Do you have a tissue?"

He handed her one. And experienced a wave of guilt at the reflection that, once Linda was gone, Caleb would benefit from his and Zady's undivided attention. And if he could trust Elaine's commitment to get together on Sunday, Caleb might finally relax and settle into his new home.

With luck, the situation with the new building would soon be resolved, as well. Then Nick and Zady could explore whatever lay between them at leisure.

He could hardly wait to be done with all this drama.

Chapter Sixteen

"It never occurred to me that my spending on clothes and toys exacerbated Bill's fear of financial instability." With Linda bouncing in her lap, Alice spoke earnestly from Zady's sofa on Saturday afternoon.

Beside her, Bill rubbed his short beard thoughtfully. "And I lost sight of what's important in our marriage. My dad went bankrupt when I was growing up. Mom had to shelve her music career for a teaching job that drained her energy."

"You learned all this in two sessions?" Zady was impressed that Franca had been willing to schedule them, and then been able to uncover so much in less than a week. And yet, one lunchtime conversation had opened Zady's eyes about Dwayne's children after years of confusion.

"We're not finished with counseling," Alice assured her. "But I feel like we're light-years from where we started."

"Also, we've worked out a schedule for the rest of our seminars," Bill said, and explained how his wife and daughter would join him part of the time. "After this month, I'm cutting back."

"And I'm starting a spending journal to curb my impulses," Alice added.

"Mommy! Daddy!" Linda burbled. "Going home?"

"You bet, sweetie," both of them said, and burst out laughing.

The front door opened to admit Nick, who carried a glossy red-and-white shopping bag from the Bear and Doll Boutique. "What am I missing? Sounds like fun!"

"We were just wrapping up," Alice said. "Where's your little boy?"

"With friends." Nick's gaze skimmed over Zady so quickly she almost missed the mischief in his expression.

They'd agreed that watching Linda trot off with her parents might be hard on Caleb. After Nick awoke a few hours ago, he'd whisked Caleb out for brunch at Waffle Heaven, then over to Zora and Lucky's house. Karen, Rod, Amber and Tiffany had asked for the children to accompany them on a planned outing to Disneyland, half an hour's drive away, which they swore was much more fun with kids along. Linda couldn't go, but Zady had urged Nick to accept for his son, and he had.

It wouldn't be Caleb's first visit, she'd learned; Nick had treated him to the amusement park a few months ago, and the preschooler had been eager to revisit his favorite rides. Zady had expected Nick to go, too, but he'd offered to pick up the mended doll and return home.

Because he understands how much I need him today.

Zady was grateful that her friend and goddaughter belonged to a happy family once more. Nevertheless, the sight of Bill beaming at his wife and the prospect of losing Linda reminded her forcefully of how far away her own happy ending was—if it ever arrived.

Having Nick around was a huge relief. And a huge temptation.

"Here's someone you've been missing." Nick handed the bag to Linda. "Her arm's back in place, good as new."

With a squeal, the girl dug through the tissue paper. "My baby!" She hugged her doll.

"I'll reimburse you." Bill launched to his feet.

Nick waved away the offer. "My son did the damage. It's on me."

With that settled, the Madisons collected their daughter's belongings, which Zady had packed earlier. After thanking her repeatedly and promising to call soon, the couple walked away with the excited child.

Through the window, Zady watched until it hurt too much. Sadly, she turned away.

"I stocked up on tissues," Nick said.

"I'm fine." She cleared her throat. "This is the right outcome."

With nothing further to say, she stood trying to figure out how to take her mind off Linda. *And off Nick.*

"Would a massage make you feel better?" he asked.

"Thanks, but I have some reading to do," Zady said.

"What sort of reading?"

"Educational reading."

"About nursing?" he asked.

"Sort of." She marched into the bedroom and would have stayed there with her book, except the sight of Linda's empty cot was too uncomfortable. Hesitantly, she ventured into the living room again. No sign of Nick.

Kicking off her slippers, Zady reclined on the couch and opened to the bookmarked page in her novel. She'd barely started reading, however, when Nick entered with a parenting magazine. As he approached, she debated whether to shield her cover, but decided that would only invite suspicion.

"That's fiction," Nick observed.

"Yes, it's a romance novel."

He tossed aside his magazine. "You said it was educational."

"It is," Zady replied. "The author is instructing us on how men ought to behave."

"That's an interesting viewpoint." Nick perched on the sofa, forcing her to scoot over. What did he aim to accomplish by crowding her? Other than raising wonderful thrills along her spine, of course.

He studied the cover. "Do women honestly believe most guys have muscles like that?"

"He's Scottish."

"Scottish men are more muscular?"

"They had to haul a lot of stuff around in the seventeenth century," Zady said. When he didn't respond, she added, "Like swords."

"I'll admit, I'm not that bulked up," Nick continued, indicating the shirtless hero. "Well, not in my arms and shoulders, but if we're discussing swords…"

"We aren't!" She chuckled.

"I'll leave you to it, then." He started to rise, but she put a hand on his arm.

"What's your hurry?"

He studied her intently. "Are you saying…?"

"Since when do heroes need an engraved invitation?"

"I think I just received one." Plucking the book from her grasp, Nick placed it on an end table. A swift movement and his strong arms surrounded her.

This man put that Scottish hero—and every other man—to shame, with his spicy scent, the glow in his eyes and the firm, slow pressure of his mouth. Gathered against Nick, Zady luxuriated in his kiss.

Sensations awoke, from a tingle in her lips to a simmering desire deep within. Winding her arms around his neck, she traced the pulse point of his throat and the sensitive coil of his ear with her tongue.

Nick's moan rippled through her. When he shifted position on the narrow couch, though, he started sliding toward the floor. They both grabbed in vain for support. Onto the carpet they tumbled, with Zady on top, barely missing the coffee table.

"We should have kept your book," Nick murmured. "Looks like we could both use instructions."

She straddled him. "Shut up and kiss me again."

He obeyed, wrapping her in his embrace. Heat flooded her, along with a powerful awareness of his arousal. Also, an awareness of the coffee table digging into her hip, and the fact that they'd be visible if anyone peered through the loosely woven front curtains. "We should move to another room."

"I agree."

As they scrambled to their feet, it occurred to Zady that this was her last chance. She could run away, cling to good judgment, play it safe.

When Nick's hand cupped hers, she got lost in his dark eyes. She meant to claim him, as he'd already claimed a part of her.

Why should Scottish women have all the fun?

IF SHE PUSHED HIM AWAY, Nick wasn't sure how he'd handle it. Zady's velvet skin and the perfume of her hair suffused him. They'd been building to this moment since he'd glimpsed her across that bleak courtyard at the motel, and his need for her had grown until he couldn't imagine wanting any other woman.

In his bedroom, he slowed their pace, gripping her wrists when she started to undress. "Let's enjoy this," he said. "We have all afternoon."

"Yes." But she seemed uncertain about what came next. What kind of man had that boyfriend of hers been, anyway?

The kind who'd cheated on his wife, and then cheated on Zady, too, Nick thought. A manipulator and, obviously, a complete fool.

He unbuttoned her blouse, uncovering a sprinkling of freckles. Kneeling as she sat on the bed, he unfastened her bra, revealing her tantalizing breasts.

She seemed to be holding her breath as he took each pink nipple between his lips and teased it until she groaned.

Zady's hands slid down his back, and she buried her face in his hair, inhaling him.

Together, they eased onto the bed. The pressure of her fingers as she unsnapped his jeans gave Nick a heady sense of lightness. He couldn't believe how lovely she was. Every perception he'd had of her intensified as he viewed Zady in a fresh glow.

She'd brought him to the edge of a place he'd never been before. Then they leaped over it, together.

THE REALITY OF NICK, his intensity and his honest caring, swept away the last of Zady's defenses. She was probably crazy, but so what? She'd discovered a love that obliterated the memory of her childish infatuation with Dwayne. Nick was a real man, not an emotional con artist.

She yielded to her desires—the desires he'd awakened. She hadn't suspected that pleasure could roll through her in waves, intensifying, ebbing, then surging to greater heights as he thrust into her. She ached for this to last forever.

Just when it seemed that it might, he drove into her, gasping, and she reached an impossible peak. Her cries mingled with Nick's as they fused. Lights swirled around them in a cloud of stars and galaxies.

He lay atop her, breathing hard. Eventually, to her regret, he rolled to the side. "That was—" he swallowed "—unbelievable."

"For me, too." As she snuggled against him, Zady tried not to think about the future or anything other than this moment. It was pure and perfect.

THEY COOKED PASTA mixed with scrambled eggs and onions for dinner, and ate it with a salad. The plain meal tasted better than it had any right to.

Neither of them spoke of changing their situation. That wasn't necessary since they already shared a house. Zady figured they'd continue to sleep separately, to set an example for Caleb. Stolen moments together would be all the sweeter.

Did she dare hope that she might someday be his little boy's stepmother and that their temporary family might become permanent? No sense pushing her luck by suggesting too much too soon.

It was nearly 11:00 p.m. when Rod and Karen brought Caleb home. They'd stayed at Disneyland to watch the fireworks, they explained. The two Adams girls excitedly described what fun they'd had.

After they left, Caleb stumbled off to put on his pajamas without protest, his head nodding as Zady helped him brush his teeth. She could have sworn he fell asleep in Nick's arms before he even reached his bed.

Tomorrow, he and Nick would reconnect with the Carrigans, while this household adjusted to its new dynamics. They'd be a threesome—with her and Nick much more than merely housemates. A new world stretched before her.

True to her resolve, Zady didn't dwell on that. Curling on the sofa beside Nick to watch a movie, she was content simply to be here and now.

SPREADSHEETS, SERIOUSLY? Nick glared at his computer. He'd been primed to expect many things from Fightin' Sam, the crusading pediatrician, in preparation for tomorrow's face-off, but this analysis of patient flow, distribution of existing personnel in offices and so on—page after page—set his head spinning.

Not in a good way, either. Nothing like yesterday with Zady.

He'd longed for a repeat after Caleb went to bed, but the movie they'd watched, *Don Juan DeMarco,* had proved less erotic than he'd anticipated when he chose it. Completely absorbing, however.

Nick stared across the kitchen toward the living room, where he could hear Caleb crashing toys into each other. Zady's soft-voiced offer to play a game met with a shouted rejection.

Perhaps it was exhaustion from the Disneyland outing that fueled Caleb's bad temper this morning. Also, he was missing his little playmate more than they'd expected, despite how often the pair had squabbled.

Zady and Nick had explained in advance that Linda was only a guest here and was about to return home. Also, they'd promised to arrange a playdate with her soon. Apparently that wasn't enough for a three-year-old.

Nick mulled over the idea of whisking the boy off early and stopping somewhere en route to the Carrigans' house. The Fullerton Arboretum might be open now.

He was looking up the website when his cell rang. Nick flinched. He wasn't on call for deliveries. *Please don't let it be...* He picked it up.

The readout read, Grandma Elaine.

Determined to be positive, he answered, "Hi, Elaine. Would you like us to come early? Caleb can't wait to see you."

"I'm sorry." Why didn't she sound sorry, then? "Bennie's not feeling well. This isn't a good day."

"What does his doctor say?" Nick demanded.

"I beg your pardon?" She spoke slowly, as if confused.

He refused to be put off easily. "If he's too unwell to have his grandson pop in, that could be cause for concern. I'll tell you what. I'll bring Caleb over to spend half an hour with you, and I'll discuss Bennie's situation with him. Perhaps we can call his doctor about adjusting his medication."

A couple of dry coughs provided Elaine a breather to cook up a reply, or so Nick assumed. "That won't work." She pronounced the words deliberately, as if reciting them. "Let me talk to my grandson. I'll reassure him."

Nick considered arguing, but he'd never won yet with Elaine. Instead, he chose a compromise. "Fine. Let's figure out how to set up a visual connection so he can see your face."

"And so you can listen in?" she responded. "I'll talk to Caleb privately. We've been very accommodating to your arrangements, Nicholas. It's the least you can do."

This was her idea of accommodating? Nevertheless, she was an old lady—well, not *that* old, at sixty-four, but people aged differently. "If you insist, but I believe you're shortchanging him."

"I'll be the judge of that."

Judge, jury and executioner, Nick thought grimly. At the entrance to the living room, he exchanged a meaningful glance with Zady, who rolled her eyes at the unspoken bad news. "Caleb," he said aloud, "Grandma Elaine wants to talk to you."

The little boy jumped up and snatched the phone from his hand. "Hi, Grandma. I went to Disneyland!"

There was a pause. Then Caleb said, "Okay," and took the phone to his room.

"What's going on?" Zady asked when they were alone.

Nick explained about Bennie being under the weather and Elaine's demand to speak privately with her grandson. "I have no idea what she's telling him and I don't like this secrecy."

"Neither do I." Her mouth pressed into a thin line.

Nick was glad she didn't criticize his handling of the interaction, because his temper was close to the boiling point. He didn't want to aim it at her, though.

And Elaine, as usual, was out of reach.

ZADY'S INSTINCTS URGED HER to prod Nick into action. However, how he chose to parent his son was a delicate matter.

Besides, what action could he take? The Carrigans weren't under his command.

When Caleb closed his door, apparently following instructions, she was glad that Nick promptly reopened it. A moment later, she heard the little boy say, "Okay, Grandma. I love you and Grandpa."

He emerged and went straight to his toys, ignoring the grown-ups. In an admirable attempt at a neutral tone, Nick asked, "What did Grandma say?"

"She said I'd be okay here with Zady."

Why me? Zady wondered.

She could hear the frustration in Nick's next question. "Did you talk to Grandpa?"

Caleb shook his head. "Grandpa's sick."

"But Grandma isn't." Zady knew she ought to stay out of this, but Elaine's comment had put her in the middle of it. "I don't understand why your grandparents won't move heaven and earth to see you. They're supposed to love you."

"And you're s'posed to love Linda!" Jumping up, Caleb fled to his room.

"I shouldn't have spoken," Zady conceded.

"No, you shouldn't." More gently, Nick said, "Taking care of my son is my responsibility."

I was hoping it was partly mine now. "All right."

"After lunch, I'll drive him to the arboretum. He ought to enjoy that, and it'll take his mind off things. First, I'd better finish plowing through the stuff Samantha Forrest sent."

They should be coping with Caleb as a couple, Zady thought. After everything they'd shared, it hurt to find they were as far apart as ever. One step forward and one step back—or was it two steps?

She retreated to her room and the hunky Scottish hero with the missing shirt. Despite his sexual prowess and heroic nature, however, he made a poor substitute for the man whose company she craved.

Chapter Seventeen

Marching along the hospital's fifth floor toward the executive suite with a small knot of doctors, Nick was conscious of the glances cast in their direction by other staff members. Maybe he should have followed his instincts and stayed home with Caleb.

His son had enjoyed yesterday's outing. "It's like a movie!" he'd cried as they strolled through a rain forest section of the arboretum, snapping pictures. At home that night, he'd been worn out, and so had Nick. Zady had exclaimed over their photos but otherwise seemed subdued.

Nick appreciated how much losing Linda must hurt, but Caleb was suffering from his little friend's absence, too. The boy needed attention after the mischief Elaine had pulled.

Nick had considered calling the Carrigans today to demand an explanation, but it might be smarter to let the matter drop. If Elaine wanted to see them, she could take the initiative. Meanwhile, three-year-olds lived mostly in the present. Without reminders, the Carrigans might slip to the back of his mind. While unfortunate, that would be preferable to this turmoil.

He'd rejected the temptation to let Caleb skip preschool and day care today. It was important to anchor the boy in his routine, and there'd been a pile of laundry to wash and grocery shopping to do. Plus, Nick's absence at this confab risked antagonizing his colleagues.

They'd rallied earlier in Samantha's pediatrics office, which had been empty for the lunch hour. She'd warned them of a range of eventualities, from her husband calling security to throw them out—unlikely—to being granted the opportunity to present a formal proposal. Setting aside a floor of the Porvamm for nonurology staff was their minimum, she'd declared.

And the maximum? Well, that was the same as the minimum, apparently.

Now, their fearless leader, her blond mane flowing behind her, strode along the corridor. With their white coats billowing in a self-made breeze, Jack and Adrienne and Jared sped in her wake, followed by Nick and a couple of pediatricians.

They marched into the executive suite's reception area. From a previous visit, Nick knew that the staff attorney occupied one of the inner offices, with the larger one assigned to Mark. Since it was lunchtime, he expected the administration secretary to be away, but there she sat, greeting them calmly.

"Dr. Rayburn's expecting you," she said. "Go on in."

He *had* been expecting his wife, Nick recalled. But the secretary didn't bat an eye about the reinforcements.

He found out why a moment later. Mark Rayburn, who rose from his desk with a smile, wasn't the only doctor awaiting them.

From nearby seats uncoiled three men: Cole Rattigan, the urology director; Owen Tartikoff, head of the fertility program; and Marshall.

Was this an ambush? Nick wondered. It sure looked like one.

THAT MORNING, THE HOUSE had echoed with Linda's absence. Rising in the predawn dimness, Zady had started to skirt the cot en route to her bathroom before realizing it was no longer there. The temporary bed was stored in the closet, the sheets washed and folded away.

No matter how strongly she believed she'd done the right thing, she missed her little girl. If only she could hold another child in her arms.

But without Linda present, Caleb had refused to let her hug him or fix his breakfast. Nick had done it—only fair, since he had Mondays off—but Zady was acutely aware of being reduced to overnight babysitter.

Not entirely, though, she gathered from Nick's sympathetic smile. The glow from that smile remained until she arrived at the office, where Marshall requested she reschedule his early-afternoon appointments. He had a couple of important meetings, he explained.

She had to bite her tongue to refrain from asking if they concerned Nick. That would be disloyal—but wasn't she being disloyal to Marshall by withholding information that might affect his program?

At lunchtime, Zady declined an invitation to accompany her fellow nurses to the cafeteria. Tension about the scene playing out in the administrator's office left her with little appetite.

In the break room, she was staring morosely at her chicken sandwich when her cell rang. It was, she saw, the hospital's day care center.

"Zady Moore," she answered.

"Thank goodness I reached you. This is Maureen Arthur." The director of the center sounded hoarse. "Is Caleb Davis with you by any chance?"

Worry darkened her vision. "No. Isn't he supposed to be there for lunch?" Nick had said he intended to stick to the boy's regular schedule.

"The van driver from the preschool checked him in on time, but nobody's seen him since," came the reply. "He should have joined his playgroup, but he's not there or in the restroom. I called Dr. Davis, but his phone went straight to voice mail."

Zady couldn't breathe. She loved that little boy. This couldn't possibly be happening.

"I ACCEPT MY share of blame for all the drama." Built like a linebacker, Mark Rayburn had no trouble dominating his office's conference table, around which the opposing groups had gathered. "If I hadn't brushed aside your concerns, this wouldn't have been necessary."

"One can hardly call it necessary." Owen Tartikoff's sardonic tone indicated his amusement as much as his disagreement. But then, having trumped the dissidents, he and his fellows had every reason to feel smug, Nick mused. "A simple email would have sufficed."

"We're way past the email stage," Samantha growled. She and Owen had had a few run-ins in the past, Nick had heard, although she wasn't directly involved in the fertility program.

"We have a, well, I guess you'd call it a compromise to propose," Mark said. "I'll let Dr. Davis—Dr. Marshall Davis—explain, since he suggested it."

All heads turned toward Nick's cousin. Rather than smirk at being singled out, Marshall folded his hands on the table and regarded them earnestly. "Until now, we hadn't formally assessed the amount of office space that will be freed up here, so I've done that."

"What is there to assess?" Samantha demanded.

"First of all, the urology program plans to concentrate our doctors in the Adams Building," Marshall said. "That means we'll be vacating three suites here."

That was their compromise? Nick wasn't impressed, and judging by the glowers of his cohorts, they shared his reaction.

Samantha voiced their skepticism. "Three more suites won't cut it."

"No, but they'll help," her husband replied. "After reviewing Marshall's figures, Cole, Owen and I agree that the urology staff should be assigned one and a half floors in the new building, with the remaining half a floor allocated to other specialties."

"Which floor?" his wife demanded. Because of the distribution of labs and other support services, the floors contained varying amounts of available space.

"We're still finalizing the layout. Let's wait until May to make that determination," Cole said. "I assure you, we'll be fair."

From the stiffening of Samantha's spine, Nick gathered that she'd prefer to argue. So would he, but they had no chance to regroup or confer. Across the table from him, Adrienne said, "Sounds okay to me."

"You'll accommodate pediatricians and neonatologists as well as OBs, right?" Jared Sellers asked.

Cole and Mark nodded. Owen folded his arms and tilted his head noncommittally. Marshall appeared relieved.

No doubt aware that she'd lost momentum, Samantha shrugged. "I'm glad we can agree in principle."

Chairs slid back on the carpet, a few knees cracked as they rose and several hands were shaken. Still irked that they'd been found out, Nick headed for the door. Just who *had* tipped off Marshall and the others?

His cousin was close behind. "All's well that ends well, eh?" Marshall said as they exited into the corridor.

"Yeah. That could have been ugly," Nick said sarcastically. "All those surgeons duking it out with their precious hands."

Marshall responded with a tight smile. "Good thing Zady spoke up."

Zady. *She'd* tipped off Marshall about the meeting, and through him, the rest of the brass. Nick's chest hurt as if he'd been punched. Damn it, he'd trusted her.

"Listen, there's something else we need to discuss," Marshall said.

What else had Zady revealed? "Okay. Just let me check my voice mail." Nick hadn't responded earlier when the phone had vibrated, and as a father, he couldn't afford to stay incommunicado for long.

He pressed the number for voice mail. And, still listening, broke into a run.

ZADY HAD READ that mothers felt guilty even when they had done nothing wrong. Her own mother was a poor example; she'd never shown any remorse for pitting her twin daughters against each other so she could remain the center of attention. However, Zady more than compensated now. Self-blame filled her as she raced from the medical building, past flower beds brimming with pansies and primroses, and through the staff entrance to the hospital.

Knowing how upset Caleb had been, she should have checked on him instead of staying in the break room. Despite an inner voice reminding her that Nick was in charge of his son, she *felt* responsible.

At the entrance to the day care center, Zady weakened with relief. Ahead, facing a couple of concerned adults, stood the small, sturdy figure of Caleb Davis.

Maureen Arthur, her short dark hair rumpled and her glasses sliding down her nose, peered toward Zady. "We were about to lock down the hospital, when a cafeteria worker brought him over."

"Oh, thank goodness." Zady issued a quick, silent prayer of thanks before adding, "The smell of food must have drawn him."

A woman wearing the yellow uniform of cafeteria staff said, "He told me he was looking for his father. Something about wanting to see his grandparents."

"He's been missing them," Zady said. "Caleb, are you okay?"

For a moment, she thought he hadn't heard her. Then he addressed Maureen. "Why did you call Auntie Zee? Where's my dad?"

Zady's face flushed. Caleb's rejection hurt, and he'd embarrassed her in front of the others. In their averted gazes, she read doubts about her relationship with the boy. And perhaps those were justified.

Don't overreact. This isn't about you.

"Caleb?" Nick's voice, thick with anxiety, rumbled from behind Zady. "Hey, little guy, you scared me. Don't ever do that again!" When his son raced forward, Nick scooped him up. "What's going on, kid? You know better than to run off."

From his position high in his father's arms, Caleb glared at Zady. "It's her fault! I had to get away from her."

Zady stood frozen. That wasn't what he'd told the cafeteria worker. But it hardly mattered, did it?

When Nick swung around, she looked to him for reassurance. Instead, his glare shocked her.

"Auntie Zee may mean well, but she isn't a very trustworthy person," he said.

What? The insult stung, badly. She had no idea where it had sprung from, but they shouldn't have this discussion in front of others.

As if things weren't bad enough, Maureen replied, "I can remove Nurse Moore as an emergency contact if you wish, Dr. Davis."

Nick blinked, perhaps recalling that he relied on Zady for overnight care. "No, that isn't necessary."

Maybe not in his view, Zady thought. But hers was changing rapidly.

Another male voice broke into her daze. "Is everything okay?" It was Marshall, from the hallway. He didn't appear to have heard the humiliating exchange, or at least, Zady hoped not.

"Fine, now," Nick said.

"Hi, Dr. Marsh!" The knife inside Zady twisted. The boy was delighted to see everyone except her.

She eased away. "I'll go finish my lunch," she muttered, and hurried off. Every muscle in her body ached, as if she'd been pummeled from all sides. And in a sense, she had been.

HE SHOULDN'T HAVE snapped at Zady in public, Nick conceded as the slim figure in the blue-flowered uniform disappeared around a corner. But she had a lot to apologize for, too.

Her betrayal had shaken him. Her spilling his confidences to Marshall had not only broken his trust in her, it had potentially harmed his colleagues. Nick hadn't decided how to explain that he was the source of the leak, but when he did, he doubted they'd ever look at him the same way again.

Meanwhile, he had a decision to make regarding Caleb. As the day care director waited, he wondered whether to sign the boy out for the rest of the day. He didn't like the idea of rewarding misbehavior, however.

Marshall resolved the matter by saying in a low, urgent voice, "I need to speak with you, Nicholas."

About the Porvamm business? Well, whatever it was, Marshall was being very insistent.

"Okay." Setting Caleb on the floor, Nick asked him, "Have you eaten?"

His son shook his head.

"I'll make sure he does," Maureen said.

"Thank you. And to everyone who was inconvenienced, I'm sorry to have put you through this," Nick said.

"I assure you, we'll review our practices so that we never lose track of a child again," the director told him.

"Good." After taking leave of his son, Nick accompanied his cousin into the hallway. "What's up?"

Marshall's stance shifted uneasily. "I'd appreciate if you'd accompany me to the next building. There's... Well, it's easier to show you."

That was odd, but Nick strode beside his cousin to the staff exit. "Don't you have patients?"

"They've been rescheduled."

Marshall must have planned ahead. Was this something else Zady had conspired in?

In the office building, they took the elevator to the sixth floor. During the short ride, Marshall uttered a few random remarks about the truce regarding office space, to which Nick responded with nods. Polite chitchat had never been his cousin's strength, and Nick was too puzzled to try to converse.

On the top floor, Marshall hastened along a hallway, clearly eager to get on with whatever he had in mind. *Curiouser and curiouser.*

He paused at a door marked Conference Room. Not another ambush! Nick gritted his teeth.

Inside, the room was empty, save for a single man. Behind the long table, a lanky figure paced by the window, hands jammed in his pockets.

With a quick intake of breath, Nick noted the graying brown hair and the slight stoop of the shoulders. Quentin Davis had aged markedly in the decades since he'd abandoned his family, but he wore a familiar wary expression. Well, he'd always been on the cusp of an excuse.

This *was* an ambush. "What the hell?" Nick asked his cousin.

Marshall spread his hands. "He begged me to arrange a meeting because you wouldn't meet him otherwise. You're free to leave, but I hope you'll let him say whatever's on his mind. It seems important to him."

"I don't appreciate the interference," Nick said flatly. How terrific—first Zady, then Marshall had let him down today.

"Ten minutes, that's all I ask." Quentin didn't attempt to draw closer.

Nick shrugged. "Might as well."

"I'll give you guys your privacy." Marshall stepped back through the open door.

"Wait!" Quentin cried. "This concerns both of you."

That appeared to surprise Marshall. "Why?"

Nick's dad clenched his hands. What on earth was such a big deal after all these years?"

"Because," he said shakily, "I'm your father, too."

Chapter Eighteen

Was this another of his father's lies or psychosis-induced delusions? But as Quentin laid out his story, there was no hint of hyperactivity about the man, and no telltale embellishments. Just simple statements that, to Nick, sounded credible.

Quentin and Adina Davis had had two sons, eleven months apart. Barely scraping up enough money for food, and living in their SUV, they hadn't planned on a second child.

Quentin's older brother, Upton, and his wife, Mildred, had had the opposite problem. Although wealthy from Upton's inventions and business, they were unable to bear children. At the encouragement of the grandparents, they proposed to adopt the older baby, Marshall.

"I'm not proud of this." Seated facing the younger men, Quentin twisted his hands atop the table. They were blue-veined and marked by age spots, although he was only in his fifties. "Upton offered to rent us an apartment and help with other expenses. In return, he and Mildred swore us to silence. No one, including you boys, was ever to know. Once the adoption went through, they arranged a new birth certificate for Marshall."

Nick's cousin held himself stiffly. *He isn't my cousin—he's my brother.* How weird was that? The guy who'd sneered at him growing up, with snide remarks about his unstable parents, had the same genetic heritage he did.

Yet Nick felt no satisfaction, only sympathy for Marshall. This disclosure might be jarring for Nick, but his entire identity hadn't just been thrown into question. "It's illegal to buy a baby," he pointed out.

His father dipped his head in acknowledgment. "That was another reason for keeping quiet."

"Why tell us now?" Marshall asked quietly.

"I've been undergoing treatment for bipolar disorder," Quentin said. "As part of my treatment, I've had to face what I'd done to you both. Marshall, I know our decision sounds selfish, but it wasn't only for our sakes. Upton and Mildred could provide you with a good home, financial support and a superior education."

"You must be aware that I'll ask my mother about this." Marshall's irregular breathing implied he had to remind himself to inhale.

"She'll be furious, but it's too late for her to try to get even." The creases deepened in Quentin's weathered face. "I haven't received money from my brother or his wife since Nick was ten."

"Since you dumped me and Mom," Nick said.

"Everything I did was for your own good, both you and Marshall," Quentin insisted. "Surely you can see that."

"Secrets and lies," Marshall retorted bitterly. "And you're springing it on us now to make yourself feel better."

The older man's shoulders slumped. "That's not my intent."

Nick tried to be fair. "I suppose you figured you were sparing Mom and me by not inflicting your troubles on us any longer when you left."

"Was I wrong?"

"And me?" Marshall demanded. "Yes, I did live a wealthier lifestyle, but because of your actions, I had no idea Aunt Adina was my birth mother. I'm not sure I ever had a private conversation with her. You took away my chance to know my real mom, and that can't be undone."

"I'm sorry," their father said. "I didn't dare speak out

while Adina was alive because Mildred continued sending her money. Since her death, well, I guess it's taken me two years to work up my nerve."

Marshall had a lot of emotional sorting-out ahead, Nick thought. By contrast, he found the revelation oddly comforting. His dad *had* put his sons first, or tried to.

Marshall pushed back his chair. "Typically, you maneuvered me into setting up this meeting."

Nick rose also. "It'll take us a while to process this, Dad." He hadn't meant to use that term of endearment, but noticing the flicker of relief in his father's eyes, he didn't regret it.

"You both have my phone number," Quentin said. "I'll be driving back to Bakersfield today. But if you have any desire to talk or—whatever—I'm available."

With brief, identical nods, the doctors Davis left the room.

"I'm sorry I dragged you to this," Marshall said. "I felt sorry for Uncle Quent and...well, I should have been honest with you. As he should have been with me." When they reached the elevator, he jabbed the button.

"Dad's good at playing on people's sympathy." Nick studied the man beside him, the cousin he'd resented for too long. In the past months, he'd gained an appreciation of Marshall's good qualities, as well as of how much they had in common. *Just as Zady urged.*

"I wish we could have been closer," Marshall said. "I was pretty snobbish toward you."

Nick had a confession to share. "Frankly, it was a good thing. Our competition inspired me to apply to medical school."

"It did?" Judging by his startled expression, Marshall was receiving his second shock of the day.

"To prove that if you could do it, so could I," Nick admitted. "Ironic, isn't it?"

A faint smile appeared. "Glad to hear I was of some use."

When the doors opened on an empty elevator, Nick seized the chance to pose another question troubling him. "If you don't mind my asking, when did Zady tip you off about our plan to ambush Dr. Rayburn today?"

Marshall's forehead furrowed. "She didn't. Mark and Owen heard it from other sources. This hospital's like a sieve."

Had Nick misunderstood the man's earlier statement? "You said it was a good thing Zady spoke up."

"Oh, that," Marshall said. "Last week, when she suggested we examine the logistics objectively, I realized I'd been overly territorial about office space."

Zady had simply tried to help, and Nick had leaped to the conclusion that she'd been a traitor. How rude he'd been to her, and in front of Caleb! He should accompany Marshall to his office right now and apologize to her.

In fact, he had more than that to apologize for, he conceded as his anger toward her yielded to remorse. He'd piled an unfair amount of responsibility on Zady for disciplining his son, then blamed her for Caleb's resentment. She deserved better—a lot better. But as he exited the elevator, his cell rang. If anything further had happened to Caleb... but the ID said Grandma Elaine. What did *she* want?

"I'd better take this." As Marshall strode away, Nick moved into an alcove for privacy. "Hello, Elaine."

"Actually, it's Bennie." The man hurried on. "We need to talk."

"Sure." Concern prompted Nick to ask, "How's your health?"

"Better," the older man said. "Listen, can you bring Caleb over? I've missed him and it's wrong, what's been going on."

"Be glad to. What exactly *is* the situation?"

"It's complicated and—" Bennie broke off. "Can't talk now. Just come over, will you?"

"You bet."

If there was trouble, perhaps Nick should leave Caleb in day care. But his son was desperate to see his grandparents.

Since Bennie had invited him, Nick decided to collect his son and head over there now. Urgent though it was, his apology to Zady would have to wait.

WHATEVER MEETING MARSHALL had attended left him unusually preoccupied that afternoon. Zady was always careful at work, but she made sure to be doubly prepared for each patient. To her boss's credit, he treated everyone without errors or omissions, but she knew him well enough to observe that, in spare moments, his mind drifted.

Meanwhile, her earlier interaction with Caleb and Nick festered. What had she done other than be the wrong person at the wrong time?

In a spare moment, Zady reviewed the list she'd jotted of essential qualities in a man. "Fresh start—no stepkids or ex-wives." Too bad she'd ignored that one.

Number 2. Never mistreated or abandoned a girlfriend. Okay, she couldn't fault Nick for whatever had gone wrong with Bethany, and as for Number 3, financial stability, he more or less qualified.

Number 4 hit her full-on. *Doesn't put me in the middle of family feuds.* That crack describing her as untrustworthy must have resulted from something involving Marshall, Caleb or Elaine, although she had no idea what.

If only Zady had heeded her own cautions. Instead, she'd fallen heart-first in love with both the man and his son. They were the family she longed for—not some vague theoretical guy and future child but real individuals. Nick and Caleb Davis.

Into her mind flashed the scene at the day care center,

the father holding the boy to his shoulder, their dark hair mingling. Both had been united in one wish: that Zady go away.

She hadn't meant to upset the child, but as with Dwayne's children, her presence had become destructive, good intentions notwithstanding. Caleb would be happier with a different sitter. Under other circumstances, Nick Davis might have been her Mr. Right, Zady thought sadly, and deleted the list. No sense saving warnings that had already failed to prevent the deepest sorrow of her life.

IN HIS BOOSTER SEAT behind Nick, Caleb vibrated with excitement as they passed the carriage-shaped mailbox. "Grandma! Grandpa!" he called as if they could hear him.

Had Nick been wrong to remove his son from the Carrigans' home? But much of the boy's distress was due to Elaine's behavior, he reminded himself, and wondered again what Bennie had been implying.

Nick halted the car in front of the portico. A couple of potted plants, possibly suggested by the Realtor to brighten the exterior, drooped from lack of watering. Not the greatest way to impress would-be buyers, he reflected as he released his son's seat belt.

Caleb pelted up the steps and rang the bell. Jumping in place, he seemed ready to explode as they waited.

When Elaine opened the door, she stared at them, speechless. Gray roots showed in her champagne-colored hair, and she wore a baggy sweat suit rather than her usual neat attire.

"Grandma!" Caleb cried. "It's us!"

"You mean Zady let you visit?" she asked.

The little boy glanced at Nick in confusion. "Dad?"

"Zady has nothing to do with this," he said. "You're the one who's been refusing to let him visit, Elaine."

"Well!" The woman's stooped frame straightened. "Thank goodness, you've come home where you belong."

She opened the door wider, and Caleb rushed to hug her. Above his head, she regarded Nick triumphantly.

Did she imagine she'd won some sort of contest? "Where's his grandfather?" Nick followed the pair into the house.

Elaine waved toward the den. "In his favorite chair, as usual."

"Can I see my room, Grandma?" Caleb asked.

She beamed. "It's waiting for you. We haven't changed a thing."

That explained why she'd refused to let Nick move the furniture. She'd intended all along for Caleb to return.

As Elaine perched on the stair lift and the little boy scampered up the steps, Nick wondered about her agenda. How could she believe he'd relinquish his son, especially since she and Bennie were in no shape to raise a child?

He proceeded to the den, where only a trace of late-afternoon sunlight penetrated the tall, curtained windows. Without the Christmas decorations, gloom pervaded the large room, partly from the darkness of the furnishings, but also from the sadness in Bennie's face.

The heavyset man rose and extended a hand. "Thank you for coming," he said as they shook. His grip was firmer than before, and his face and neck less puffy.

"I can't tell you how much I appreciate your call." Following Bennie's example, Nick sank into a chair. "Please fill me in."

Keeping a wary eye on the hallway, Bennie said, "I can no longer accept how irrational Elaine's become. She's been playing games with the real estate agent, changing appointments at the last minute, like she did with you. When the director of the assisted living facility called and asked me why we hadn't finished filling out the application, it forced me to face that she's been lying about our plans. To everyone, including me."

Nick recalled the behavioral changes he'd noticed—the evasiveness, the occasional slurred word and the deliberate manner of speech. Possible diagnoses ran through his mind. Alzheimer's or another form of dementia? Mental illness, including paranoia, could strike a person even in their mid-sixties, and that might explain her fixation on Zady as the enemy. "Has she been evaluated by a physician?"

"I've urged her to consult her doctor. But when she does go, she makes excuses for not taking me, so I don't know what they talk about." Bennie kept his voice low. "I discovered she has pain pills from several physicians. It may have begun as a way to treat her arthritis, but I think she's addicted."

"And she's doctor shopping." Nick had read that as many as one in five patients who'd been prescribed painkillers consulted multiple doctors, lying about their treatment in order to get additional drugs. He'd also learned that addiction among baby boomers was a growing problem and was tricky to spot, since the symptoms differed from those displayed by younger people abusing drugs. "What does she expect to accomplish?"

"Last night, she let it slip." Bennie shivered. "She has this fantasy that if she can get rid of Zady, you and Caleb will both move in here."

"I would never do that," Nick blurted. The idea of raising his son in this house alongside the Carrigans was preposterous.

"I know," Bennie said. "That's when I called her sister in Ohio. She and her husband are flying out tomorrow, and we'll coordinate with her doctor to do whatever it takes. Put her in rehab, move me to assisted living and so on. But I couldn't bear to let that happen without first hugging Caleb. I love that boy."

Nick laid his hand on the old man's arm. "He loves you, too, Bennie. Don't worry. Wherever you are, I'll bring him to visit."

"You're a good man," Bennie said.

From upstairs echoed Elaine's screech. "Don't talk about that witch! I don't care how funny she is, she's evil!"

Bennie pressed his hand to his forehead. "Caleb must have mentioned something positive about Zady."

They'd both done her a great injustice, Nick thought, guilt rushing in as he remembered how he'd treated her. But his immediate concern was for his son. "I'll go fetch him."

As he rose, small footsteps thumped down the stairs. The boy raced into the room, tears streaking his cheeks. "Daddy! Don't make me stay here!"

"Of course not." Nick knelt to clasp his son.

Caleb clung to him. "Grandma's acting weird."

"You didn't do anything wrong," Bennie assured him. "Elaine's sick."

"I am not!" Elaine had made surprisingly good time descending the stairs, perhaps powered by adrenaline.

With his father for support, Caleb swung to face her. "You scared me."

Emotions fleeted across her lined face. "I didn't mean to yell at you, sweetheart."

"Can we go home, Daddy?" Caleb asked.

"Sure. Just hug your grandpa first." Nick steered the little boy in Bennie's direction. "He's been waiting for you."

Holding up his arms, Caleb went to his grandfather. The old man bent to clasp him, his cheeks, too, glistening with tears.

Elaine peered at Nick in confusion. "I'm sorry I shouted at him. It's that woman's fault."

"Zady has done nothing but try to help Caleb and me," Nick retorted. "You need to deal with your problems and stopping blaming her." *And so do I.*

Wriggling away from his grandfather, Caleb reclaimed Nick's hand. "Let's go, Daddy."

"Goodbye," Nick told them. "I'll be in touch."

Bennie nodded. Elaine appeared dazed.

The crisis wouldn't be easily resolved, Nick reflected as he took his son outside. But perhaps today's visit had shaken Elaine enough to make her more receptive to treatment. Bennie and their relatives would have to do the rest.

"I don't live here anymore," Caleb said as Nick strapped him into the car seat.

"No. You live with me and Zady."

The boy took a deep breath. "Daddy, don't ever go away."

Nick bent down, embracing the child of his heart. "I won't. I promise."

An hour later, nearing home, he recalled that he was responsible for dinner tonight. At the supermarket, he bought take-out roast chicken and vegetables, along with a bouquet of spring flowers tied with a pretty ribbon.

He hoped that would make up for how he'd treated Zady, although it was only a start. While he was dwelling on his own need for loyalty, he'd betrayed *her* trust in him.

As he drove onto their street, the single-story house with its eggshell-blue paint and rosebushes welcomed them. "We're home," Caleb said.

"Yes, we are."

They clomped into the house, wreathed in the scents of roast chicken and flowers. There was a stillness in the air that felt unnatural, although Nick couldn't pinpoint why. "Auntie Zee!" the little boy called.

From her bedroom, Zady emerged. Her face was pale beneath the freckles. "Oh, hi. Where've you been?"

"We saw Grandma and Grandma." Caleb ran over. "Grandma acted funny."

"Funny how?"

"I'll explain later," Nick promised. "We brought dinner."

"Thanks, but I'm eating at my sister's."

That was when it hit him what was wrong. The usual scattering of Zady's possessions—a magazine on the coffee table, a decorative plate she'd hung near the kitchen—were gone. And a couple of cardboard boxes, closed and sealed, waited by the door.

She was leaving.

Chapter Nineteen

Another few minutes and Zady would have been gone, permitting father and son to enjoy their dinner undisturbed. Mercifully, she'd located a refuge. Gossip about the incident at the day care center had reached her sister, and when Zady called, Zora had immediately offered the use of a cot in the twins' nursery for a long as she liked.

She'd accepted with gratitude.

Nick's shocked expression and the flowers in his hands told Zady that he'd relented toward her. But fundamentally, nothing had changed. She'd taken a risk, and, as she'd feared all along, it had blown up in her face.

This was a good time to leave, in view of Caleb's high spirits. Seeing the Carrigans had been exactly what he needed. Unusually exuberant, he ran through the house, greeting everything. "Hi, kitchen!" His voice drifted to her. "Hi, yard!" He flew briefly into sight before vanishing into his bedroom, where she could hear him greeting each of his stuffed animals by name.

Nick shifted his sack of dinner onto a table. "These are for you." He held out the flowers. "With an apology."

Zady accepted them and took a sniff. "They're beautiful."

Nick's pleading gaze fixed on her. "You have every right to be angry. I had no business blaming you and embarrassing you. I thought you'd tipped off Marshall about our meeting today. It was a misunderstanding that I deeply regret, and I'll apologize again in front of the day care staff." He appeared to have run out of breath.

If only she could stay, but that would be wrong. They'd

both end up miserable, especially her. Rather than argue, Zady asked, "What's up with Caleb's grandparents?"

"Bennie asked us to come. Apparently, Elaine's addicted to painkillers. She's been lying about things and had a crazy idea that if you left, Caleb and I would move in with them." Nick swallowed. "Of course not. Our place is here with you."

If only that was true. "I'm afraid that doesn't apply to Caleb. He's had a hard time, and my presence isn't helping, it's hurting."

Nick moved across the living room toward her. He reached out as if to take her hands, but she lifted the bouquet to hold him at bay.

Despite her pain, she drank him in—his rumpled hair, the appealing end-of-day stubble on his cheeks—and her heart twisted. She loved him, but it wasn't enough.

"Elaine pitted him against you," Nick went on. "It was so devious that I missed it. She turned this into a you-versus-her situation for Caleb. Now that's finished."

"But it worked. And it worked because I stepped in here blithely assuming, at some level, that this was my ready-made family. That I could become his mother." Just as she'd imagined she could be a second mother to Dwayne's children. "Well, to him, I'm not and I never will be."

"Don't say that."

"For me to hold on would be selfish. Caleb's welfare comes first. My absence will be the greatest gift I can give him, and you."

There it was, flat-out reality. No use denying it any longer.

NICK ADMIRED ZADY'S insistence on protecting Caleb. But how could he accept the searing prospect of a future without her, especially when he knew she belonged here?

All his life, perhaps as a result of his father's abandonment, Nick had demanded absolute loyalty from those close to him. Rigidly, he'd perceived betrayal in every corner. Now he saw how unreasonable he'd been. And in the process, he'd hurt the woman he loved.

"I can't lose you," Nick burst out. "If you feel you have to move elsewhere for a while, let's stay close. Even if I can't have you one hundred percent, don't throw away what we've shared. You can come back whenever you're ready."

If he dared hope she might rethink her decision, her next words shook him.

"Hanging on to each other wouldn't be fair to Caleb," Zady said. "He needs a mom. There must be another woman out there who'd be right for him *and* you. Once I'm out of the picture, you'll have a chance to find her."

She hurried off, the flowers in her arms.

Gripped by longing, Nick had no idea what to do next. He was still standing there when Caleb trotted out. "Where's Auntie Zee?"

"She's…packing."

The little boy stared at him reproachfully. "What did you say?"

"I tried to stop her." Phrasing to avoid implying his son was at fault, Nick said, "She believes we'd be happier without her."

"Why?"

He'd run out of evasions. "You'd better ask her."

With a determined expression, Caleb wheeled and stomped toward Zady's room. Nick decided to allow them a few moments of privacy.

DISCOVERING LINDA'S SECOND-FAVORITE doll under the bed nearly proved Zady's undoing. Fighting sobs, she cradled the babylike figure. Would she ever have a child to keep?

A tap at the entrance drew her attention to Caleb's small figure. He glared at her. *Not again,* she thought wearily.

"Don't worry, little guy," she said. "I'm moving out."

His gaze fixed on the doll. "You're going to stay with Linda?"

"No, Linda lives with her mommy and daddy. I'll return this to her later." Zady tucked the toy into her suitcase. "I'll miss you a whole lot, Caleb."

"Then why are you going?"

She sank onto the edge of the bed, too overwhelmed to spin an excuse. "Because I can see how miserable I make you. You tried to run away because of me."

His eyes widened. "No, I didn't. Not really."

"You told everybody you hate me," Zady pointed out. "That your problems are my fault."

He ventured closer, bewilderment coloring his expression. This was a complicated situation for a little boy to process, she realized.

"Are you mad at me?" he asked.

"No, Caleb." Zady ached to gather him in her arms. "If I had a magic wand, I'd wave it right now and be your mommy forever. But a long time ago, I tried to create a home for some other children and they ended up hating me, too. I've learned my lesson. I love you too much to stick around and upset you."

His eyes glittered. "I'm sorry I was mean. Please don't leave."

Zady wasn't sure she dared trust this sudden declaration. Perhaps Nick had influenced his son. "You might change your mind."

Caleb's onrush caught her off guard. Zady barely maintained her balance on the bed as he climbed onto her lap. He wrapped his arms around her, burrowing into her shoulder. "Those other children were stupid. I love you, Auntie Zee."

Cradling the boy, she rocked him gently. "I love you, too, Caleb."

She hadn't heard Nick enter until his voice rumbled

through her. "I knew there was something I left out. Zady, I love you, too. I want to marry you. If you aren't ready for a commitment, I'll understand. But I'm asking you anyway."

"If I'm not ready for a commitment?" she repeated. He had it backward. What she'd feared was a repeat of her huge mistake with Dwayne. That she risked hanging on, hoping and struggling, opening her heart and being left with nothing but regret.

An armful of flowers and an apology didn't mean much. But here he was, eyes dark with emotion, begging to share his life with her.

Or was she interpreting his words to suit her fantasies? Zady studied Nick blurrily, uncertain that she'd heard correctly.

"Would you repeat the part about wanting to marry me?" she asked.

Wriggling out of her grasp, Caleb plopped onto the floor, where he sank to one knee like the hero of the romantic movie they'd watched. Nick followed suit. Father and son knelt there, the smile playing around Nick's mouth tempered by uncertainty.

"Will you marry me?" he asked.

"Me, too?" Caleb chimed in.

Zady had to push through a lump in her throat to answer. "Do you both promise to love me forever?"

Two dark heads nodded vigorously. Zady let her tears flow—but this time, they were tears of happiness.

"Then, yes," she said. "We'll be a family."

Joy glowed in Nick's face as he rose. Caleb, however, seemed dissatisfied. "Dad," he muttered. "Where's the ring?"

"Oops." Nick strode over to the bouquet Zady had placed on her night table, and removed the rainbow ribbon. "Can we tie this on your finger for now?"

"No!" Caleb said. "She's s'posed to get a ring."

"And she should, I agree." Producing his phone from his pocket, Nick tapped it a few times. Into the room played the tinny notes of "Here Comes the Bride."

"It's a ringtone," he explained playfully.

"Dad, that's lame!"

Zady shook with silent laughter. "It's okay," she managed to say.

"No, it's not," Nick said. "When we all have a day off, let's go to a jewelry store and pick out a ring."

"A sparkly one!" Caleb commanded.

"It will be," his father promised. "It'll be everything your new mom ever dreamed of."

Zady knew that couldn't be true. She already had everything she'd dreamed of, right here.

"MARSHALL'S YOUR BROTHER?" Zady said as they sat on the patio in the cool evening, after an excited Caleb had finally fallen asleep and Nick had filled her in about the events of the day. "What an amazing development."

Nick's hand cupped hers on the armrest. "It'll take a while to get used to the idea. Luckily, we've dropped our old antagonism. He's a good guy, even if he is kind of a stuffed shirt."

"And you're completely without fault," she teased. "Like me."

"I guess that makes us the perfect couple."

Zady closed her eyes, feeling the mild breeze of a March evening and inhaling the scents of jasmine and lemon flowers from a neighbor's yard. She luxuriated in the warmth of Nick's grip.

When she'd shared the good news with her sister, Zora's response had been, "I wondered how long it would take you guys to figure out you were in love." She'd instantly accepted Zady's request to serve as her matron of honor.

Her eyes reopened as she considered another implication of Nick's revelation. "Any chance you'll ask Marshall to be best man at our wedding?"

"Don't you think that might be overdoing it?"

"No."

Nick chuckled. "Neither do I. Sure, I'll ask him."

She decided not to inquire whether his father would be invited. That might still be a sore subject. "And your son will be the cutest little ring bearer ever."

"*Our* son," Nick corrected.

Zady's heart swelled. "Our son."

"Think Linda will be available as flower girl?"

"I hope so!" She grinned at him. "You're really getting involved in this wedding idea."

"Oh, I have lots of ideas," Nick replied cheerily. "Even more than that shirtless Scottish guy, I'll bet."

"Prove it," Zady said.

And he did.

* * * * *

Staten

When her old hall clock chimed eleven times, Staten Kirkland left Quinn O'Grady's bed. While she slept, he dressed in the shadows, watching her with only the light of the full moon. She'd given him what he needed tonight, and, as always, he felt as if he'd given her nothing.

Walking out to her porch, he studied the newly washed earth, thinking of how empty his life was except for these few hours he shared with Quinn. He'd never love her or anyone, but he wished he could do something for her. Thanks to hard work and inherited land, he was a rich man. She was making a go of her farm, but barely. He could help her if she'd let him. But he knew she'd never let him.

As he pulled on his boots, he thought of a dozen things he could do around the place. Like fixing that old tractor out in the mud or modernizing her irrigation system. The tractor had been sitting out by the road for months. If she'd accept his help, it wouldn't take him an hour to pull the old John Deere out and get the engine running again.

Only, she wouldn't accept anything from him. He knew better than to ask.

He wasn't even sure they were friends some days. Maybe they were more. Maybe less. He looked down at his palm, remembering how she'd rubbed cream on it and worried that all they had in common was loss and the need, now and then, to touch another human being.

The screen door creaked. He turned as Quinn, wrapped in an old quilt, moved out into the night.

"I didn't mean to wake you," he said as she tiptoed across the snow-dusted porch. "I need to get back. Got eighty new yearlings coming in early." He never apologized for leaving, and he wasn't now. He was simply stating facts. With the cattle rustling going on and his plan to enlarge his herd, he might have to hire more men. As always, he felt as though he needed to be on his land and on alert.

She nodded and moved to stand in front of him.

Staten waited. They never touched after they made love. He usually left without a word, but tonight she obviously had something she wanted to say.

Another thing he probably did wrong, he thought. He never complimented hcr, never kissed her on the mouth, never said any words after he touched her. If she didn't make little sounds of pleasure now and then, he wouldn't have been sure he satisfied her.

Now, standing so close to her, he felt more a stranger than a lover. He knew the smell of her skin, but he had no idea what she was thinking most of the time. She knew quilting and how to make soap from her lavender. She played the piano like an angel and didn't even own a TV. He knew ranching and watched from his recliner every game the Dallas Cowboys played.

If they ever spent over an hour talking they'd probably figure out they had nothing in common. He'd played every sport in high school, and she'd played in both the orchestra and the band. He'd collected most of his college hours online, and she'd gone all the way to New York to school. But they'd loved the same person. Amalah had been Quinn's best friend and his one love. Only, they rarely talked about how they felt. Not anymore. Not ever really. It was too painful, he guessed, for both of them.

Tonight the air was so still, moisture hung like invisible

lace. She looked to be closer to her twenties than her forties. Quinn had her own quiet kind of beauty. She always had, and he guessed she still would even when she was old.

To his surprise, she leaned in and kissed his mouth.

He watched her. "You want more?" he finally asked, figuring it was probably the dumbest thing to say to a naked woman standing two inches away from him. He had no idea what *more* would be. They always had sex once, if they had it at all, when he knocked on her door. Sometimes neither made the first move, and they just cuddled on the couch and held each other. Quinn wasn't a passionate woman. What they did was just satisfying a need that they both had now and then.

She kissed him again without saying a word. When her cheek brushed against his stubbled chin, it was wet and tasted newborn like the rain.

Slowly, Staten moved his hands under her blanket and circled her warm body, then he pulled her closer and kissed her fully like he hadn't kissed a woman since his wife died.

Her lips were soft and inviting. When he opened her mouth and invaded, it felt far more intimate than anything they had ever done, but he didn't stop. She wanted this from him, and he had no intention of denying her. No one would ever know that she was the thread that kept him together some days.

When he finally broke the kiss, Quinn was out of breath. She pressed her forehead against his jaw and he waited.

"From now on," she whispered so low he felt her words more than heard them, "when you come to see me, I need you to kiss me goodbye before you go. If I'm asleep, wake me. You don't have to say a word, but you have to kiss me."

She'd never asked him for anything. He had no intention of saying no. His hand spread across the small of her back and pulled her hard against him. "I won't forget if that's what you want." He could feel her heart pounding and knew her asking had not come easy.

She nodded. "It's what I want."

He brushed his lips over hers, loving the way she sighed as if wanting more before she pulled away.

"Good night," she said as though rationing pleasure. Stepping inside, she closed the screen door between them.

Raking his hair back, he put on his hat as he watched her fade into the shadows. The need to return was already building in him. "I'll be back Friday night if it's all right. It'll be late, I've got to visit with my grandmother and do her list of chores before I'll be free. If you like, I could bring barbecue for supper?" He felt as if he was rambling, but something needed to be said, and he had no idea what.

"And vegetables," she suggested.

He nodded. She wanted a meal, not just the meat. "I'll have them toss in sweet potato fries and okra."

She held the blanket tight as if he might see her body. She didn't meet his eyes when he added, "I enjoyed kissing you, Quinn. I look forward to doing so again."

With her head down, she nodded as she vanished into the darkness without a word.

He walked off the porch, deciding if he lived to be a hundred he'd never understand Quinn. As far as he knew, she'd never had a boyfriend when they were in school. And his wife had never told him about Quinn dating anyone special when she went to New York to that fancy music school. Now, in her forties, she'd never had a date, much less a lover that he knew of. But she hadn't been a virgin when they'd made love the first time.

Asking her about her love life seemed far too personal a question.

Climbing into his truck, he forced his thoughts toward problems at the ranch. He needed to hire men; they'd lost three cattle to rustlers this month. As he planned the coming day, Staten did what he always did: he pushed Quinn to a corner of his mind, where she'd wait until he saw her again.

As he passed through the little town of Crossroads, all the businesses were closed up tight except for a gas station that stayed open twenty-four hours to handle the few travelers needing to refuel or brave enough to sample their food.

Half a block away from the station was his grandmother's bungalow, dark amid the cluster of senior citizens' homes. One huge light in the middle of all the little homes shone a low glow on to the porch of each house. The tiny white cottages reminded him of a circle of wagons camped just off the main road. She'd lived fifty years on Kirkland land, but when Staten's granddad, her husband, had died, she'd wanted to move to town. She'd been a teacher in her early years and said she needed to be with her friends in the retirement community, not alone in the big house on the ranch.

He swore without anger, remembering all her instructions the day she moved to town. She wanted her only grandson to drop by every week to switch out batteries, screw in lightbulbs and reprogram the TV that she'd spent the week messing up. He didn't mind dropping by. Besides his father, who considered his home—when he wasn't in Washington—to be Dallas, Granny was the only family Staten had.

A quarter mile past the one main street of Crossroads, his truck lights flashed across four teenagers walking along the road between the Catholic church and the gas station.

Three boys and a girl. Fifteen or sixteen, Staten guessed.

For a moment the memory of Randall came to mind. He'd been about their age when he'd crashed, and he'd worn the same type of blue-and-white letter jacket that two of the boys wore tonight.

Staten slowed as he passed them. "You kids need a ride?" The lights were still on at the church, and a few cars were in the parking lot. Saturday night, Staten remembered. Members of 4-H would probably be working in the basement on projects.

One kid waved. A tall Hispanic boy named Lucas, whom he thought was the oldest son of the head wrangler on the Collins Ranch. Reyes was his last name, and Staten remembered the boy being one of a dozen young kids who were often hired part-time at the ranch.

Staten had heard the kid was almost as good a wrangler as his father. The magic of working with horses must have been passed down from father to son, along with the height. Young Reyes might be lean but, thanks to working, he would be in better shape than either of the football boys. When Lucas Reyes finished high school, he'd have no trouble hiring on at any of the big ranches, including the Double K.

"No, we're fine, Mr. Kirkland," the Reyes boy said politely. "We're just walking down to the station for a Coke. Reid Collins's brother is picking us up soon."

"No crime in that, mister," a redheaded kid in a letter jacket answered. His words came fast and clipped, reminding Staten of how his son had sounded.

Volume from a boy trying to prove he was a man, Staten thought.

He couldn't see the faces of the two boys with letter jackets, but the girl kept her head up. "We've been working on a project for the fair," she answered politely. "I'm Lauren Brigman, Mr. Kirkland."

Staten nodded. *Sheriff Brigman's daughter, I remember you.* She knew enough to be polite, but it was none of his business. "Good evening, Lauren," he said. "Nice to see you again. Good luck with the project."

When he pulled away, he shook his head. Normally, he wouldn't have bothered to stop. This might be small-town

Texas, but they were not his problem. If he saw the Reyes boy again, he would apologize.

Staten swore. At this rate he'd turn into a nosy old man by forty-five. It didn't seem that long ago that he and Amalah used to walk up to the gas station after meetings at the church.

Hell, maybe Quinn asking to kiss him had rattled him more than he thought. He needed to get his head straight. She was just a friend. A woman he turned to when the storms came. Nothing more. That was the way they both wanted it.

Until he made it back to her porch next Friday night, he had a truckload of trouble at the ranch to worry about.

Lauren

A MIDNIGHT MOON blinked its way between storm clouds as Lauren Brigman cleaned the mud off her shoes. The guys had gone inside the gas station for Cokes. She didn't really want anything to drink, but it was either walk over with the others after working on their fair projects or stay back at the church and talk to Mrs. Patterson.

Somewhere Mrs. Patterson had gotten the idea that since Lauren didn't have a mother around, she should take every opportunity to have a "girl talk" with the sheriff's daughter.

Lauren wanted to tell the old woman that she had known all the facts of life by the age of seven, and she really did not need a buddy to share her teenage years with. Besides, her mother lived in Dallas. It wasn't like she'd died. She'd just left. Just because she couldn't stand the sight of Lauren's dad didn't mean she didn't call and talk to Lauren almost every week. Maybe Mom had just gotten tired of the sheriff's nightly lectures. Lauren had heard every one of Pop's talks so many times that she had them memorized in alphabetical order.

Her grades put her at the top of the sophomore class, and she saw herself bound for college in less than three years. Lauren had no intention of getting pregnant, or doing drugs, or any of the other fearful situations Mrs. Patterson and her father had hinted might befall her. Her pop didn't even want her dating until she was sixteen, and, judging from the boys she knew in high school, she'd just as soon go dateless until eighteen. Maybe college would have better pickings. Some of these guys were so dumb she was surprised they got their cowboy hats on straight every morning.

Reid Collins walked out from the gas station first with a can of Coke in each hand. "I bought you one even though you said you didn't want anything to drink," he announced as he neared. "Want to lean on me while you clean your shoes?"

Lauren rolled her eyes. Since he'd grown a few inches and started working out, Reid thought he was God's gift to girls.

"Why?" she asked as she tossed the stick. "I have a brick wall to lean on. And don't get any ideas we're on a date, Reid, just because I walked over here with you."

"I don't date sophomores," he snapped. "I'm on first string, you know. I could probably date any senior I want to. Besides, you're like a little sister, Lauren. We've known each other since you were in the first grade."

She thought of mentioning that playing first string on a football team that only had forty players total, including the coaches and water boy, wasn't any great accomplishment, but arguing with Reid would rot her brain. He'd been born rich, and he'd thought he knew everything since he cleared the birth canal. She feared his disease was terminal.

"If you're cold, I'll let you wear my football jacket." When she didn't comment, he bragged, "I had to reorder a bigger size after a month of working out."

She hated to, but if she didn't compliment him soon, he'd never stop begging. "You look great in the jacket, Reid.

Half the seniors on the team aren't as big as you." There was nothing wrong with Reid from the neck down. In a few years he'd be a knockout with the Collins good looks and trademark rusty hair, not quite brown, not quite red. But he still wouldn't interest her.

"So, when I get my driver's license next month, do you want to take a ride?"

Lauren laughed. "You've been asking that since I was in the third grade and you got your first bike. The answer is still no. We're friends, Reid. We'll always be friends, I'm guessing."

He smiled a smile that looked as if he'd been practicing. "I know, Lauren, but I keep wanting to give you a chance now and then. You know, some guys don't want to date the sheriff's daughter, and I hate to point it out, babe, but if you don't fill out some, it's going to be bad news in college." He had the nerve to point at her chest.

"I know." She managed to pull off a sad look. "Having my father is a cross I have to bear. Half the guys in town are afraid of him. Like he might arrest them for talking to me. Which he might." She had no intention of discussing her lack of curves with Reid.

"No, it's not fear of him, exactly," Reid corrected. "I think it's more the bullet holes they're afraid of. Every time a guy looks at you, your old man starts patting his service weapon. Nerve-racking habit, if you ask me. From the looks of it, I seem to be the only one he'll let stand beside you, and that's just because our dads are friends."

She grinned. Reid was spoiled and conceited and self-centered, but he was right. They'd probably always be friends. Her dad was the sheriff, and his was the mayor of Crossroads, even though he lived five miles from town on one of the first ranches established near Ransom Canyon.

With her luck, Reid would be the only guy in the state that her father would let her date. Grumpy old Pop had what she called Terminal Cop Disease. Her father thought everyone, except his few friends, was most likely a criminal, anyone under thirty should be stopped and searched, and anyone who'd ever smoked pot could not be trusted.

Tim O'Grady, Reid's eternal shadow, walked out of the station with a huge frozen drink. The clear cup showed off its red-and-yellow layers of cherry-and-pineapple-flavored sugar.

Where Reid was balanced in his build, Tim was lanky, disjointed. He seemed to be made of mismatched parts. His arms were too long. His feet seemed too big, and his wired smile barely fit in his mouth. When he took a deep draw on his drink, he staggered and held his forehead from the brain freeze.

Lauren laughed as he danced around like a puppet with his strings crossed. Timothy, as the teachers called him, was always good for a laugh. He had the depth of cheap paint but the imagination of a natural-born storyteller.

"Maybe I shouldn't have gotten an icy drink on such a cold night," he mumbled between gulps. "If I freeze from the inside out, put me up on Main Street as a statue."

Lauren giggled.

Lucas Reyes was the last of their small group to come outside. Lucas hadn't bought anything, but he evidently was avoiding standing outside with her. She'd known Lucas Reyes for a few years, maybe longer, but he never talked to her. Like Reid and Tim, he was a year ahead of her, but since he rarely talked, she usually only noticed him as a background person in her world.

Unlike them, Lucas didn't have a family name following him around opening doors for a hundred miles.

They all four lived east of Crossroads along the rambling canyon called Ransom Canyon. Lauren and her father lived in one of a cluster of houses near the lake, as did Tim's parents. Reid's family ranch was five miles farther out. She had no idea where Lucas's family lived. Maybe on the Collins Ranch. His father worked on the Bar W, which had been in the Collins family for over a hundred years. The area around the headquarters looked like a small village.

Reid repeated the plan. "My brother said he'd drop Sharon off and be back for us. But if they get busy doing their thing it could be an hour. We might as well walk back and sit on the church steps."

"Great fun," Tim complained. "Everything's closed. It's freezing out here, and I swear this town is so dead somebody should bury it."

"We could start walking toward home," Lauren suggested as she pulled a tiny flashlight from her key chain. The canyon lake wasn't more than a mile. If they walked they wouldn't be so cold. She could probably be home before Reid's dumb brother could get his lips off Sharon. If rumors were true, Sharon had very kissable lips, among other body parts.

"Better than standing around here," Reid said as Tim kicked mud toward the building. "I'd rather be walking than sitting. Plus, if we go back to the church, Mrs. Patterson will probably come out to keep us company."

Without a vote, they started walking. Lauren didn't like the idea of stumbling into mud holes now covered up by a dusting of snow along the side of the road, but it sounded better than standing out front of the gas station. Besides, the moon offered enough light, making the tiny flashlight her father insisted she carry worthless.

Within a few yards, Reid and Tim had fallen behind and were lighting up a smoke. To her surprise, Lucas stayed beside her.

"You don't smoke?" she asked, not really expecting him to answer.

"No, can't afford the habit," he said, surprising her. "I've got plans, and they don't include lung cancer."

Maybe the dark night made it easier to talk, or maybe Lauren didn't want to feel so alone in the shadows. "I was starting to think you were a mute. We've had a few classes together, and you've never said a word. Even tonight you were the only one who didn't talk about your project."

Lucas shrugged. "Didn't see the point. I'm just entering for the prize money, not trying to save the world or build a better tomorrow."

She giggled.

He laughed, too, realizing he'd just made fun of the whole point of the projects. "Plus," he added, "there's just not much opportunity to get a word in around those two." He nodded his head at the two letter jackets falling farther behind as a cloud of smoke haloed above them.

She saw his point. The pair trailed them by maybe twenty feet or more, and both were talking about football. Neither seemed to require a listener.

"Why do you hang out with them?" she asked. Lucas didn't seem to fit. Studious and quiet, he hadn't gone out for sports or joined many clubs that she knew about. "Jocks usually hang out together."

"I wanted to work on my project tonight, and Reid offered me a ride. Listening to football talk beats walking in this weather."

Lauren tripped into a pothole. Lucas's hand shot out and caught her in the darkness. He steadied her, then let go.

"Thanks. You saved my life," she joked.

"Hardly, but if I had, you'd owe me a blood debt."

"Would I have to pay?"

"Of course. It would be a point of honor. You'd have to save me or be doomed to a coward's hell."

"Lucky you just kept me from tripping, or I'd be following you around for years waiting to repay the debt." She rubbed her arm where he'd touched her. He was stronger than she'd thought he would be. "You lift weights?"

The soft laughter came again. "Yeah, it's called work. Until I was sixteen, I spent the summers and every weekend working on Reid's father's ranch. Once I was old enough, I signed up at the Kirkland place to cowboy when they need extras. Every dime I make is going to college tuition in a year. That's why I don't have a car yet. When I get to college, I won't need it, and the money will go toward books."

"But you're just a junior. You've still got a year and a half of high school."

"I've got it worked out so I can graduate early. High school's a waste of time. I've got plans. I can make a hundred-fifty a day working, and my dad says he thinks I'll be able to cowboy every day I'm not in school this spring and all summer."

She tripped again, and his hand steadied her once more. Maybe it was her imagination, but she swore he held on a little longer than necessary.

"You're an interesting guy, Lucas Reyes."

"I will be," he said. "Once I'm in college, I can still come home and work breaks and weekends. I'm thinking I can take a few online classes during the summer, live at home and save enough to pay for the next year. I'm going to Tech no matter what it takes."

"You planning on getting through college in three years, too?"

He shook his head. "Don't know if I can. But I'll have the degree, whatever it is, before I'm twenty-two."

No one her age had ever talked of the future like that. Like they were just passing through this time in their life and something yet to come mattered far more. "When you are somebody, I think I'd like to be your friend."

"I hope we will be more than that, Lauren." His words were so low, she wasn't sure she heard them.

"Hey, you two deadbeats up there!" Reid yelled. "I got an idea."

Lauren didn't want the conversation with Lucas to end, but if she ignored Reid he'd just get louder. "What?"

Reid ran up between them and put an arm over both her and Lucas's shoulders. "How about we break into the Gypsy House? I hear it's haunted by Gypsies who died a hundred years ago."

Tim caught up to them. As always, he agreed with Reid. "Look over there in the trees. The place is just waiting for us. Heard if you rattle a Gypsy's bones, the dead will speak to you." Tim's eyes glowed in the moonlight. "I had a cousin once who said he heard voices in that old place, and no one was there but him."

"This is not a good idea." Lauren tried to back away, but Reid held her shoulder tight.

"Come on, Lauren, for once in your life, do something that's not safe. No one's lived in the old place for years. How much trouble can we get into?"

Tim's imagination had gone wild. According to him all kinds of things could happen. They might find a body. Ghosts could run them out, or the spirit of a Gypsy might take over their minds. Who knew, zombies might sleep in the rubble of old houses.

Lauren rolled her eyes. She didn't want to think of the zombies getting Tim. A walking dead with braces was too much.

"It's just a rotting old house," Lucas said so low no one heard but Lauren. "There's probably rats or rotten floors. It's an accident waiting to happen. How about you come back in the daylight, Reid, if you really want to explore the place?"

"We're all going, now," Reid announced, as he shoved Lauren off the road and into the trees that blocked the view of the old homestead from passing cars. "Think of the story we'll have to tell everyone Monday. We will have explored a haunted house and lived to tell the tale."

Reason told her to protest more strongly, but at fifteen, reason wasn't as intense as the possibility of an adventure. Just once, she'd have a story to tell. Just this once...her father wouldn't find out.

They rattled across the rotting porch steps fighting tumbleweeds that stood like flimsy guards around the place. The door was locked and boarded up. The smell of decay hung in the foggy air, and a tree branch scraped against one side of the house as if whispering for them to stay back.

The old place didn't look like much. It might have been the remains of an early settlement, built solid to face the winters with no style or charm. Odds were, Gypsies never even lived in it. It appeared to be a half dugout with a second floor built on years later. The first floor was planted down into the earth a few feet, so the second-floor windows were just above their heads, giving the place the look of a house that had been stepped on by a giant.

Everyone called it the Gypsy House because a group of hippies had squatted there in the seventies. They'd painted a peace sign on one wall, but it had faded and been rained on until it almost looked like a witching sign. No one remembered when the hippies had moved on or who owned the house now, but somewhere in its past a family named Stanley must have lived there because old-timers called it the Stanley house.

"I heard devil worshippers lived here years ago." Tim began making scary-movie-soundtrack noises. "Body parts are probably scattered in the basement. They say once Satan moves in, only the blood of a virgin will wash the place clean."

Reid's laughter sounded nervous. "That leaves me out."

Tim jabbed his friend. "You wish. I say you'll be the first to scream when a dead hand, not connected to a body, touches you."

"Shut up, Tim." Reid's uneasy voice echoed in the night.

"You're freaking me out. Besides, there is no basement. It's just a half dugout built into the ground, so we'll find no buried bodies."

Lauren screamed as Reid kicked a low window in, and all the guys laughed.

"You go first, Lucas," Reid ordered. "I'll stand guard."

To Lauren's surprise, Lucas slipped into the space. His feet hit the ground with a thud somewhere in the blackness.

"You next, Tim," Reid announced as if he were the commander.

"Nope. I'll go after you." All Tim's laughter had disappeared. Apparently he'd frightened himself.

"I'll go." Lauren suddenly wanted this entire adventure to be over with. With her luck, animals were wintering in the old place.

"I'll help you down." Reid lowered her into the window space.

As she moved through total darkness, her feet wouldn't quite touch the bottom. For a moment she just hung, afraid to tell Reid to drop her.

Then she felt Lucas's hands at her waist. Slowly he took her weight.

"I'm in," she called back to Reid. He let her hands go, and she dropped against Lucas.

"You all right?" Lucas whispered near her hair.

"This was a dumb idea."

She felt him laugh more than she heard it. "That you talking or the Gypsy's advice? Of all the brains dropping in here tonight, yours would probably be the most interesting to take over, so watch out. A ghost might just climb in your head and let free all the secret thoughts you keep inside, Lauren."

He pulled her a foot into the blackness as a letter jacket dropped through the window. His hands circled her waist. She could feel him breathing as Reid finally landed, cussing the darkness. For a moment it seemed all right for Lucas to stay close; then in a blink, he was gone from her side.

Now the tiny flashlight offered Lauren some much-needed light. The house was empty except for an old wire bed frame and a few broken stools. With Reid in the lead, they moved up rickety stairs to the second floor, where shadowy light came from big dirty windows.

Tim hesitated when the floor's boards began to rock as if the entire second story were on some kind of seesaw. He backed down the steps a few feet, letting the others go first. "I don't know if this second story will hold us all." Fear rattled in his voice.

Reid laughed and teased Tim as he stomped across the second floor, making the entire room buck and pitch. "Come on up, Tim. This place is better than a fun house."

Stepping hesitantly on the upstairs floor, Lauren felt Lucas just behind her and knew he was watching over her.

Tim dropped down a few more steps, not wanting to even try.

Lucas backed against the wall between the windows, his hand still brushing Lauren's waist to keep her steady as Reid jumped to make the floor shake. The whole house seemed to moan in pain, like a hundred-year-old man standing up one arthritic joint at a time.

When Reid yelled for Tim to join them, Tim started back up the broken stairs, just before the second floor buckled and crumbled. Tim dropped out of sight as rotten lumber pinned him halfway between floors.

His scream of pain ended Reid's laughter.

In a blink, dust and boards flew as pieces of the roof rained down on them and the second floor vanished below them, board by rotting board.

COMING NEXT MONTH FROM

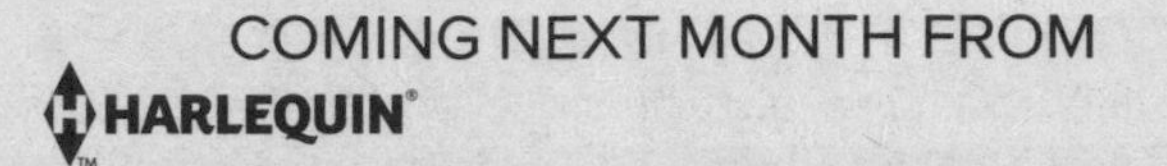

American Romance

Available October 6, 2015

#1565 HER RODEO HERO

Cowboys in Uniform • by Pamela Britton

After an accident, Natalie Goodman is looking to start over, but she needs Colt Reynolds's help. The rodeo cowboy tries everything to resist falling for the beauty, but he's no match for her sweet kisses...

#1566 A COWBOY'S CHRISTMAS REUNION

The Boones of Texas • by Sasha Summers

Hunter Boone broke Joselyn Stephens's heart years ago. Now Josie has a chance at happiness, but she refuses to come between Hunter and his son—no matter how much she wishes she could be part of their family.

#1567 A HUSBAND IN WYOMING

The Marshall Brothers • by Lynnette Kent

Reporter Jess Granger is determined to unearth the truth about artist-turned-rancher Dylan Marshall. But the closer she gets to the taciturn cowboy, the more she wonders if what she's found instead...is a Wyoming husband.

#1568 MISTLETOE RODEO

Welcome to Ramblewood • by Amanda Renee

Handsome bull rider Chase Langtry just wants to be left alone after his dismal showing at the National Finals, but reporter Nola West is determined to get the scoop...and the man!

This Christmas, can a single-dad cowboy reclaim the woman from his past?

Read on for a sneak preview of A COWBOY'S CHRISTMAS REUNION, the first book in new author Sasha Summers*'s miniseries,* ***THE BOONES OF TEXAS!***

She'd know that butt anywhere. Hunter Boone.

In eleven years, his derriere hadn't changed much. And, apparently, the view still managed to take her breath away.

"Need some help with that, Josie?" Her father's voice made her wince.

She was clutching a tray of her dad's famous German breakfast kolaches and hiding behind the display counter. Why was she—a rational, professional woman—ducking behind a bakery counter? Because *he'd* walked in.

She shot her father a look as she said, "Thanks, Dad. I've got it." Taking a deep breath, she stood slowly and slid the tray into the display cabinet with care.

"Josie? Josie Stephens?" a high-pitched voice asked. "Oh my God, look at you. Why, you haven't changed since high school."

Josie glanced at the woman but couldn't place her, so she smiled and said, "Thanks. You, too."

That was when her gaze wandered to Hunter. He was waiting. And, from the look on his face, he *knew* Josie had no idea who the woman was.

"So it's true?" the woman continued. "Your dad said you were coming to help him, but I couldn't imagine you back *here*. We *all* know how much you hated Stonewall Crossing." Josie remembered her then. Winnie Michaels. "What did you call it, redneck hell—right?" Winnie kept going, teasing—but with a definite edge. "Guess hell froze over."

"Kind of hard to say no when your dad needs you," Josie answered, forcing herself not to snap.

Her father jumped to her defense. "She wasn't about to let her old man try to run this place on his own."

"It's kinda weird to see the two of you standing here." Winnie glanced back and forth between Josie and Hunter. "I mean, without having your tongues down each other's throats and all."

Hunter wasn't smiling anymore. "I've gotta get these to the boys."

Josie saw him take the huge box by the register. A swift kick of disappointment prompted her to blurt out, "Too bad, Hunter. If I remember it correctly, you knew how to kiss a girl."

"If you remember? Ouch." His eyes swept her face, lingering on her lips. "Have fun while you're back in hell, Jo. I'll see you around."

HAREXP0915

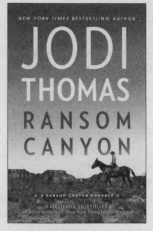